Claimed by Rage

Brutal Beauty
Book One

Misti Wilds

Claimed by Rage

Copyright © 2025 by Misti Wilds

Cover Design: Raven Ink Covers

Paperback ISBN: 979-8-9902695-2-1

All rights reserved.

Misti Wilds asserts the moral right to be identified as the author of this work.

This novel is entirely a work of fiction. The names, characters and incidents portrayed in it are the work of the author's imagination. Any resemblance to actual persons, living or dead, events or localities is entirely coincidental.

Designations used by companies to distinguish their products are often claimed as trademarks. All brand names and product names used in this book and on its cover are trade names, service marks, trademarks and registered trademarks of their respective owners. The publishers and the book are not associated with any product or vendor mentioned in this book. None of the companies referenced within the book have endorsed the book.

No part of this book may be reproduced in any form or by any electronic or mechanical means, including information storage and retrieval systems, without written permission from the author, except for the use of brief quotations in a book review.

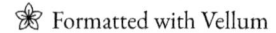

❦ Formatted with Vellum

Author's Note

Claimed by Rage is a dark, why choose, mafia romance with mature themes woven throughout the book. If you are familiar with my work, this series is darker than the *Baranova Bratva* duet, so please check all content notes and warnings on my website: https://mistiwilds.com/

This book ends on a cliffhanger that leads directly into book two, *Tempted to Rebel.*

Chapter 1

Celia

There are a few key things a working woman needs to keep her going when her employees call out sick for the third time this week: a double shot of espresso, a fine-tipped French manicure, and thigh-quivering orgasms to keep the stress at bay.

But that doesn't mean she needs them *all at once.*

Caffeine and adrenaline surge through my veins in a heady cocktail of *too much* as my very stubborn, very delinquent *not-boyfriend* nudges my thighs apart with his shoulders. I knock over a jar of pens as he slides my ass to the edge of my desk. "*Rage*," I hiss, digging my nails into his scalp. No matter how many times I pull out his hair, he keeps coming back every other morning, a lazy smirk on his face as he sits me on top of my desk and makes me ride his face.

It's not my idea, *I promise.*

He huffs, his breath hot against my panties. "I told you to stop wearing these."

"And I told you—*ohhh*."

His tongue feels just as wide as his shoulders as he swipes it against me, wetting my panties like a fucking animal. My face flames as he groans, no doubt tasting my desire. He may act like an animal, but I'm the bitch in heat who *likes* it.

And he fucking knows it.

Rage nips my clit through the fabric, making me buck against his face. *Fuck*. It hurts, but only in the way that makes everything else dial up a notch. The tension. The thrill. The *need* pulsing between us.

As much as I claim that he's the one addicted, the counterargument that I'm *not* is lost in these moments, the little punches of breath, the shuffle of our clothes, the frantic way we touch each other.

Because that's how it always is: frantic, needy, insatiable. There's no love here, but there's *something*. That something keeps him coming back and me, well, *coming*.

He presses a rough kiss against my inner thigh and slides my panties down my legs. "Don't wear these next time, Celia. I mean it."

I roll my eyes—or I try to. They clench shut the moment he buries his face in my pussy. Pleasure zings up my spine and shoots down to my toes all at once, each insistent swipe of his tongue powerful and purposeful. He's a man on a mission, and he knows exactly how to claim victory. "R-rage," I cry, biting my lip. Resistance may be futile, but I have to save *some* of my dignity. "We can't do this. I'm *working*."

The burly man shoots me a quick look, like he

doesn't believe me, and hooks my calves over his shoulders, the soft fabric of his dress shirt warm and inviting. One thing I've always admired about him, not that I'd ever admit it, is his attire. The man doesn't go cheap, and it shows in both texture and appearance, all of his shirts and slacks tailor-made to fit his muscled frame, stitched together with expertise that makes me jealous.

I'd kill for that kind of skill.

My breath hitches as he licks my slit from stem to stern, hooking the tip of his tongue over my clit at the last second. He chuckles as my legs seize, then pushes the flat of his palm against my inner thighs, widening my stance as he dips his tongue inside my heat.

I grab the back of his giant, arrogant head and pull him closer, hoping he suffocates while he's down there.

Yeah, I guess we're doing this. *Again.*

I should have said no the first time he showed up at my door. Hell, *before* then. The very first night we met at that ridiculously-exclusive club, I let him seduce me in the middle of a crowded room. *Stupid,* I now realize, quivering against his skilled tongue as he works my body into a frenzy. This is the game we play every few days: how quickly can I come on his wicked tongue?

He has to be keeping track with how often he checks the Rolex strapped to his wrist.

With each expert flick of his tongue, shame curls heavy inside my chest, making it harder to breathe. I shouldn't let him keep touching me like this, *here,* at my workplace. It's not right. I'm not some horny teenager working a retail shift—I'm the owner of this boutique. I can't have men walking in here to tongue-fuck me all hours of the day. People will *find out*. People will *see*.

It's only a matter of time before someone walks in—

The jingle of bells at the front door makes my stomach drop. Rage is usually good with timing, arriving just after the morning rush when the shop is quiet. But today, he arrived late. It's too close to the next wave of customers. People will stop to browse the entire street of boutiques and cafes, mine included, any second now.

The bells over the door jingle a second time, and someone clears their throat out on the shop floor.

No, not in any second, *right now*.

Panic beats wildly in my chest. "Rage. Stop. There's a customer—"

He presses his tongue flat against my clit, swiping with slow, lazy strokes, unhurried in the slightest. I grab his hair and *pull*—he grunts, spreading my thighs wider apart to slip two thick fingers inside my molten core.

I gasp in a breath and screw my eyes shut as he works me slow and steady, curling his fingers to tease an orgasm from me one stroke at a time. I come just as slowly as he works my body. A ripple of pleasure pulses from my core to my limbs, leaving me boneless and sex-drunk as he pulls back to stare at me.

Licking my desire from his knuckles, he hums happily. "You taste like honey, *krosotka*. Sticky and sweet."

My face burns. The problem isn't just Rage—it's his brothers, too. The three of them have been paying me visits throughout the day, each one with their own MO.

Rage likes to taste me. Rebel likes to touch me. Ruin likes to watch me. It's only been two weeks, and they're already tearing down the structure and routine I've carefully crafted in my life and creating space for themselves to fit.

I used to be civilized. I'd have sex at home, in bed, instead of wherever the hell the mood strikes. I'd be able to look my partner in the eyes and hold love in my heart while we *made love*—but nothing about these men is *loving*.

They take what they want, when they want.

The only blessing is that they take turns. Rage is a morning man, appearing while I'm at work and disappearing within an hour. Rebel likes to appear in the evenings, drinking my best coffee or lounging on my couch by the time I make it home. But Ruin is the true wild card—I never know where or when he'll strike. His brothers, I can predict pretty well. Ruin is another story entirely, appearing out of thin air at all hours of the day, demanding that I touch myself... while he watches.

Sometimes, in the moments before sunrise when I'm finally alone, I tell myself that it's all one crazy dream. That I'm still Celia Monrovia, a loveless, sexless divorcée who puts on a pretty smile while her heart secretly cracks into sharp little pieces.

But then our new routine starts all over again, and Rage reminds me that this impossible situation is very real and *very* dirty.

I take a deep breath as I come back into my body. That's Rage's cue to help me up. He puts me back on my feet and straightens my skirt, as though that makes me modest again.

There's nothing modest about what we just did. What we *keep* doing.

Clearing my throat, I adjust my hair clip in the mirror. "You should leave. There are customers waiting." I nod towards the back exit, determined not to look directly at him. I might combust from the lust burning in his gaze. I haven't reciprocated his oral advances—not even once. He hasn't asked.

I haven't offered.

"Don't do this again, Rage. Not this close to the lunch rush." I exit the *employees only* section and return to the sales floor, smiling at three new customers and praying they don't notice the scent of *wet pussy* lingering around me.

I move behind the counter to ring up one of the ladies. "Oh, I love this top. Did you see that we carry it in blue? It's right over here—"

Her gaze drifts from the garment in my hands to my right, the tiniest gasp passing her lips. Her expression softens immediately, her posture shifting as she pushes out her chest and juts out her hip. She's older than me by a few years, maybe a decade at most, but when it comes to desire, age doesn't matter. People have the same tricks and tells when we see something—or someone—we like.

My smile freezes in place, my skin tingling as I imagine Rage running his hands over my body. He might as well be—I can feel his eyes roaming my curves like he didn't just feel me up two minutes ago. I told him to go out the back door, didn't I? What the hell is he doing up front?

"Ma'am?" I try to get her attention. "Did you want to see this in blue? It would look great with your skin tone."

She turns her gaze back to me slowly. "That's... not necessary. Just ring it up, please."

As I'm folding the garments into her bag, she slinks toward Rage. I stare at one of the mirrors across the room and catch a side-view of him leaning against the wall, arms crossed, a scowl twitching onto his lips as the woman approaches him. He's probably annoyed that she's blocking his view.

I'm still wondering why the hell he hasn't left yet.

I set the brunette's bag aside while the next customer comes to the counter. While I chat with her and ring up her items, the brunette tries to start small talk with Rage. He doesn't respond. I'm not even sure he gives her a pitying glance.

That's how all three of them are—laser-focused on me.

What a fucking *blessing*.

I roll my eyes before I catch myself, and the customer with me frowns. "Excuse me?"

Shit.

"I'm sorry, I'm—that wasn't meant for you." I force a smile. "My *brother* won't leave," I lie, raising my voice to make sure Rage can hear me. We're in no way related, but I'd rather people think my brother Mikhail pays me regular visits than Mr. Tall, Tattooed, and Temperamental. "He really needs to listen when I tell him that I'm *working*."

The woman glances between the two of us, but I can tell she doesn't want to get involved. She grabs her bags and heads out the door without another word. The third customer leaves without buying anything.

I wait for the first customer to leave, the brunette with a big smile and bigger tits, but she pulls out a pen from her purse and grabs Rage's hand, scrawling something on his wrist. Her smile is seriously *huge*—too much teeth, not enough lip—as she blows across Rage's wrist to set the ink. I'm pretty sure she grazes his knuckles against her boobs—*ugh*—before letting go. Then she takes her sweet ass time meandering to the door, fondling racks of clothes and casting furtive glances in Rage's direction every few seconds.

I glare daggers at her back the entire time, hoping she'll turn around to see me and get the hint that she's not welcome back if she's gonna hit on strangers in the shop, but she doesn't spare me a single glance.

That's probably for the best. I'm not on my best behavior today.

Once the door closes behind her, I turn my ire onto the real problem. "Listen, *asshole*, you can't just—" I gasp as Rage closes the distance between us in three long strides. Flinching back, I stumble against the front counter, the words I mean to say sticking in my throat. He slams his palm against the wall beside my ear, the blue ink on his wrist catching my eye. Turning my head, I ignore the heat of his stare and read the message.

Ten numbers, followed by a perfect heart stamp.

I roll my eyes. *Of course* he'd get her number. Now he can add her pussy to the all-you-can-eat buffet: open for breakfast *and* dinner.

Rage flexes hard enough that I can see a thick vein pulsing up his forearm. He clips each word between clenched teeth. "Don't roll your eyes at me, Celia."

I push against his chest, but he doesn't budge. With a huff, I push harder. "Then stop being a fucking *man* and get off of me. I told you to leave."

Snatching my wrists, he pins them together over my head. "You *also* said that I was your brother, you fucking liar." He exhales hotly, dipping his face into the curve of my neck. His lips brush the shell of my ear. "You think pretending to be my sister will keep me from touching you? Keep me from *fucking* you?" Shifting his weight, he keeps one hand on my wrists while the other reaches down and fists the bottom of my dress. "Nothing will keep me from you, *krosotka*, especially not something as weak as a *lie*." He abandons the fabric to shove his hand between my thighs, mirroring how he touched me earlier. The gentleness is gone, replaced with something harsher. Anger? Annoyance? Is he actually upset about this?

I'm the one who has every right to being upset!

My body is still slick from his tongue, making the swirl of his fingers over my clit a smooth glide. He presses down hard, and I cry out as pleasure-pain *zings* up my spine.

My eyes fly open as he works my body and touches me exactly how I like, rimming my clit instead of pushing against it head-on. I bite my lip to keep from moaning. Panic mixes with pleasure as people continue walking by the front windows, some glancing inside, most walking right on by.

Keep walking, I pray, *don't see me like this.*

If anyone catches me getting fingered behind the counter, I'm screwed. This isn't a franchise I'm running—it's high-end, personalized, with the prices to match. My clientele can make or break anyone in the city with the right word to the right people. No one can know that I'm fucking around with a man like Rage.

No one.

Nothing about my livelihood or its fragility breaks through Rage's determination. "Your body sings for me, Beauty, and I'll play its song any fucking time I please." He presses an open-mouthed kiss to my neck, lacking finesse as he skims me with his teeth. "Now, say thank you."

My clit pulses with desire as he pinches it between his fingers. "F-for what?"

"For making you come."

I dig my fingernails into my palms and shake my head. "I'm not coming." But *dear God*, do I want to. I can feel it building deep inside, threatening to pull me over the edge.

He pulls back to glare into my eyes, finally letting up on the assault on my clit. We stare at each other for a heartbeat while I try to take back control over my body. Steady my breathing. Stop sweating. Ignore the ache.

When he suddenly arches his fingers and plunges three inside, I keen like a wild animal.

"Yes, you are."

I'm so wet that he glides inside without any resistance. With a hard press of his palm, he grinds into my clit and knocks the air from my lungs. Pain lances through me. *It hurts,* yet it feels *really* good. No part of this should make me even hotter, but somehow Rage lights my body on fire every time we're near each other. Anger. Desire. Fear. Heart racing, blood pumping, body shaking—all of it, because of Rage.

I think I hate him for it.

His mouth descends over mine, claiming my lips in a kiss that's *hungry.* He sinks deeper, all the way down to the knuckle, not shy about fondling me in public. With a groan, he forces his tongue past my lips on his conquest to victory—the finish line in sight. My body trembles as I near my breaking point, and he knows it.

Rage breaks the kiss to growl harshly in my ear, sounding as ragged and raw as I feel. "You want my cock, don't you, Beauty? Say it. Say that you want me to fuck you right here, right now, for all your fucking customers to see."

That's the thing he doesn't understand. Here in the waking world, I'm not the mystery woman from the club. I don't have on a mask, and I don't go by the name Beauty. He's mixing the two women up and claiming both in the process.

But Celia Monrovia isn't his. She's *mine.*

I sharpen my resolve to a fine point, wielding it like a

spear that I can plunge straight into his heart. "Fuck you," I hiss, finally mustering the strength to break free from his grasp. I dig my nails into his neck and shove, but he still doesn't move, groaning like he likes it—like I'm fisting his cock instead of scoring the fine tips of my manicure into his throat. "I don't want you *or* your cock."

The problem is that he hasn't stopped—his fingers are buried deep inside of me, determined to wring an orgasm from my body. He touches me however he pleases, thinking that I enjoy it.

The sick part is, I kind of do.

My knees buckle as he keeps going, curling his fingers in my heat, feeling how fucking *drenched* I am, both of us hearing it loud and clear as his movements build into a rhythm—*plunge, curl, retreat.*

A whimper catches in my throat, burning as much as the liquid heat inside me, both of them threatening to break free. I'm close—*so fucking close*—and I fight to keep it locked up tight. I don't want to give him another piece of me, no matter how small.

He doesn't deserve it.

Rage's onyx eyes burn with equal parts fury and desire as I delay the inevitable. "You might lie to yourself, Celia Monrovia, but your body tells the truth. You want me. You want my brothers. You want *all of us.*" His shoulder dips as he shifts the angle of his wrist, shoving the three fingers deeper, grunting as he hits something *delicious.* My breaths come out as these tiny puffs of air, and when he flicks his fingertips *faster,* hitting that perfect spot that makes me see stars, I cry out, my body seizing as the dam breaks. White hot *everything* tears through my body, too much, too fast, too overwhelming, consuming more than I've ever felt before, more than I've thought possible.

I *hate* how he makes me feel so... *helpless.*

"That's it, beautiful, come all over my fingers." He wraps his other hand around my throat and brushes his thumb over my pulse point, staring deeply into my eyes as tremors pulse through my body, his pupils blown so wide that all I see are endless pools of black.

If I believed in eternity, this is where I would find it —no end, no beginning, just floating in a moonless sea of shadows without a single guiding star to light my way home.

When he suddenly removes his fingers from my core, I cry out from the loss, my hips chasing his retreat. Embarrassment flares in my chest at the visceral reaction, my neck flushing pink as he admires his glistening fingers in the light. His smile curves, all harsh lines and sex appeal, as he sucks them into his mouth one by one, cleaning the mess—*my mess*—from his fingers.

The phone number on his wrist is smeared, illegible now that the ink has rubbed off on my thighs. He licks that too, catching a trail of my desire that slipped past his wrist, removing the other woman's mark almost entirely. All that's left is the fuzzy outline of the heart.

A tendril of something cool and soothing curls inside my chest until he swallows, groaning like a man on the verge of coming. I watch his Adam's apple bob, my mouth falling open as he smirks and licks his shiny lips. Wanton need courses through my veins, burning away my resolve *not to enjoy this* one heartbeat at a time. That's another thing about Rage—some primal part of me recognizes the primal parts of him, making it easy to overlook the strings attached to every kiss, every touch, every taste.

Nothing with this man is freely given. My mind understands that, but my body has yet to catch up.

The bells over the door jingle, but even then, he doesn't tear his gaze away. "You want me." His dark eyes flash silver as he brushes the pad of his thumb across the seam of my lips, smearing what little remains of his spit and my arousal, then pressing harder, seeking entrance. "The proof is right here. Taste how much you want me, *krosotka*."

I jerk my head away. "No."

Rage's nostrils flare and he descends on me again, gripping my chin to turn my face back toward his. "You don't get to tell me no."

There isn't much I can hear over my hammering heart, but I'd recognize the *click* of a gun cocking anywhere. "Get your fucking hands off her."

Rage bears down on me for one more intense second before lifting his gaze to look at whoever's got the gun. Whatever he sees pisses him off even more than I did. "Point that thing somewhere else," he growls, "before I smash your pretty boy brains all over the floor."

I can hear the exasperation in the man's voice—*my*

brother's voice, I realize—as he chuffs. "You'd be dead before you could get close enough."

Rage body-blocks me from my brother, effectively cutting me off from the conversation. More importantly, from the path of the bullet. My brother wouldn't shoot me—but he sure as hell would shoot a man touching me without my consent. If Mikhail has been watching, I'm not sure what he would have seen: a woman being given all the attention she wants, or someone being forced to like it?

The way adrenaline buzzes through my body makes the truth fuzzy. I don't know which is true.

I run a hand through my tousled hair. "Settle down, boys. I'm *fine*."

Neither of them moves. It's like I hadn't even spoken.

"Mikhail—" I peer around Rage's bulging bicep to look at my brother... and immediately regret it. His eyes are narrowed into slits—at Rage, yes, but also at *me*. He turns his steely gaze on me in a heartbeat, the scowl on his lips carved so deep that he looks ten, twenty years older.

Like our father.

The realization hits me like a punch to the gut, knocking the air from my lungs. The resemblance is striking. Our father was many things before he died, and *unhappy* is only the tip of a very deep, depressing iceberg.

I can't be the reason my brother is unhappy. *I can't.*

But it isn't really *my* fault, is it?

Rage is clearly the problem. Like my brother, he

doesn't do well with hiding his emotions. I see them flicker across his features, the clear, murderous intent snapping into place in an instant. I have no doubt that Rage would kill any man who gets in his way of claiming me—my brother included.

But Mikhail would kill for me just as quickly.

The tension in the room rebuilds, only this time it's between Rage and Mikhail. Moving through it is like like treading through water, each small step becoming a fight. Against my better judgement. Against my brother. Against all sense and sanity.

When I take Rage's hand, the clench of his jaw eases, but he keeps his gaze glued to the gun. "Hey," I murmur, gentle with my movements, my words. "It's okay. It's my brother. He won't hurt me."

Mikhail makes this sound, something between a whine and a warning. "*Celia*, I swear to God, get over here!"

That's what I should do. Retreat. It's what I've wanted ever since Rage walked onto the shop floor instead of out the back door—distance. Space to breathe. Time to think.

I have none of those things whenever Rage is around, and my brother's presence doesn't change that. Mikhail won't shoot while I'm standing so close to Rage. He's not as good of a shot as he claims, preferring knives as his weapon of choice, and it's in close-quarters like this when it becomes most apparent.

He won't shoot until I'm far enough away for the bullet to clear me.

I glance up at Mikhail. This is the first time I've seen him in weeks. I don't linger, because one look at the fury in his eyes tells me everything I need to know: despite coming to my rescue today, he's still pissed at me for ignoring him over the past few weeks.

Well, I'm still furious, too.

I feel the anger like a second heartbeat all the way from my head to my toes. It pulses through me like lava, making me feel violated from within. I don't normally get angry like this but when your brother and his mafia buddies hold a wedding party hostage and terrorize the guests for hours of ruthless interrogations, you get a little frustrated.

For the first time in my life, that anger and frustration overpowers all other emotions. I might be annoyed with Rage's persistence in making me his, but I'm *furious* with Mikhail for acting like what he did on his wedding day was okay.

When our eyes meet, I see my own staring back at me. Being twins means that we share a lot of physical traits, from our chestnut brown hair to the same tip to our noses. But in this, we will *always* differ.

I will never agree with being part of the bratva if it means terrorizing innocent people, regardless of the *why*.

"Go home, Mikhail."

He freezes, the hard line of his mouth pressing tighter, nearly disappearing altogether. "He's bothering you, Celia."

I know that Mikhail coming to my rescue is likely some kind of divine intervention. A sign from God that

Rage is just as bad as I think he is—that I should walk away right here, right now, and let my brother splatter his brains all over my boutique. I would finally escape his eyes—his tongue—his wicked claim over my heart.

However.

What my brother doesn't know is that Rage isn't one man—he's a package deal. There are *three* of them itching to get inside me, and if Mikhail shoots Rage today, he'll have two more psychopaths to contend with.

As pissed as I am at Mikhail, I'd rather he not die at my expense.

"I can handle this. Go home to Valentina."

It's no secret that the bratva's Queen is finally home where she belongs after her unexpected disappearance—I've heard whispers of her return throughout the shop as gossip trades hands over shifting hangers and clutched handbags. Mikhail should be with her right now, not with me.

Mikhail finally shifts his gaze, looking between me and Rage. "I'll go when he goes," he says gruffly, "not a moment before." His warm brown eyes pierce mine, screaming *I'm not leaving you alone with this asshole.*

For that, I *am* grateful.

When I turn back to Rage, he's not staring at the gun anymore. There's the slightest curve to his lips, a confident smirk in place that makes *another* kind of heat rush through me. My face warms all over again as he reaches up to touch the pink flush blooming across my cheeks.

I cringe away from his touch, my lips twisting into a grimace. "Don't read into this." The words rush out as one long string of syllables. "I don't want your blood all over my floor."

"Mhm." Rage's grip tightens as he holds me steady and ducks his head toward mine. "I think you just chose me, *krosotka*," he rumbles, the tips of our noses brushing, "and that's the hottest fucking thing I've ever seen." He devours my mouth in a searing kiss, one that steals the breath from my lungs. His tongue slips between my lips, and I can taste it—the desire he took from me, spilling back inside my mouth. He groans, suddenly pulling my hand to his crotch to feel the thick outline of his cock, hard and hot and eager, and he cups my palm around his length, forcing me to touch him, *to feel him*, to acknowledge how much he wants me, even now, with a gun aimed at his head.

Mikhail curses behind us. "For fuck's sake, man, get the hell off of her!"

I pull away first, not wanting to linger on the hummingbird flutter of my heart or the way his hard length feels rocking into my palm. *Jesus*, the heat of him is gonna imprint on my brain.

Thankfully, Rage decides to play nice. He chuckles and presses a hard kiss to my forehead. "Don't worry, I'm fully loaded for you anytime, anyplace." He winks as he saunters away, clapping Mikhail on the shoulder as he walks past him to the exit. "Good to see you, brother."

Mikhail's face twists. "I am *not* your brother."

The bells over the door jingle as Rage leaves, but I don't miss the way he hovers outside, watching me through the massive front windows.

My brother glares at me, tapping the butt of his gun against his thigh in short, jerky bursts. "You have the *worst* taste in men." He glares out the window at Rage. "Do you need me to take care of him?"

The light, fluttering feeling in my chest deflates instantly, my hands balling into fists. I'm not ready to admit that Rage makes me feel good—physically, at least —but the crash back to reality hits hard, like a sledgehammer to the gut. Bile rises in the back of my throat, and when I look at my brother, I see him for what he is.

He's no longer *only* Mikhail Monrovia, the man who has kept our family safe since Dad died, but one of the bratva's *vors*, a captain willing to get his hands dirty to *keep* me safe, even now, a decade later.

He would kill a man like it's barely worth the time it takes to consider doing it. That's who he is now. Bratva-made, like most of the men in this city.

I'm pretty sure he's only asking because he knows that if he kills Rage without my consent, I'll never forgive him.

The weight of it all crushes me. "No." I shake my head. I don't want any more death, not even for a man like Rage, but I don't dare tell my brother that. I don't want to pick a fight, not after the insane highs and lows over the past hour. My heart can only handle so much. "I'll take care of him."

Mikhail doesn't buy it, but at least he doesn't argue. "Fine. But Celia?" He tucks his gun into a holster hidden beneath his suit jacket. "Grow up and stop ignoring me." His eyes narrow, a lock of his chestnut hair falling across his forehead. "You're bratva whether you like it or not. You can't wish it away on some shooting fucking star." Thrusting his hand out toward Rage, still lingering outside, he huffs. "Case in point. Do you know who he is? *Really* know? Because he's not the kind of guy I thought I'd find you trading spit with."

I don't know specifics. Rage doesn't really talk so much as he takes. But I don't want Mikhail to spoon-feed me information about my latest hookup. "I told you, I'll handle it." It's no secret that Rage, Rebel, and Ruin are bratva—I see it in their tattoos, in the way the world bends to their will, the fine lines of their muscles, honed into weapons. It means that I made a huge mistake dancing with them at the club two weeks ago, but I couldn't help it.

For the first time in years, someone wanted *me*.

My brother wouldn't understand how, at that exact moment, nothing else mattered.

Chapter 2

Celia

My home has always been a picture of perfection both inside and out. Pristine white walls match the decor: sleek and shiny, with hints of silver and sparkle strategically placed to catch rays of sunlight in the warmth of dusk and dawn. The flowerbeds outside are much the same, filled with local greenery that rotates every few months as the seasons change. Strangers and friends alike know at least one thing: Celia Monrovia keeps a tidy home.

Not even Rebel can change that.

Every time he misplaces a throw blanket, leaves the TV remote out, or rifles through my cabinets for something to entertain himself, I put everything back into its proper place. Some may call it a compulsion, but my mother would call it a homemaker's duty, and that's how I choose to see it.

A perfect home means a perfect life.

That's what I tell myself as I drive up the slope and

park beside Rebel's motorcycle. It doesn't fit here, much like the rest of him. All tattoos and smoke, filling my home with something dark and disorderly—out of place for a cookie-cutter suburban.

Yet he makes himself at home even when I'm not around, becoming more in-tune with my belongings than even my ex-husband was. Rebel has spent countless hours rummaging through my cabinets, drawers, and closets, like he's looking for something. A secret. An affair. Something broken that I've swept under the rug.

He won't find anything, because I have nothing to hide.

As I round the sidewalk from the front to the side door, I catch glimpses of his presence. The open windows, spilling warm light into the yard. The middle drawer in the antique china cabinet, angled open on the right side. The swivel armchairs in the living room, facing the windows instead of the coffee table in the center of the room. Despite the disarray, passerby still have the opportunity to glimpse the picture I've painted, pristine white and perfect, not a single speck of dust, dirt, or decay. It's what my mother advised after my divorce settled.

Show them how strong you are in the aftermath, and everyone will forget you were ever weak in the first place.

I hover outside the kitchen door as I catch Rebel within, doing what he does best: snooping. He hops up on the kitchen counter and reaches for the cabinet above the fridge, the edge of his t-shirt lifting to expose a sliver of skin over his hips. He goes straight for the liquor, unscrewing the cap on a half-empty bottle of vodka and taking a swig. Or two. Or *three*. He holds the bottle by the neck with one hand and continues rummaging with the other, sorting through what little remains from my ex-husband's liquor stash. When Rebel closes the cabinet and reaches for the one beside it, I roll my eyes and push open the door. "There's nothing interesting up there, Rebel, I promise."

I drop my keys into the wooden bowl on the bar, frowning at his own set already nestled snugly within. It's like he *wants* to live here. Nothing about Rebel screams *domesticated*, though. He's all dark tattoos and lean muscle, black skinny jeans slung low over his hips, a charcoal gray v-neck exposing the intricate ink curving across his chest. Despite sharing midnight hair and dark eyes with his brothers, he stands out by the glint of metal looped around his bottom lip and the soft beanie slung over his head.

That, and the distinct *dick piercing* I remember rubbing against my tongue that night I sucked him off at the club.

He doesn't have the grace to pretend he isn't snooping. Flicking his gaze in my direction, he slips something silver inside his front pocket before hopping off the counter. "Everything here is interesting, baby." He sets the vodka down on the counter before slinking toward me, wrapping his arms around my waist like vines. "It's yours."

The sincerity in his eyes *almost* makes me believe him.

I settle my hands over his hips and take a deep breath. Even this part is foreign: the sweet *welcome home*. My heart aches for the little things it's missed from my marriage—things that I haven't lost, but things that I never *had*. This is one of them.

Rebel's lips brush my cheek as he bends down to my height. With only a few inches between us, he doesn't have to stoop far. "Missed you today."

There's no telling how long he's been waiting for me, only that this has become routine just as much as Rage's morning visits at the boutique. I never gave Rebel a house key; he finds a way inside on his own, likely breaking a lock in the process. He dips lower and mouths a tender spot on my neck, humming against my skin. "You feel tense. Rough day?"

A shiver rolls down my spine as he sucks the mark he left yesterday, pulling blood to the surface to darken it some more. That's the thing with these men—they enjoy marking their territory. "You could say that." Rage was rougher than usual today, not stopping after his morning snack, breaking routine to get on my nerves and take more than was on offer. The memory of his fingers pulsing inside my heat forces a blush to my cheeks. "I think I made your brother mad."

Rebel scoffs, lifting his head to peer into my eyes. His lips shine with saliva, the snakebite gleaming silver in the light. "Rage is always mad. I swear he was born with a huge stick up his ass." Rolling his eyes, he pulls me away from the kitchen and into the hallway, toward the stairs to the second level. "C'mon, let's strip you outta these clothes."

"I can do it myself."

He keeps a hand wrapped around mine as he leads me up the stairs. When we reach the landing, he spins us and pins me to the wall, crowding me with his warmth, his scent. The glint of mischief in his eyes is the only warning I get before he dips, sealing his lips over mine. I can feel the smirk in his kiss, the way he buries a piece of himself within everything he does, including this.

If Rage's kisses are an all-consuming fire, Rebel's are the smoke that lingers long after he's gone.

"It's more fun when I watch," he murmurs, sucking my bottom lip between his. With a groan, he pulls back completely, leaving me dazed as he gestures toward the bedroom. "After you, beautiful."

The only sound accompanying the change from my wraparound dress into pajamas is the rustle of clothing. Rebel remains silent as he watches me, dark eyes hooded with a longing that's palpable. I can taste it in the remnants of his kiss, see it in the pitched tent of his jeans, feel it when he leans back on the bed, the long length of his body screaming *fuck me*.

I slip into the bathroom instead of climbing into his lap and dry humping him into oblivion. I resist, because I can't give in to these men. Little things like tolerating their break-ins and tantrums, sure, I can handle that. But seeking out the warmth of their bodies? The sting of their touch?

My nipples harden to sharp peaks as a shiver rolls down my spine. I'm still strung out from Rage's advances earlier in the day—*always wet now*, it seems—and I go through the motions of my nighttime routine to try and break out of it. I remove my makeup, scrub my face, brush my hair and teeth, check my cuticles, hop into the shower, whatever I can do to delay walking back into the bedroom.

I know what's waiting for me, and it's a *very* bad idea.

Everything about these brothers screams *bad fucking idea*.

By the time I finally muster up the courage to face Rebel, he's no longer in the bedroom. Darkness has fallen outside, which means that much like the last rays of sunlight, he's gone, off to God-knows-where to do God-knows-what. He's left the two bedside lamps on and a crudely-made sandwich on a plate.

A smarter woman would have reservations, a fear of poison or drugs or hidden razor blades, and throw the sandwich away, but I don't. I devour it in two minutes flat, grateful that he sliced a fresh tomato and added pepper jack cheese. It's not gourmet, and *God*, my mother would lose her shit if she knew I was eating not just a cold-cut sandwich, but a sandwich *in bed*, but this is what my life has become.

I'm no longer cooking elaborate meals every night. Instead, I'm letting a stranger feed me scraps from the fridge.

Exhaustion creeps in far too quickly. I've got orders to place and clients to contact and groceries to buy, but I slip into a light sleep easily, like my body is ready for something my mind is not. It's in these half moments, the ones where I'm sort of in my body but sort of not, that are the most dangerous.

It's when *he* arrives.

The third brother, his face and body covered in little more than black leather, always appears in my doorway as a shadow. At first, I think he's just that: a trick of the light. A figment of my imagination. Nothing to worry about.

Except then he moves.

If death has a personification, I imagine that it's Ruin. Moving through the shadows like ink, slowly bleeding from one to the next, so gentle that everything still feels like a dream. Yet, your body begins to react. It knows that something is near—something potentially dangerous—but the way he moves is breathtakingly beautiful, languid, graceful, soothing... how can something so magnificent be anything other than *welcome*?

He stands at the foot of my bed, staring.

This is how the night always begins.

Slowly, he reaches out a leather gloved hand, lifting the sheets to expose my feet, my legs. He starts there, brushing his fingertips against the tips of my toes, the arch of my foot, gliding gently across my body with a lover's touch. It's only when he reaches my calves that he hooks around them, palming my muscles, rubbing now, soothing the aches of the day away. My eyes flutter—open, closed, doesn't matter—because now I can feel him. Now, I know that this isn't a dream, that he's here with me.

Inside my bedroom. Inside my mind.

His breathing is steady until he bends my knees, lifting them higher on the mattress, his movements louder, his touch persistent. If I spread my legs to quicken things along, he freezes in place.

Only when I settle back into the sheets does he continue. He likes me pliant, but not willing. Clothed, but not covered. Trapped, but not chained.

He works the blankets up over my waist, pinning me with their weight on my torso and his hands on either side. Breathing heavy, he exhales harsh against the black mask covering his entire face. *Staring.*

"Were you good girl today, *krosotka?*" His Russian accent is thicker than his brothers' and always present. "Or did you let them touch you?"

I bite my lip as he runs a gloved palm up my inner thigh, spreading my legs wider, making room for him. He already knows the answer: I couldn't stop Rage from touching me if I tried, and Rebel keeps his kisses above-the-waist. Each man's touch is different, and Ruin is no exception. Our eyes lock through the slits in his mask, the sight of their irises—not quite black like his brothers', but a deep ocean blue—becoming as achingly familiar as his touch. Featherlight, then not. Imaginary, then real.

Ruin pushes up my nightgown and shoves it beneath the wad of blankets across my waist. He drags his palm over my stomach, leaving sparks in its wake. I drag in a deep breath and try to stay still as he inches closer to where I want him most. His hand hovers over my mound, fingers twitching, before pulling back and reaching into his pocket. The ache between my thighs sharpens as he reveals a switchblade and flicks it open with a snap of his wrist. I can't see Ruin's face, but I picture it all the same, blending his brothers' features to come up with my best guess. Does he bite his bottom lip as he slices through my panties? Is there a divot between his brows as he concentrates on the task? Or are his lips parted in silent rapture as he pulls the fabric away to bare my body to him?

His voice crackles when he speaks, each word sharp as a knife's edge. "Show me."

My face flames as I wriggle my arms down the sides of my body, reaching for the place between us. He keeps his palms pressed tight to my knees, pinning them in an awkward angle that dips them into the mattress while lifting my hips closer toward him. I squirm to free my right hand from the blankets, and the first punch of cool air hits hard. My hand shakes as I brush over my swollen clit, the needy ache burrowed deep inside me sparking at first touch. It's the ache that Rage planted this morning, embers of his touch seared into the deepest parts of me. The same one that Rebel unknowingly tended, the long lines of his body and soft licks of his tongue fanning the flames.

Under a moonlit sky, it's Ruin's turn to crack me open and draw my desire out, to make me feel the weight of my body's betrayal and the force of its release. He's the one who shatters my resolve, bending me to his will with simple commands and promises of pleasure.

Ruin exhales harshly as he dips lower, applying more

pressure to my knees as he leans in for a closer look. "Keep going."

Biting my lip, I dip my fingers between my folds, knowing that he's watching them slip inside, seeing my desire coat my fingers as I push and pull, teasing him as much as I'm teasing myself. Tension coils tight inside my abdomen as I pull them out and twirl the pads of my fingers over my clit. It's not the same bruising intensity of Rage's touch, but it doesn't have to be. My toes curl, my breath catching in my throat. Heat blooms deep inside my body, and I catch myself moaning as I swipe across my bundle of nerves, faster, harder, needing the release. Knowing it's close—that Ruin needs it, too, needs to see it. Feel it. Experience the crash with me.

His weight shifts on the bed and suddenly it's not just my hand between my thighs, but his, too, his palm cupping mine as he crawls on top of me. Normal men might grind their dicks against my pussy, but not Ruin— he pushes the heel of my hand into my clit and shoves my fingers inside my heat, the feel of warm leather against my skin making my moans deeper, louder, frantic as his fingers join my own. I can't tell which are mine and which are his, but there are *so many* now, the wet suction drawing them all in. He leans on his forearm beside my head, the feel of his hot breath lost behind his mask, but I can *hear* it—the heavy panting, the way he growls as my hips buck up into our hands, the tortured sound catching in his throat as he comes in his pants before I've even toppled over the edge.

But these moments are never about his pleasure,

they're about mine. How many times can I come in an hour? How loud can I moan, and at what pitch? Which are better—the breathless, high-pitched whines or the deep, long moans that reverberate around my ribs?

Rebel may search my house for answers, but Ruin searches my body, piecing me together like a puzzle, each orgasm a mere flip of a piece to reveal the picture hidden underneath.

It's something that Rage, for all his righteous declarations of possession, doesn't understand.

You can't claim something without understanding it.

I want Ruin to kiss me, but he never does. Once sated, the ache of lust morphs into an ache of longing—for tender moments, warm breaths against pillows, the shift of skin against skin as our legs tangle in the sheets, the caress of morning light across our cheekbones, whispers of affection that go beyond the needs of the flesh.

But those pieces are the ones Ruin doesn't know how to give, much how I wouldn't know how to ask.

I fall asleep to the feel of his body weight over mine, his hand pressed firmly against my pussy, his face hovering over mine as he watches my consciousness slip away.

When morning comes, I'm always alone, gifted a few hours' peace where I can try to detangle my thoughts. My body wars with my mind as I peer in the vanity mirror and take stock of the marks the men have left. Fingertip bruises on my thighs, a deep hickey along the column of my throat, a flush across my chest, the remnants of last night still slick in the curve between my thigh and my sex.

A shiver rolls down my spine, my eyes delighting in the traces of them that remain. A body that's been touched—devoured—is a welcome sight.

But my stomach twists at the implications behind it. Their touch doesn't come free. This isn't a relationship, but an *ownership*. A way to claim my body as theirs and ward off others' attention.

To leave me alone with no one but them for comfort, and the comfort they provide is only skin-deep.

Something gold and gleaming on my dresser catches in the morning light. Even before turning my head, I know what it is. Still, I stare at the envelope like it's an unknown—like it could be anything else. I dream of other possibilities, imagining winter galas bathed in faux fur coats and glittering crystal curtains, or a new bride's luxurious wedding deep in the heart of snow-tipped mountain ranges, or perhaps a sudden, spur of the moment getaway vacation to the Bahamas where the sea and salt are my only company.

But the vision shifts every time, fading back into the grim reality of vaulted ceilings shrouded in darkness, masked dancers grinding their bodies against one another, deep crimson silks draped over beams and cascading down walls. I know what I'll find, because I've been there. *Midnight* is the dirtiest secret of the city—but once you've tasted it, once you've experienced the rush, it gets into your bloodstream.

Shit like that is hard to shake.

As I tear open the envelope and finger the thick cardstock inside, a rush of excitement washes over me. The rules of the club state that all guests must remain anonymous, utilizing code names and masks to remain secret to one another. That in itself is a thrill. It's easy to get caught up in that—the surreal atmosphere, the way everything feels like a dream. But now that my persona *Beauty* has been claimed by three mafia men, alongside that excitement comes dread.

Because in the light of day, only one truth remains: if I don't break free now, I'll be theirs forever.

Theirs to own.

Theirs to steal.

Theirs to break.

Chapter 3

Rage

There are few problems I can't solve with my fists. Taking things, breaking things... it's all the same, with the same result, as long as I get my hands dirty.

Things always go my way.

That's why Celia is an enigma. I've touched her. Tasted her. *Fucked her.* And yet... she still resists being mine.

I roll my shirt cuffs higher over my forearms, controlling my breathing as I ignore the pleading stare from the man strapped to the rickety metal chair in front of me. Jimmy's one of our worst men, stuck on the front lines doing grunt work that even a ten year old should be able to handle, yet somehow, he always manages to fuck up the job.

The only reason he isn't dead yet is because of some S-tier sheer fucking luck, but my patience is running thin. "I don't tolerate failure," I remind him, tilting my head to the side until my neck cracks with several short *pops*. "You know this, Jimmy."

If there weren't a gag in his mouth, I'd have to hear the same old whimpering sob story he tells me every time he ends up in the chair. His car broke down. He got mugged. His gun jammed. He ran out of ammo. His shoelace was untied. Different lies, same story.

There's only one part I care about: he didn't get the job done.

I level him with a stare that does exactly as it's intended: makes the man quake in his tiny fucking boots. "How many times are we gonna play this game, hm? How long has it been, now? Five, six years? No, that can't be right." Placing my hand on the back of his chair, I lean in close and get a good look at his eyes.

Clear as a summer sky. Sweaty in his armpits and across his shoulders, but that started when I entered the room, not before. Twitchy with his fingers, but he's always like that. He's still little more than half a shit stain wrapped in a body, but at least he's not huffing our product.

Jimmy recoils away from me, not that he can go far. The ropes binding his arms and legs to the metal chair creak as he shifts his weight. I'm used to this part, too, the part where he flinches like a little bitch when I close in.

Heat rushes from my chest to my throat, making it hard to swallow. There's always a part of me that *hates* men like Jimmy. Spineless, brainless, pieces of shit that do more harm than good. Still, this part is routine, too. I always get a little worked up when men don't face the consequences of their actions head on.

My next words are trapped behind the steel clench of my jaw. It takes genuine effort to unhinge and *breathe*. I must not do a good job of looking sane and sober, because Jimmy flinches again, harder this time. My temper flares hot. "If you've been fucking up that long…" I point my fingers at his temple and mimic placing a gun to his head. "Your brains would have splattered this wall a long fucking time ago, Jimmy." I dig my fingertips into his temple, twisting them as I push hard, *harder*, until he makes a choked, strangled sound in the back of his throat.

When I pull back, his skin's an angry red and his eyes bug out of his head, but it's not enough.

It never is.

The first punch lands square against his jaw. His head snaps back, a pained grunt pouring into the gag between his teeth. The second one reverberates up my arm, tingling my nerves in a shockwave that makes my jaw clench harder. On the third, his tooth splits the skin around my knuckles, and I *hate* him for it.

When I touch my girl later and see this stupid fucking cut from Jimmy's stupid fucking teeth, he'll be closer to her than he ever has the right to be.

And that makes me *livid*.

Despite my name, it's rare for me to lose control. To really *let go* and pummel my opponents with all of the fury I keep locked up tight. Ever since I was old enough to make a fist, I've been warned about the dangers of striking out in anger. My mother, in particular, tried to soothe the beast when it was still a cub thrashing against its cage. She used to brush her palms over my knuckles and murmur a soft *shh* against my temple, attempting to calm the creature within.

When she died, no one stepped up to take her place.

My inner beast quickly grew claws and teeth, earning me a reputation within the bratva as a brawler. A demon. Tearing through his targets with a ferocity that astounded even the oldest, hardest men within the bratva's ranks.

Most people pull their punches.

I learned early on how stupid that was.

The feel of Jimmy's face beneath my fist becomes a rhythm as consistent as the pulse in my veins. I don't stop, because I'm *angry*. It burns through my body like a poison, familiar in the way that it claims me much as I claim it. Harnessing that anger is what got me to where I am today: it's power as much as it is poison. Most people don't understand that. Anger is fuel. It's a weapon. A *friend*.

Jimmy moans, the sound as pathetic as he is. I sneer as I take in the swollen bruises all over his face, hideous and malformed and downright *revolting*. Just like he is. I loosen my fist and stretch my fingers, knowing that they're hot and bruised, too, as angry as I feel inside. "Fail me again, Jimmy," I warn, "and it won't be my fists kissing your face next time."

From the shadows in the back of the room, my brother Ruin emerges, slinking forward into the light. Jimmy can't see for shit with swollen eyelids and broken sockets, but he flinches anyway—they always do when Ruin appears from thin air. That's part of his charm, I suppose, the way he can pull the fear from people's hearts. It radiates from their bodies in this sickening cold that swallows the world whole in something bitter and gray.

If anger is my motivator, fear is my brother's. He eats that shit up with a cracked-out smile and a pleased hum in his throat.

Crazy bastard.

"Keep him alive," I remind Ruin, "but make sure he tells us everything. Go slow." There's zero chance that Jimmy isn't pulling some shit, and I need to know what it is before it blows up in our fucking faces.

Even shit stains like him can create ripples in the system if they thrash around long enough.

Ruin tears the gag from Jimmy's mouth. He likes to hear them scream.

"W-wait," Jimmy slurs, "I'll talk." When my brother grabs a pair of metal cutters, his voice pitches higher. "*I'll talk.*"

Sighing, I step aside and roll my shoulders back. Tension pulls in my back, and I grab the half-empty bottle of vodka from the table littered with various tools and instruments. Popping the cork, I chug a few swallows and let the burn settle over the thrum of rage still pulsing deep. It'll take a minute to rein it back in. Being around *fucking Jimmy* doesn't help. The whimpering alone is enough to make me wanna bash his skull in. "I know you will, Jimmy." I smack his cheek and grip tight, dragging his eyes back to mine. "You don't have a choice anymore."

I leave my brother to his work. We've been doing this long enough that he knows not to kill Jimmy too quickly —first, we need all the intel in his puny fucking brain, and *then* Ruin can carve him up all he wants.

There are five cells we've built into the basement beneath the club, each one a concrete box meant to hold prisoners for as long as we need. Collecting things—intel, money, bribes—is part of the business. Collecting *people* is part of it, too, and the reason for the raucous upstairs. I can hear the laughter as I bound up the stairs to the main level. Each step forces another cinch of my mask into place, burying the rage beneath a layer of charm and charisma a club owner needs to keep his cattle in check.

Dangle carrots, not guns, to appeal to the stock.

With Celia knowing my identity, *more or less*, I don't need to wear a physical mask tonight. The warm air upstairs is already tinged with the sting of booze and haze of cologne that comes with the party, and I dart into my family's private suite in the back to freshen up before Celia arrives.

I can't cover the bruises or cuts on my knuckles, but I dab them with antiseptic to keep them clean and wrap them in loose bindings. If Celia is observant, she'll notice —maybe even ask questions.

I won't lie to her about it if she does, but I'm hoping

it won't come to that. The last thing I want is *fucking Jimmy* on my mind when I'm with her.

As I swipe loose strands of hair from my eyes and slick them back into position, I catch a glimpse of myself in the mirror. Color has risen to my cheeks, stray flecks of Jimmy's blood dotting my arms and neck. Mutely, I wash them off at the sink, pat myself dry, and take a deep, sobering breath.

If Celia isn't already waiting for me at the front, she'll arrive any minute. I instructed Rebel to keep her occupied until I was finished downstairs, so if he has any fucking sense, he'll have listened and kept her away from the crowds. I'm not opposed to people seeing her—but if they touch one fucking hair on her head, they're fucking *dead*. I clench my jaw as an image of her smiling at a faceless man surfaces to the front of my mind.

She wouldn't dare.

Except...

I didn't visit her this morning, so I have no clue what kind of mood she's in. Will she be happy to see me? My chest swoops at the thought of her rushing to me, leaping up on her tiptoes to greet me with a kiss. *As it should be.* But knowing Celia, what I want isn't what she'll give me. She could be a moody bitch tonight. She could make everything smooth as fucking sandpaper solely because she's stubborn as hell and doesn't want to give in.

Even if she doesn't admit it, she's already mine.

We've been playing this back-and-forth game for weeks now, and although the resistance to my affections is expected, even appreciated at times, when we're in front of the club or the bratva, the last thing I want is a challenge.

I want a woman clinging to my arm—*begging* for my mouth on hers—with every goddamn breath she takes.

Instead, I have the most stubborn, resistant woman on the face of the earth.

If I can't keep my woman on my arm and her attitude in check, who will trust me to keep the club—and its surrounding streets—clamped tight in my fist? As archaic as the notion is about women being suppliant and subservient, there's a reason for it. People expect bratva women to serve their men and spread their legs —*willingly*.

Claiming Celia as my future bride makes sense to everyone except her. She's bratva-born and raised, despite her resistance to her family ties, and returning Celia to the fold will be the ultimate show of strength and stability that the bratva sorely needs after all the shit that went down with our *pakhan* and his queen.

We need to show that the Baranova Bratva is unified, strong, and not a force to be fucking messed with.

Which is why my future wife *has* to be Celia.

She's the most resilient woman I fucking know.

So when I push through the back doors and spot her across the room with her arm looped through another man's, at first, I'm grateful that Rebel is doing his job. But then she laughs, tipping her head back to reveal the column of her throat, and squeezes the man's bicep.

She isn't usually that receptive to any of my brothers.

Rebel is grinning down at her in that wolfish way men do when they find something pretty they think they can devour, but the cut of his jaw is all wrong. I step closer to find that his shoulders are too bulky and broad, then his legs too tall, and his suit too loose. His grip on her waist is too polite, even, with how gentle he's holding her. He's being careful. Claiming her in a show of light touches and lingering conversation, but not *claiming her* like Rebel would. My younger brother would snake his arms around her waist and bury his face in her neck for the thrill of having her all to himself.

The man on Celia's arm is *not* my brother.

And he's touching what's *mine*.

Both of my fists curl as I storm across the room, determined to cut them off. They've begun following the steady trail of people heading to the playrooms at the back of the club—likely intending to join the fray.

The mere idea of another man than me or my brothers undressing Celia, paying her compliments, eying her perfect skin, touching the swell of her cheek or worse, *actually fucking kissing her*, sends me into a fury stronger than *fucking Jimmy's* pathetic whimpering ever could.

If we're playing a game to see whose lap she'll sit on tonight, willingly or otherwise, there's only one possible victor, and he's standing right fucking here. Convincing the room—and the idiot hooked to her side—is the easy part. Convincing *Celia* that she's mine, however, is the challenge.

But I know one thing for certain: failure isn't a fucking option. Celia Monrovia will understand not only that she's *mine*, but she'll know what that means by the end of the night.

No matter how much it fucking hurts to swallow.

Chapter 4

Celia

The last thing I'm expecting at the stroke of midnight is for a limo to idle on the street in front of my house. It sits there for an entire minute, the exhaust curling in the air, bright headlights beaming down the empty lane. I stare at it from my front window for a long time, knowing that it's lost. It *has* to be on the wrong street. At the wrong house. *On the wrong planet.*

Because there's no way in hell that a *limo* is picking me up for a scandalous night at a sex club.

But then the back door opens and a man pops out. Not just any man, but a *huge* one. Despite the chilly winter air, he's wearing a short-sleeved t-shirt and jeans, as unbothered by the cold as a bear preparing for hibernation. A tuft of dark chest hair peeks out the collar of his shirt, and when his gaze lands on me—or more likely, the house—I imagine sharp canines and glowing orange eyes to complete the look. It only takes him one second to make a decision, suddenly pushing himself up the arched driveway that meets my front walkway, then up the three tiny porch steps that meet my front door. He disappears from view as he knocks on the door.

I stand motionless at the window, because umm —*what the fuck?*

"Celia Monrovia," the man rumbles, his voice deep enough that my breath catches, "I know you're in there."

My heartbeat kicks into overdrive. I open my mouth but no sound comes out. This must be what hyperventilating feels like. My body starts to shake, and my breaths turn into these tiny little puffs of air. "I need—"

The man pounds his fist against the door, and I picture those bright, orange eyes flashing.

"—a minute!"

"We don't *have* a minute, princess," the stranger growls. "We're late."

Drawing up every ounce of strength I have, I force my feet to move toward the door. Unlocking the deadbolt, I pop it open and the man shoves it open wider with the flat of his palm. His eyes lock onto my dress first —a jet black, lacy number that dips low in the front *and* the back—and his scowl, already cutting across his face, somehow digs deeper. "You're wearing *that*?"

A flash of hot embarrassment whips inside my chest. I bought this dress after my divorce finalized—something sultry and seductive and *new.* The opposite of what I used to wear. "What's wrong with my dress?" I brush my palms down the sides, fingering the high slit up my thigh. My heartbeat throbs under the bear's intense stare.

Not orange eyes like I imagined—but a deep, mahogany brown.

"Are my panties showing?" I didn't actually check if they were visible. Carefully, I spin in a tight circle and let the skirt swish around my legs, the click of my heels helping settle my nerves.

If there's one thing I understand in life, it's fashion. The way a dress hugs a woman's body should be intimate, and I tailored this dress to perfection the moment I bought it, spending hours earlier this afternoon adjusting those alterations now that I've gone up a few sizes since the divorce. My boobs are bigger, my hips wider, my thighs thicker. I had to undo the cinches I originally made in the waistline, and I was self-conscious about it with each pull of the needle.

But you know what?

I still look *damn* good.

It's enough to make me laugh, full and bitter, as I shake my hair loose from the bun behind my head. It cascades down my back in a tumble of soft curls that I *know* look and smell amazing.

After all, *looks* are what I do for a living, so *fuck* this guy's opinion. "I know I look good," I huff, grabbing my clutch from the side table and shoving it against his chest, "or else your jaw wouldn't be on the fucking floor."

Truthfully, his jaw is clenched so tightly that his teeth might crack from the pressure, but the remark hits its target. As his neck flushes an angry red and his pulse point throbs obscenely fast, for a split second, it's almost like Rage is standing in front of me. But that isn't quite right—this man is taller, broader, with way more muscles and a few years of experience on Rage. Silver hair peppers his temples, and the wrinkles around his mouth are clearly from frowning way too often to be healthy. A scar cuts through both of his lips from top to bottom on the right side, curving around his chin until it tapers off over the bend.

Our eyes meet and although this man isn't Rage, I can see the resemblance. "Are you Rage's dad?"

His dark eyes narrow and his glare turns venomous. "Get in the car, princess."

It's my turn to glare. "*Princess?*"

He grabs my wrist and pulls me through the door, slamming it shut behind us. I stumble down the steps as he drags me along behind him, walking way too fast for the heels strapped to my feet. I'll break an ankle at this rate. As we approach the dip of the driveway and the long, arching walk down the hill to the street, I pull him back with all my strength. "Hey, wait—"

My heel catches and I tumble forward, my heart leaping to my throat.

I haven't fallen down in years, especially not in heels.

I shut my eyes to brace myself for the impact, but when I don't feel the stinging pain of concrete scrapes or rattled bones, I pry them back open to find the bear staring back at me.

Storm clouds. A thousand shades of gold rolling into each other, all at once separate but whole. Chaos contained. The buildup before the thunder or the downpour of rain.

A shiver runs down my spine as the stranger breaks our gaze to stare at my feet. No, *glare* at them. With a grunt, he loops his arm behind my knees and lifts me into the air, holding me tight to his chest as he barrels down my driveway to the limo still idling in wait for us. "We're *late*," he repeats, even surlier than the first time he said it. He cracks the car door open with one hand and thrusts my body inside head-first, tossing me through the air to the nearest bench seat. The bounce, while not exactly painful, knocks my brain around my skull.

I choke on a *scream* as my blood boils. "Who the hell do you think you are?" If Rage finds out he handled me like this—

I nearly scream a second time. There's no way in hell I'm broaching *that* subject with an egomaniac like Rage.

The bear-man ducks inside and shuts the door, taking the seat furthest from me before rapping his knuckles on the opaque divider between us and the driver. The limo lurches ahead—I didn't even know a luxury vehicle could do that—as we peel away from my street and off into the city. Even though I'm not blindfolded for the journey, I might as well be because the windows are blacked out. I can't see a damned thing. The window controls are useless, too, clicking without actually working.

I'm being treated like a child—a *secret love child* being ferried from one underground bunker to the next.

"If you're Rage's dad, you did a shit job raising him." I lift my hair from my neck and fan myself, my temper making my body flare hot. "He's an asshole, but at least now I know where he gets it from."

The man ignores me, staring at the blacked out windows like he can see the future within his reflection. His jaw tics and he folds his hands in his lap, grasping them tightly together. Scars crisscross his knuckles, tearing through weathered, black and grey tattoos that wrap around his fingers and across the backs of his palms. Definitely older than Rage, but just as angry as him.

The apple doesn't fall far from the tree.

"You know, he manhandles me like that too." I rub my wrist where this guy pulled me after him, soothing the aching skin with the pads of my thumbs. "Pushes me around. Puts his hands on my—" I cut myself off from saying *ass*, but I could say a lot of body parts, and it would all be true.

Rage touches me *everywhere*.

The sound Rage's dad makes is a pained, whining twinge in his throat. "Why are you telling me this?"

I shrug one shoulder and tug the hair still bunched in my hands. "You should feel bad that you created a monster."

Rage's dad exhales slowly, pulling his eyes away from the window to stare at my outstretched foot. The strap of one of my heels broke in the struggle down the driveway, its buckle useless now. I dig the heel into the floor and pry it off my foot, kicking it across the limo. It clunks against the leather seat and bounces back to the floor.

Slowly, the man lifts his gaze inch by inch up my body, starting with the burgundy polish on my toes, over the curve of my calf, up the length of my newly-shaved thigh, to the spot where my skin meets the hem of my dress. His gaze lingers there while his lips move. "I'm not Rage's father."

My cheeks flush, the unwelcome lump in my throat making it hard to swallow. "Oh."

He stares at my thigh for another heartbeat before reaching for a compartment in the base of his bench seat, next to where he's seated. After a moment of rustling through whatever's inside the secret compartment, he pulls out a pair of heels strapped together. They're identical to mine—black, low to the ground—but with a slightly thinner heel. The arch of the shoe still holds that layer of gloss that screams *new*, the designer's metallic gold logo glinting in the light. Brand fucking new. He unclasps them from each other and sets one on the bench beside him. "But you're right." The golden storm in his eyes turns dark. "Rage's dad *is* a bastard. That, unfortunately, passed to all of his sons." He exhales heavily, his gaze returning to my bare foot. "Lift your foot." Patting his thigh—his *very thick* thigh—he invites me to set it down on top of him.

I shouldn't give this stranger any part of me.

But I hold my foot over his thigh anyway, and he gently sweeps the heel into place and clasps three tiny, bright red buckles. They stand out against the black but go well with my polish, and when I straighten my foot to admire the look of them together, I catch the red sole of the shoe.

Expensive heels.

That, I can appreciate.

We follow the same motions with my other foot, but before he clasps the heel in place a second time, he thumbs the arch of my foot in a way that makes my eyes roll back, a moan building in my chest. I twitch against his hold and bite my lip as he does it again. His hands are rough against my skin, calloused from years of use doing God knows what, but *holy shit*, do I *so* not care.

He's giving my pedicurist a run for her money.

The scar on his lips pulls as they twitch, but as soon as I think he's going to crack a smile, he shuts it down. Dropping my foot without bothering to clasp the final strap, he glares—first at my foot, then burning a trail up my body, his scowl deepening with each passing second.

I clasp the damn strap myself. "What's your problem?"

His glare snaps up to my face. He chews on his response for a few seconds before choosing to ignore my question and pulls something from his back pocket. Tossing it my direction, he folds his arms across his broad chest and turns his icy stare out the window.

I lift the strip of fabric and roll my eyes.

It's a fucking blindfold.

"I'm *not* putting this on." I mirror his posture, crossing my arms over my chest.

He clenches his jaw. "Put it on."

"No."

Sighing, he pinches the bridge of his nose. "If you don't put that on, I can't take you inside. You know the rules."

The rules state that I'm supposed to be transported with my eyes covered and wrists bound the entire time. A limo ride and personal pick up, no matter how surly the escort, is definitely beyond the realm of *normal procedure*. "I think we're a little past the rules, don't you?"

"Some rules can be bent. Not this one. Put the blindfold on, Celia."

I wind the fabric around my fingers. "What happens if I don't?"

A muscle in his jaw tics. "Then you'll find out how well I can tie knots." He glances over at me. "Because I won't be bending *any* of the rules."

∽

My grumpy chauffeur disappears as soon as he ushers me inside the club. He pulls the blindfold from my eyes with a snap of his wrist then disappears into the crowd, blending in easily with all of the other well-dressed guests. After anticipating seeing Rage again, I'm expecting him to be waiting for me the moment I step out of the limo.

In the end, I'm left completely alone—but that's exactly what I want.

I need time to enact my plan for the night.

Shaking off what happened in the limo is easy the moment I take my first step into the room. The heels are sublime. I'll admit it. They fit like a glove and have just enough cushion that I know I won't blister by the end of the night, no matter how new they are, and I can tell by the glances I'm getting that they're doing their job.

I'm drop-dead gorgeous in these fucking things.

I smile at whoever glances in my direction before realizing that I need to be selective. I don't want just *anyone's* attention—I need an alpha. Someone who threatens Rage's self-proclaimed authority over me. But most importantly, it needs to be someone who simply *isn't him*.

I keep an eye out as I wander the room, familiarizing myself with not only the landscape, but the people as well. Part of me looks for my best friend Lilith, hoping for an anchor to keep me steady throughout the night, but deep down, I know that if I find her, I'll have to steer clear. She has more questions than answers about how Rage and Rebel tag-teamed me in the middle of this very room at the last event, and I don't want to give her *more* fuel for her inevitable interrogation.

No, I can't cling to what's familiar and safe tonight. I need to be daring. I need to not only step out of my comfort zone, but leap way the hell over the line.

A stranger notices me from the side of the room, but I quickly turn away. I need to be the one taking initiative. I need to pick someone—*anyone*—that fits the agenda.

Someone who not only makes Rage mad, but *really* pisses him the hell off. Someone who threatens Rage's masculinity by simply existing.

I spin around to head back toward the bar when I stumble into someone, their cologne instantly washing over me. It's a deep, woodsy scent—not too much alcohol, not too in-your-face, but just the right kind of scent that screams decent money.

One glance at his chiseled jawline and a quick squeeze of his bicep seals the deal. He's the one.

I fake stumbling into him, square against his chest. "Oh! I'm so sorry." I put on a small smile as he catches me, his hands falling to my waist. *Bingo.* "I wasn't looking where I was going. Lost in the lights, and all." I wind my fingers around the collar of his shirt and pull myself up, tugging him down closer to me at the same time. The crisp, white dress shirt with the first three—no, four—buttons undone, and an exposed triangle of tanned skin that *begs* to be touched makes this seduction even easier. He *wants* to be noticed. "Thank you for saving me."

The surprise on his face quickly melts into charm. "It's my pleasure, beautiful. Are you new here? It can be a lot to take in your first time."

I'm not new, exactly, but he doesn't need to know that.

"It's my first time," I lie, biting my bottom lip. "I'm a little nervous."

His hand wraps around mine and pulls it to his lips. I pray he gets a big whiff of my perfume—I put on a special pheromone blend for the night. If I can dance with this man, maybe kiss him a little, then Rage, Rebel, and Ruin can get an eyeful of what Beauty looks like when she's *not* theirs to torment.

"Maybe I can help with that. Would you like to join

me for the night? I can show you around, give you a tour."

"That would be wonderful! Your date won't mind?"

Doesn't hurt to check if I have competition for his attention.

He shakes his head. "I'm all yours tonight. What's your name?"

I introduce myself as Beauty, while he tells me his name is Goliath.

My laugh is genuine. "I can't imagine what they were thinking, giving you that codename. I'm sure you know how the story goes. Goliath was taken out by a single stone. You don't seem like you'd go down so easily."

The curve to his lips mirrors the glint in his eye. A hint of wickedness that somehow feels like a promise. "Trust me, whoever decides the names for these events does their homework. I haven't met a single person whose name didn't fit." He inclines his head toward me. "Yours is spot on, gorgeous."

My chest tightens, my smile following suit. I know what he sees—I'm good at dolling myself up. I always have been. Perfect, silky hair flowing past my shoulders, the glint of diamonds catching in the light and bringing the eye to the tip of my cleavage. Long legs, high cheekbones, warm brown eyes highlighted with a stripe of glitter and smoke with a killer winged eyeliner—I'm a fucking package. I always have been, truth be told. I'm used to being beautiful.

I used to believe it, too, but now I'm not so sure.

The things we put on display can't all be truths. Lies

are woven throughout every image, every persona, because the truth is often much uglier than we ever want to admit.

Goliath gives me a charming smile that, once upon a time, would have made my knees go weak. But now, I see it for what it is: another front, *another lie*. I understand it, because when I smile back, I'm doing the exact same.

Playing the game.

"Let's get you a drink." He leads me to the bar, where he downs a bourbon in record time, and I have a straight shot of vodka. His eyebrows shoot up when he sees me take the shot without flinching.

I have two more before the alcohol really kicks in.

"You're good at that."

Embarrassment makes me blush. "I'm Russian," I explain, "vodka's like water to us."

"Russian, huh? I'd started to think that there were only Russian men in the city. I've yet to meet a Russian woman since I moved here."

"Maybe you're looking in the wrong places."

He licks his lips, crystal blue eyes traveling down my body. "Maybe I found the best one."

Warmth pools in my belly, but it's the alcohol talking, not Goliath. Drinking while on a mission isn't the best idea, but neither is hooking up with strangers in a secret club in the first place. I'm 0 for 2 in this place.

"Dance with me?" I slide my palm up Goliath's forearm. "I won't trip this time, I promise."

His hand finds my hip. "Our tour isn't over. This is just the first stop."

Impatience pricks my skin like needles. I didn't want this to take all night. I need Rage to see me having a good time with another man, that's it. "Can't it wait? I'd really like to dance."

Goliath leans closer, even though I can hear him just fine from where he's standing. "Look around. Do you see many people dancing?"

I glance up and scan the room. Although a few couples and throuples are moving to the beat on the ballroom floor, most of them are flocking to the sets of doors at the left side of the room. The crowd is thinner than the last time I was here, making me feel more vulnerable and exposed than before. Especially because I'm with a stranger.

"What's over there?" I ask, staring as people disappear into the side rooms. Neon lights shine brightly overhead, including one of those curvy script signs reading *The Playroom* in hot pink. I have a feeling I know what's behind those closed doors, but I play dumb. "Is that a show or something?"

"Something like that."

I like Goliath's evasive answer even less than the lingering hand on my hip. "Tell me what it is."

He slips his hand in mine and tugs me away from the bar without paying. "Why don't I show you instead? If you don't like it, we can come back out to dance."

My heartbeat picks up tempo. If Rage, Rebel, and Ruin run this club—which I suspect they do—there's no telling what's on the other side of those doors. I'm expecting copious amounts of sex from a name like *The*

Playroom, but it could be anything. A burlesque show, a torture room, group showers, *golden* showers, you name it. Maybe each night has a different theme.

The notion that any of those boys would be scheduling strip teases and themed group events is damn near hilarious, though.

Determination keeps me glued to Goliath's side as we cross the room. The hairs on the back of my neck stand at attention the closer we get to our destination, and a pit in my stomach weighs me down. Heat and fire lick at my heels, spurring me to walk faster, as I realize how dangerous this really is. Playing with these brothers' vices, their desires. They won't take kindly to me playing with another man outside our little foursome.

My heart races as the back of my neck tingles. It's just a feeling of unease, like the churn of my stomach, but now more than ever I *feel* that I'm being watched.

As Goliath and I reach the doors to the Playroom, I can hear someone approaching from behind—*fast*. Heavy footfalls thud across the hardwood, making me flinch before I can catch myself. If Goliath notices, he doesn't react, reaching for the door handle to usher us inside.

He never makes it.

Strong arms wrap around my waist and pull me back, out of Goliath's grip. Rage's voice rumbles in my ear, low enough that only I can hear. "Find something you like, Beauty?" He palms my stomach greedily, twisting the soft fabric of my dress against his hands, before raising his palm to cup my breast. Squeezing, he exhales hot against my neck. "You look fucking gorgeous, and instead of wrapping that tight little body on *my* arm, I find you with—" he breaks off with a snarl—"*someone fucking else.*"

His body shakes with anger, his hands rough as he feels me up. My breath catches as he kneads pain into my muscle and bone, one hand crushing my hip, the other slipping past the deep V of my neckline to palm my naked tit. Heat blossoms deep within me, and I recoil from the sensation, from the way he makes me feel.

Tight. Hot. Aching.

Goliath turns then, his face pure surprise as he realizes I'm no longer standing beside him. His smile freezes on his face as his gaze lands on me, then on Rage, and finally on the two of us together. "Excuse me," he snaps, voice turning cold in an instant, "that's *my* date."

Bile rises to the back of my throat at the thought of *another* man claiming me so easily. I suppose it's my fault—I'm the one who led him on. *But still*, I'm not some shiny toy to pass around and shove your dick into when you get bored. Anger flares inside my chest, but it gets caught in my throat as I choke on a needy, pained whine, Rage's knuckles pinching my nipple *hard*. Stars dance in the corners of my eyes, and I have to grab Rage's arm banded around my stomach to stay upright.

The sharp points of Rage's teeth scrape against the side of my throat. "Yours? Because she feels like *mine.*" He growls, something deep and menacing unlocking inside his chest.

Goliath visibly pales. "Hey, man, my bad. I didn't know she already had someone."

Rage barks a laugh, making me flinch. "Oh, she has someone. Three someones, actually. But right now, she's mine and mine alone, and you fucking *touched her*." He clicks his tongue against his teeth. "In *my* club. On *my* floor." His grip tightens, and I cry out at the force of it. Sharp pain drills down into my hip and shoots into my chest, both of his hands squeezing. At the sound, presses a kiss to my temple but doesn't lighten his grip.

I know I'll have bruises the exact size and shape of his hands.

Goliath looks over our shoulders, his throat clicking as he swallows. "I, um, I didn't mean—I'm gonna go," he says lamely, already sidestepping away from us. But he only takes one step before Rage lunges for him, shoving me against another hard body as he slams his fist into Goliath's face.

A scream catches in my throat, my heart pumping on overdrive.

"Easy there, beautiful," a voice purrs in my ear. A new set of arms wrap around my waist, but this man is at ease behind me, locking me in without the show of force Rage used. He hums as he holds me, kissing the hickey on my neck from yesterday. "Missed you today."

My body trembles with a rush of relief. *Rebel*. The most sane one of them all. I grab his hand and hold on tight, unable to tear my gaze away from the way Rage's body moves. The muscles in his shoulders ripple as he throws Goliath to the ground. The muscles in his forearms are flexed, his fists tight, as he stomps on Goliath's leg to keep him from scrambling away.

While Rage's victim howls in pain, Rebel chuckles in my ear.

"Buckle up, baby. Rage is gonna fight for every—" Rebel kisses my neck—"last—" slides his warm hand inside the slit on my skirt—"inch—" and pants in my ear —"of you."

A moan falls from my lips as Rebel slips his fingers inside my panties, but it's not his touch that I'm focused on.

It's Rage. The roar of his anger touches mine, breathing new life into my body, making my blood warm and my heart race. I was already strung out on nerves and adrenaline, but *this*—this is something different, something more primal, something more dangerous.

Because while I should be revolted by how Rage touches me like he owns me, it's the way he moves with such conviction and confidence as he beats the shit out of someone who touched me that reaches the deepest scars around my heart and *squeezes*.

This isn't a man staking his claim for all the world to witness.

It's the promise of him keeping it.

Chapter 5

Rebel

Rage likes to talk big about responsibility and our duty to the bratva. I get it—the man's spent over a decade climbing the ranks of power. When you're in that deep, it's hard not to be a *yes man* to whatever the boss asks. Running a club like *Midnight* comes from one of those *yes, sir* moments with our *pakhan*. It fronts as a VIP exclusive, sexy rager of a party, but we funnel various things through our clientele like drugs or dirty money. Rage thinks this place is our responsibility, a repayment toward the organization that took us in when we were unruly teenagers left to fend for ourselves.

But *this man* right here, the one knocking his fists into some other guy's teeth, is the one I recognize. Not the guy who's responsible and loyal and all that other boring shit, but the one who will snap someone's neck for looking at us funny, who wields his body like the weapon he's spent years at the gym creating.

Violence is a language of its own—and Rage is fucking fluent.

Our girl's cheeks flush deep crimson as she stares at my older brother. I understand that, too. He's fucking ripped on account of how often he pumps iron, building muscles in places that should be illegal. His dress shirt pulls across his shoulders with each swing of his arm, and it's a shame that the damn thing won't rip apart.

Because our girl? She's *salivating*.

"Like what you see?" I tease, humming in her ear. Celia is wet as *fuck*, already drenching her panties. My fingers glide smoothly over her clit, and she gasps, clutching my forearm tightly. She shakes her head, sending a wave of her sweet conditioner into my face, and I inhale *deep*. Spending my evenings with her has given me a hard-on for all things *Celia*, including the fucking smell of her hair. What was the name of that bottle, again? *Passionate Peach?* I make a mental note to check her shower the next time I'm digging through her bathroom.

"He's a—*oh god*," she keens, tossing her head back onto my shoulder. There's this little divot between her eyebrows as she worries her lip between her teeth.

I chuckle as I press the flat of my fingertip against her clit, feeling it pulse. "Well, I wouldn't call him *that*—it'll go straight to his head." She buries her face in my neck, but I click my tongue. "No, baby, you can't hide. Not from this. *Look.*" I have to remove my hand from her panties—a fucking *travesty*—to reach up and grab her chin. I turn her face back toward Rage so that we can watch the masterpiece unfold. "It's a work of art, you know. The way he moves. Watch how he overpowers the other guy."

Rage has flipped the man onto his back and stomped on his fingers, no doubt breaking a few of them, but what draws my attention isn't the poor man suffering a beat-down, it's the total domination my brother has over him. That's what I want Celia to focus on, too. "Look at how strong he is, Celia. He's a protector. He's keeping you safe from bad men." I nod toward Rage, watching as he kicks the guy's side, likely bruising a vital organ or something. He kneels, pushing his knee into his victim's chest to keep him pressed flat to the floor, and returns to punching the guy's face. I'll have to step in soon, but for now, I brush my fingers over the column of Celia's throat, admiring how warm she is to the touch.

"He *is* the bad guy," she chokes out, struggling to free herself from my hold. "That other guy wasn't going to do anything."

I scoff. "You can be pretty all you want, Celia, but you *have* to be smart. He was going to take you into the Playroom and fuck you raw even if you begged him not to. Is that what you wanted? Some random guy's dick tearing into your sweet, soft cunt?" The thought of it makes my taste go sour. "He wouldn't have cared if you said no or fought him off. I bet he has STDs too." My lip curls. I have no idea if any of this is true, but it feels true enough.

Any man who isn't me or my brothers is a threat to

Celia's wellbeing, and they're fucking scum no matter what they do.

Celia shakes her head. "You're wrong. The only man forcing himself on me is Rage." A shiver runs down her body as she whispers a small *and you.*

This is the closest I've come to Celia's pussy—*ever.* I'm nearly offended at the insinuation that my hand buried between her velvet thighs is *normal* for us, but, well, not offended enough to care. I haven't asked Rage what he does when he visits her in the mornings, but I would know if he were fucking her. He'd have this post-sex glow that's impossible to ignore by the sheer fucking magnitude of his ego. But I might as well ask—"has he fucked you, Celia?"

She squirms in my arms. "Not since that first night, no."

Ah, she means the first time she came to *Midnight.* She wanted all three of us then—a drastic change to her attitude now. It's like she got her first taste and decided we weren't what she wanted after all. But that's too fucking bad, because she made addicts out of the three of us. We can't go back.

Neither can she.

Even if she denies it, I've seen the way she looks at me, like she's one second away from jumping my bones. I like to think that it's because of my charm and sex appeal, but I'd be an idiot to discount my brothers' hands in her desire. *Literally.* If they're getting her off without shoving their dicks inside of her, it's no wonder the girl is cock-starved.

But if she had tried to fuck any one of us, we would have let her. So why the hell did she approach someone at the club instead?

"You know that *this*—" I dig my boner into her ass— "is all yours, baby. Why go after someone else?" I glare at the sack of meat on the floor. He wouldn't get her off before himself, that's for damn sure. It's like Celia was trying to piss us off—

Ah.

"It wasn't about sex," I realize, grinning. "You don't actually want to fuck him."

The relief I feel is surprising, but I don't focus on it for too long. The man on the ground has stopped moving and groaning, which means it's time for Rage to stop fucking his shit up. "Brother," I call out, shuffling closer with Celia, "turn around. She's right here waiting for you."

Celia jerks her head back and digs her nails into my arms to try and pry me loose, but although I'm not as strong as Rage, I'm still stronger than her. I can hold her down just as easily as my brothers—or, well, close enough. They may have the muscles, but I have the stamina to outlast them all.

"I am *not* waiting for him!"

It's like her voice breaks Rage out of a daze. He rises to his feet and turns toward us, his body coiled tight, and closes what little distance remains. His hands are the first part of him to touch our Beauty as he cups her face. The bruising along his swollen knuckles stands out against her honeyed skin. When he brushes his thumbs over her cheeks, he leaves smears of blood in their wake. He exhales harshly as he stares into her eyes, and without warning, he slams his body into hers—*ours*—and claims her mouth as his own.

She makes this outraged sound, but he swallows it down with a groan of his own. My arms are stuck between their bodies with no hope of pulling them free, so I do what I do best: I meddle.

"Let him in, beautiful. He needs you."

Her body goes rigid, and I try not to roll my eyes. They're both wound tight like they're the ones fighting each other, when all they need to do is give in. My hands are locked in place, so I kiss the curve of her neck instead of running them down her body like I desperately want to.

There's a creamy fucking pussy waiting for my touch.

"I know you like how strong he is," I murmur, licking salt from her skin. "Touch him, baby, feel his strength. Put your hand on him."

When she moves her arm, it's a stiff, jerking motion, but her hand lands on his bicep.

"Good, now rub his muscles. They worked so hard to protect you."

I know that Rage wasn't in full protection mode like I'd told her—he was staking his claim as much as anything. Making a point to the club—and to Celia— that she's off-limits. But in the end, he still saved her from a lousy-ass time getting fondled by some rich dude with too much pride and not enough sense. She has to understand that. We are here for her in every possible way, and I don't even know what those all are yet. I just know that it's true.

We'd do damn near anything for this girl.

I don't think she's learned that lesson, though.

Celia follows my instructions, however, rubbing her palm up and down Rage's arm in these slow, hard, tense strokes, and as his muscles relax, so does her touch. Their kiss shifts before my eyes, becoming less like two walls slamming together. They soften in tiny increments, first with their touch, then with their kiss. He reins in some of his residual anger and softens his kiss, and she parts her lips to meet him. Her hand travels up his arm to his broad shoulders, and he slides his bruised fingers into her hair.

My cock is rock fucking hard wedged against her ass. I could cut diamonds with this fucking thing. A ripple of jealousy for my brother makes it hard to swallow, but I know I'll get my turn. First, they need to work out whatever the hell is going on between them, or else Ruin and I don't stand a chance.

Rage could ruin this entire operation before we've even started running with it.

For now, all I can do is encourage the two of them. "That's it, baby, doesn't that feel good?"

She moans, and *god,* do I wish it were for me.

They kiss for a few heated minutes, until finally Rage pulls away. There's this dazed look in his eyes, almost like he hasn't gotten enough sleep. Celia is heavy in my arms, and I push her into my brother's. "Take her," I tell him, "and be gentle."

I don't think he knows how to be gentle, but he needs to try. Just like she needs to stop fighting him so damn much.

The spell breaks over both of them the minute I release her, and she backpedals into my chest. "I'm not going anywhere with him," she declares, an edge to her voice that I thought Rage had kissed out of her.

Rage responds in kind, his jaw clenching as hard as his fists. "Yes you are. You're mine for the night."

"I don't belong to anyone!" Celia pushes away from both of us. "That's the fucking point! I get to choose who I'm with, and I'm sure as hell not choosing the two of you!"

"It's too fucking late for that," Rage hisses, "because you *already* chose us. Or do you need a reminder of what that looks like?" All the tenderness in his gaze sharpens in an instant, the little lovestruck smile on his face replaced with something sinister. "Yeah, I think you do."

Celia backpedals straight into our youngest brother, Ruin. She shrieks as she collides with his chest, suddenly blocked on three sides. I don't know when Ruin arrived to our little party, but he appeared at the perfect moment, like he always does. The fucker has a knack for timing.

"Put her on her knees." Rage snaps open his belt with a jerk of his wrist. "She can choke on my cock until the lesson sinks in."

"You'll blow your load before then," I warn, shivering as excitement *zings* down my spine. It's like electricity whenever Celia gets her mouth on you. I know for a fact that Rage will come way too soon if she puts in the work. Hell, even if she *doesn't*. The man is strung so tight that an accidental graze might set him off.

But I know the look in his eye; this isn't about busting a nut. It's about the promise we made to each other, right here on the dance floor. Celia may not realize that she made a promise that night she declared she was ours, but she will after this.

As Rage unzips his fly and shoves his pants over his hips, he continues the micro-lecture he's probably been practicing all day. "Promises are kept in this family, and you made a promise, *krosotka*." He drops the waistband of his boxers beneath his ballsack, cradling both it and his cock for maximum leverage.

Celia's eyes widen as she stares at his dick. I'm not sure if she's seen it before, but she sure as hell is seeing it now. "I'm not part of your family!" She fights Ruin's grip on her shoulders as he pushes her down to her knees, the *thud* of bone on hardwood loud enough to gather a few stares.

We had already attracted an audience with the sudden beat-down, but now we're attracting even hungrier gazes. Since we're right beside the Playroom, we also catch those leaving for refreshments or fresh air—meaning, all eyes are *literally* on us.

My blood pulses hard through my veins, making my cock twitch. *Fuck.* I want her to suck *me* off. Fuckfuckfuck. I study her position to see if I can snake my way into there, but between Ruin's death grip on her shoulders and Rage's cock smacking against her cheek, there's little room for me.

A familiar grunt from over my shoulder makes me bark out a laugh on account of how surprised I am to hear it. My oldest brother isn't actually Rage—it's Thanatos, our half-brother. He's the last person I expected to find down here. He hates the club. It was an act of God that he agreed to picking Celia up tonight. "Come to watch our pretty girl get on her knees?" I lick my lips as Rage fists Celia's hair and presses his cock against the seam of her lips.

She isn't letting him in.

"She looks good, doesn't she?" I hum appreciatively, palming my dick through my jeans. She always looks good, but on her knees like that, with a pretty pink flush trailing down her neck and across the swell of her tits? She's a fucking *vision*.

If even Thanatos can see that, then all hope isn't lost for him, after all. The perpetual bachelor is picky as fuck about his women. Says they're too clingy, like he's some kind of cat that only wants petted every few days.

Fuck *that*.

Celia can pet me all fucking day and night.

Finally, Rage breaks past Celia's jaw and slides his cock into her mouth. He goes straight for the throat, making her eyes bulge. Shit, he's going rough from the start. I spare Than a quick smile before stepping closer. If Rage keeps going like that, he'll choke her until she passes out.

As I kneel beside our girl, I glance up at my brothers

and admire the view. Rage to her front. Ruin at her back. Me, on one side, and Than on the other.

It's not what usually constitutes as family, but hey, that normal bullshit is overrated anyway.

As Celia struggles to breathe, I brush my hand over her hair and tell her how good of a job she's doing, and *fuck,* this whole scenario is gonna make me come. In two seconds flat, I'm convinced—*nothing* can top coaching your girl through swallowing your brother's dick.

Normal is so fucking overrated.

Chapter 6

Celia

A RINGING in my ears drowns out the rest of the room. The whispers coming from all sides. The steady clicking of heels as people draw closer. The heat of Ruin's hands on my shoulders, pinning me down. All at once, my senses go into overdrive and it's like I can feel everything, from the bass pulsing through the floorboards to the heat radiating from the salty tip of Rage's cock as he pushes it against my lips. The ringing helps—it gives me something sharp to focus on.

My scalp burns as Rage tightens his grip on my hair and thrusts his hips, scraping his cock against my teeth.

"*Open up,*" he grinds out, jaw clenched even tighter than when he found me with another man. In fact, that's how I would describe Rage to anyone listening to the woman forced on her knees. *Tighter. Harder. Crueler.* Somehow, this rejection stings him even more than the first.

If it's a game of egos that these brothers play, Rage is winning by a landslide.

The brief moment when we kissed—*really* kissed, without all the anger in the way—he seemed... different. Calmer. *Gentle.*

But there's nothing gentle about the flash of his teeth as he bares them at me, or the yank of his fingers in my hair, or the *smack* of his cock against my cheek, my lips, my nose.

It's humiliating, being on display. I don't know how I found power in it before, because this?

This is *cruel*.

Rage hisses, bumping his cock against my teeth a third time. "Open *up*, Celia."

I shake my head, ignoring the sharp spike of pain behind my eyes, and press my lips tighter together. Glaring at him, I hope he gets the hint.

Over my dead fucking body.

A shudder rolls down Rage's spine, subtle enough that I barely catch it. He inhales once, quickly, and holds it. Seconds pass as we stare at one another, until finally, he licks his lips and rocks on his heels. "You taste good, you know," he rasps, thrusting into the soft pillow of my cheek. "Every morning, you taste like peaches at first. Sweet and soft on my lips." Groaning, he strokes his thick shaft with his free hand. "But then comes the *cream*. You get so wet for me, Beauty, and you taste even better at the end. Less sweet..." He bites his bottom lip as he strokes again, this time slower, punching the tip of his cock over my lips. "...more *heat*. You're like fire on my tongue." His eyes flash silver as they flick down to my thighs. "If I taste you now, I know what I'll find, and it won't be *sweet*."

The scent of his arousal sends mine into a spiral, pooling between my thighs as something hot, liquid, *aching*. I burn from the inside out, the flush on my cheeks spreading down my neck.

Rage's lips curve into a satisfied smirk, but he doesn't say anything else, basking in his triumph.

He's turned me on, and he knows my body's tells.

My thighs shake, and I shut my eyes to block out the arousal pulsing through my veins. The ringing in my ears intensifies until it's *screaming*.

Someone grips my chin and tilts my face up. *Rage*. It has to be him. His voice rumbles in my ears from all around, enveloping me. "Look at the man who owns you, Beauty."

My eyes snap open with a gasp, and Rage plunges his cock inside my mouth. "That's it," he grunts, pushing the back of my head to lodge himself deeper, "let me in, and you'll earn a reward."

I glare at him as he fucks my mouth with short, hard thrusts and dig my nails into his thighs. He groans like the pain turns him on, not breaking his rhythm in the slightest. It strikes me then that he isn't wearing a mask— and neither is Rebel. They aren't concerned for their anonymity or their reputations, so why would they ever care about mine?

The truth hurts, but so does the way Rage pushes against the back of my throat, insisting that there's more room for him in there. I shake my head as best I can, but

Rage is having *none* of that. He stalls at the back of my throat long enough to make me choke.

Tears sting my eyes as I realize *I can't breathe.*

Tipping my head back, Rage readjusts the angle so that his cock presses even harder against the threshold, seeking entrance where none have gone before. His jaw ticks, like he has a right to be angry about any of this.

A shadow shifts by my side, making me flinch. Rebel's face comes into focus a second later, his touch gentle as he brushes his hand over my hair. "Let him in, beautiful. He needs you. Can't you feel how much he needs you?"

Rage's cock throbs against my tongue.

A whimper catches in my throat, blocked by the giant fucking dick trying to force its way inside. I can't do this. I jerk my head back and forth, tears slipping down my cheeks. This is *insane.* I didn't ask for any of this.

Promises are kept in this family, and you made a promise, krosotka.

These brothers are fucking *delusional.*

Rebel's touch is soft as he palms my throat, rubbing it soothingly. "Let him in," he coaxes, "relax your throat."

I turn my glare on Rebel's stupid fucking snakebite, wishing I could rip it out with my teeth. There's no way in hell I'm letting in *more* of Rage's—

My eyes widen as Rage *pushes*, and in my desperate attempt to breathe, I open my throat and do the impossible: I let him in. It feels like something's going down the wrong pipe, but Rage persists, cutting off my air as he bottoms out. Although Rebel's palm massages my throat lovingly, Rage's grip on my hair is painfully tight. One brother hell-bent on praise, the other on punishment.

Black spots dance in my vision. *This is it.* I'm going to die by dick asphyxiation. Sorry, Mom, I know you tried your best to raise a good daughter, but she's gonna have the words *Death by Dick* engraved on her tombstone.

"Breathe through your nose," Rebel murmurs, his eyes transfixed by the stretch of my lips around his brother's cock. "You can do this. He *needs* you to, baby, or he'll hurt you." He turns a quick glare onto his brother. "The last thing we want is your pain."

My eyes lock with Rage's, and all I see is *red*. Specks of it on his cheeks. In the whites of his eyes. The flush crawling up his neck. If beating someone bloody wasn't enough to prove to the whole world that *I am his*, then choking me on the his manhood will surely make his claim crystal clear.

This isn't a man concerned about my pain.

This is a man who wants to own that part of me, too.

I smack Rage's thighs with all my strength, which proves to be damn near zero, and scream as loud as I can. The dark spots in my vision turn into waves, and suddenly the pressure in my throat finally lets up. I choke on air and saliva as Rage pulls his dick from my mouth, my throat and eyes burning as I gasp in as much air as possible.

The oxygen rushes to my brain, and my resolve snaps into place. If this is a game of who can last the longest, I can win. Fixing my stare on Rage, I pop open my mouth and loll out my tongue, hoping it looks inviting.

His dick twitches hard in his hand, and then he's punching forward to bury himself to the hilt again. Before he can shove it to the back, I snap my jaw closed, tasting copper on my tongue.

Rage's groan is deep, tearing from his chest like I've tapped into something primal. A heated shiver rolls down my spine, pulsing straight to my clit. I swallow the mix of saliva and blood while Rage switches his grip and cups my face with both hands. "Can you taste it now, *krosotka*? Can you taste *my* fire?" With another groan, he jerks his hips and dislodges my teeth. The bitter tang of metal fills my mouth as he fucks my face at a brutal pace, no longer digging into my throat but battering it every few seconds as he hammers inside my mouth.

My cheeks burn from his hot hands and heavy grip. My jaw aches from keeping it open so damned long. Spit drips down my chin and drops onto my chest. My pussy flutters like a damn butterfly, all hot and bothered and gasping for air. She's *drenched*. Swollen to the point of aching. Needy. A whine catches in my throat as pleasure pulses through me, and if it isn't already humiliating enough, Rebel hears it.

"That's it, beautiful," he coos, palming my heavy tit in his hand and squeezing. "It feels good, doesn't it? Look at what you do to him. He's falling apart for you."

I can't look. I *won't* look. There's some part of me that knows watching Rage come undone will unhook the latch keeping my baser impulses at bay.

I might start asking for the brothers' dicks if it feels like *this*.

Hot. Achy. Needy. *So fucking good.*

Shame flares inside my heart, but not at what Rage is doing to me. Not at the crowd for watching, or at Ruin for holding me down, or at Rebel for thinking he's doing me a favor by talking me through it.

The shame comes from how much I *like* this.

Rebel mouths the hickey on my neck as he slips his hand inside my dress and pinches my nipple between his knuckles. White hot desire pulses through my body. I've never experienced anything like this before. The rush of power from having a man so strung out that he *has* to have me and the distinct lack of power to stop it coalesce in a bittersweet paradox.

It's heavy, hot, painful... but exhilarating. I've never seen so much red before, and as another drop of saliva slides down my chin and drops onto my chest, I imagine that it's red, too. As dark as my nail polish, or as bright as the buckles on my new heels.

Maybe all Rage knows *is* red, so he paints the world in shades of crimson, claiming it one tainted piece at a time.

If there's one piece of me he can have, it's that piece —the anger, overflowing with so much red that it *hurts.*

I hate the way he makes me feel so *raw.*

From the way his eyes burn into mine, I know that he feels it, too. *The hate.* Neither of us can control how we react to each other.

In this moment, he's a man possessed by a hunger he can't satisfy on his own.

It's just as Rebel said—Rage *needs* me.

His thrusts are animalistic, the sounds he makes matching the furious way he claims my mouth. I'm forced to breathe through my nose—a new skill I haven't mastered—and pray that it ends soon.

Because as much as I hate him for doing this to me, I might hate myself for enjoying it, too.

My ex-husband was never like this. Passion was a word that neither of us knew inside our bedroom walls. We'd try—to spice things up, to have a baby, to make things click between us—but the sex was either too slow, or too dry, or too mechanical to get things moving in the right direction.

Nothing about Rage, Rebel, or Ruin is *dry* or *mechanical*. It's instinctive, flowing through their veins as a part of who they are.

Animals. Fiends. Monsters.

They're the opposite of what I've been told to look for in a husband. Of the kind of men who protect and serve and secure. Good men of faith and family. The kind you can take home to your mother on the first date.

Then again, maybe I'm not the kind of woman you should take home to meet the family. Not anymore. These men aren't dating me—they're devouring me.

There must be a reason for that.

Rage's eyes spark like embers trying to ignite, and I can taste it. The fire. His cock swells against my tongue, the salt of precum making me tremble. He makes this sound in the back of his throat, a soft moan that no man his size should be capable of, and satisfaction thrums through me like the first hit of a heady drug claiming its next addict.

I did that.

My body satisfies him in a way that others can't. He chose *me* for this, not any of the countless other women in the club eager to sit on his lap and ride him until dawn.

A switch flips inside of me, and I wrap my palms around his muscled thighs and drag him deeper, hollowing out my cheeks and *sucking*.

My ex would have shut his eyes by now, but Rage's jaw unhinges as he stares at his Beauty. He buries his fingers in my hair but doesn't force himself deeper this time, allowing me to work his length my own way. I suck on the tip, flicking my tongue beneath the head. Then I bury him in the pocket of my cheek, testing his size before wrapping my palm around his spit-slicked shaft and stroking.

When he moans, I do the same, pulling him deep again.

Broken Russian phrases fly past his lips and with three short thrusts, he swells to bursting, shooting jets of cum against the roof of my mouth, covering my tongue, filling me so full that I can't hold it. I pull back, and the floodgates open. Cum coats his cock and slips past my lips, sliding down my chin. I can't swallow—never have —and my failure stains my skin with his seed.

"Oh, no," Rage rumbles, catching my chin in his iron

grip. "You will swallow, or I will push every last drop inside your pussy." His cock twitches with anticipation, another bead of cum leaking from the tip.

Ice cold dread pools in my gut, making me shiver. He came inside me last time. It was a huge mistake—one I had to rectify with a trip to the pharmacist the next day.

Having Rage's cum—or his brothers'—anywhere *other* than my mouth will be a big problem.

But Rage catches my shiver and his smile spreads into a grin. "You like that?"

My eyes widen. *Oh, no.* I shake my head and swallow the half-load still inside my mouth.

He latches onto the idea, though, still grinning as he collects the spillage from my chin onto his finger and crudely scrapes it back onto the tip of his cock. "Does the memory of my cum warming you up make you hot?" He holds the base of his shaft while I stare at the cream meant for me. "Or is it the thought of my baby inside of you that you like so much?"

I don't answer—*can't answer*—because I'm frozen shut. My heart, my lungs, all of it shutting down at the mention of a baby.

There's nothing I want more than a beautiful baby of my own.

But there's nothing more terrifying than having Rage as the father.

Thankfully, he doesn't press the subject, already tapping the tip of his cock against my lips. "Open up, *krosotka*, and accept your gift."

I move mechanically, all of the excitement and

tension from earlier disappearing in a heartbeat. Wrapping my lips around him is easy, but swallowing is harder. He rolls his cock around my mouth to get it nice and wet, then squeezes and gives himself one long, final stroke to get as much of his cum into my mouth as possible. A tear slides down my cheek as I obey and swallow, trying not to gag as I feel it sliding down my esophagus.

"Next time, I'll make a direct deposit. Right here—" He palms my throat lovingly—"or *here*." He presses the flat of his other palm against my stomach, pressing down firmly. A shudder rolls through him, but he keeps his eyes locked on mine the entire time.

There's a fire in their depths, burning hot enough that it ignites the ache in my soul.

"That wouldn't be so bad..." he murmurs, brushing his lips over mine, "would it?"

I swallow hard, knowing that if I'm not careful, I'll give too much away. If Rage finds out that I want a baby, he'll do everything in his power to give me one.

Of his.

"I don't want to have children, Rage." The lie feels like shrapnel burrowing inside my soul, scoring deep enough to bleed eternally. "I've never wanted to have children."

His lips press into a firm line, still close enough that I can feel it. "That's too bad."

My exhale rushes from my lungs as soon as Rage pulls back. *Thank God.* It worked.

"I'm planning on having *many* children, and there's only one woman I'd ever accept as their mother." Rage's cock is still out, thickening the longer I stare at it. *A weapon*. That's what it is. Threatening to give me everything I've ever wanted—*at a price.*

The scariest part is, if it comes down to either having Rage's baby or not having a baby at all, I might be willing to pay it.

I might become his after all.

Chapter 7

Celia

Rage leaves me on my knees.

It takes me a few seconds to process his retreat, and by then, Rebel has already lifted me back to my feet. He presses a kiss to my hair and tells me that I did *so good*, but I barely hear it.

I'm staring across the room as Rage allows a pretty woman in silver glasses and a sexy, scarlet blazer to apply antiseptic to his hands and wrap them tightly in gauze and these long, thin strips of bandages that wind around his knuckles. He bends to her ear and says something, to which she nods and disappears into a back hallway. I wonder if she's his real girlfriend—if I'm just the side piece he uses to satisfy sexual urges she refuses to indulge.

Maybe they match on a mental level, when all Rage and I feel for one another is physical.

My stomach twists into knots, but I'm not sure why. It's not like I'm *not* being tossed between him and his brothers on a daily basis, so why shouldn't he have someone else on the side?

I've got three men lined up and ready to go at a moment's notice.

That's what I tell myself as I watch Rage tour the room, shaking hands with well-dressed men in masks, clapping others on the back as he passes, smiling at ladies in sheer dresses and lingerie. "What is he doing?" I ask, following Rebel's patient lead to a high-top bar backlit with ice blue neon lights. It's the same one Goliath brought me to, but everything feels different now, like I'm in an alternate dimension. That *can't* have been tonight. Can it?

I glance away from the bar to find Rage again. He *can't* be working the room. Rage has about as much charisma as a turd left to dry on the asphalt in the middle of a blazing hot summer. Which means, *none at all.*

Rebel orders us drinks and plops me down on a padded bar stool, swiveling it so that I can't watch Rage's reflection in the twenty-foot wide mirror overlooking the bar. He tuts as he slides my dress off my thighs and inspects the red, angry skin across both my kneecaps. "He's being an ass," Rebel finally answers.

"That's his default."

Rebel's iron eyes flick up to mine. "It doesn't have to be."

I snort aloud just as the bartender sets two drinks beside us. The liquid is clear with a single, large sphere of ice nestled inside. Rebel lifts his glass to his lips and takes a half sip. I've seen the man drink half a bottle in the time it takes to boil a box of pasta—he's holding himself back right now.

I don't bother with the pretense, downing my drink before I can even taste the alcohol on my tongue. Despite the icy chill, it goes down smooth. *Vodka*. Go figure.

He frowns but lifts his hand and gestures for another one. "I'm serious. You two could be good together."

The statement burns more than the drink. "I *seriously* doubt that." I brave a glance at my knees and wince. Not only are they swollen and red, but they're bruised, too. Was it from the initial fall, or did Ruin hold me down while his brother face-fucked me? In the moment, I was too focused on not choking to death to pay much attention to my knees, but now I'm paying for it.

I have a feeling I'll keep paying for things I haven't asked for.

"Why? Because he pushes you?" Rebel taps the edge of his glass with his fingertip. "You push right back." The bright lights around the room glint off the piercing in his bottom lip, and my gaze wanders the contours of his face. He's not as sharp-boned as his brother, lacking the hard ridges of his cheekbones and the permanent five o'clock shadow, but he's no less handsome. *Pretty*, even, with curved eyelashes and thick eyebrows. But the unkempt wildness to his hair and the heavy tattoos crawling up his neck give him an edge that Rage lacks.

I take a sip of my drink and it dawns on me that I shouldn't be sitting here at all. I should be *running*. Far the fuck away. I could blame the twinging ache in my knees for my lack of desire to hightail it out of here, but that wouldn't be the truth.

I'm not ready to leave yet. Not until I've made my point clear.

"He can't control me," I murmur around a swallow. This time it burns, sending a shudder down my spine. "He wants to, but he can't. I won't let him."

The look Rebel gives me is hard to decipher. "I don't want him to hurt you."

Rolling my eyes, I gesture broadly to my aching knees. "Too late for that."

"I don't want him to hurt you any *more*," he says slowly, like he's trying to let the words sink in. It's too bad, because I won't let them.

All Rage does is hurt me. Even when he's wringing the best orgasm of my life out of me, it *hurts*. Physically. Mentally. It's like he's chipping off pieces of me and stashing them in a jar with his name scrawled across the lid.

He'll claim every broken piece of me just so that he can say the word *mine*.

Shaking my head, I blow out a heavy exhale. "Even when he's..." *Soft* isn't the right word. "*Less agitated*, he's impossible to deal with." I swivel my chair back toward the mirror and scour its reflection for any sign of the man in question. "You saw how he kissed me, Rebel. There was nothing kind about it. He doesn't know how to do anything without making it about *him*." I crinkle my nose as I catch a whiff of dick-breath. I definitely need to wash my mouth out.

Rebel turns me back toward him with a hand on my thigh. He rubs his thumb in an arch across my skin, staring into my eyes with an openness that makes my insides squirm. Whereas Rage's walls are made of ten-inch steel, Rebel's look like they're made out of the thinnest layer of glass. He draws a small breath that pulls me closer. "I need you to give him a chance, baby, or we won't get ours."

I turn my head away, my cheeks suddenly hot. My pulse races, memories of my time with Rebel rushing to the surface. Those are much more tender than anything Rage has given me, even when Rebel has my back pressed against the wall and my wrists trapped in his hands. He coaxes pleasure from my body in a way that's endearing, like he's savoring it as much as I am. We haven't gotten very far—second base, if we're being technical, and only with our hands. Rebel's lips never venture lower than the curve of my neck.

When I imagine the future I could have with these men, it's Rebel that I picture the most.

If there's anyone deserving of the title *father*, none of them really qualify, but I could see Rebel getting there.

"Do you want kids?" I ask suddenly, cringing as the words leave my mouth. "Um, never mind, please don't answer that."

Rebel licks his lips and leans even closer, his breath ghosting across my cheek. I can feel the smile on his lips as he murmurs, "do you want me to, baby?"

I swallow hard. "I don't know."

Would it change anything if he said yes?

He chuckles, palming my chin to turn my face toward his. There's a sparkle in his eye that's impossible to miss. He looks damn near *gleeful*. "You told Rage that you didn't want kids. I heard you say it." His tongue sneaks past the seam of his lips to taste mine, and he groans. "Did you *lie*, pretty girl?" The next rumble in his chest is deep, making my toes curl. "Did you say that just to piss him off, or is the thought of having his baby *that* repulsive?" He inhales sharply. "Would you rather have mine?"

The ache in my chest throbs, and I jerk back on impulse. This has gotten *way* too complicated, *way* too fast. "I—I don't know," I stammer, tears stinging my eyes. *Fuck.* I do *not* want to talk about babies tonight. They make my brain go haywire. "That's not what I meant."

"Mhm." Rebel doesn't sound convinced, but he also doesn't seem too concerned about the way my voice shakes, either. So much for being the *kind* brother. "Think about it, beautiful, because one of us is gonna knock you up eventually. If you have any protests, now is the time to voice them."

I gape at his stupidly arrogant smirk as he takes another sip of his drink. "Excuse me?"

"You heard me."

"I am *not* getting pregnant!" My heart *swoops* nonetheless, clinging to the idea no matter how foolish it is. I should have never brought this up in the first place, but my mouth ran ahead of my brain. "Rage just—the things he said—" My frown runs deep. "I am *never* having children with *any* of you. There! Decision made." I slam my heels back on the floor and wince at the sting in my knees.

Rebel chuckles to himself as I walk away, but he doesn't try to stop me.

Asshole.

I wander the room in a daze, all too conscious of the eyes following my every move. It isn't just the fact that I can feel Rebel and Rage's stares, it's everyone else's. The room has a thousand eyes, and at least half of them are trained on me. A shudder runs down my spine and bile rises to the back of my throat.

If I vomit, will Rage get pissed that my body rejected his seed?

It's tempting to shove my finger down my throat just to spite him.

When I glance up from the fuzzy spot in the distance that I've been moving toward, I catch Rage's dazzling smile as he talks to someone else. He might be holding a conversation with them with his lips, but his eyes are having an entirely different discussion with me.

They scream, *you have nowhere to hide.*

Yeah, fat fucking chance. I strut past the obnoxiously bright *restrooms* sign and march ahead of the line, daring the ladies waiting to stop me. When they don't, I laugh. I guess getting face-fucked has *one* benefit for the night.

I splash water in my face and stare at my reflection for a long time. Long enough that at least five women come and go, each one making a point to look me up and down as they fix their lipstick or wash their hands. If my friend Lilith were here, she'd have stormed into the bathroom behind me and demanded to know what the hell I was doing, letting a man force himself on me like that.

But Lilith isn't here, or else she would have stopped the *sexual assault* from happening in the first place. The phrase churns my stomach hard enough that I bolt past a woman on her way to the stall and expel every last ounce from my gut into the bowl. I groan as it flushes automatically. I'd get on my knees and hug the rim, but one, that's super fucking gross, and two, the thought of getting on my knees again makes me wanna hurl a second time. I wipe my mouth with a few squares of toilet paper and flush that, too, before standing on shaking legs.

As I stand in front of the mirror this time, I hardly recognize myself. The woman staring back at me is pale, her mascara smeared across her cheeks, her lipstick a mere whisper of color. I tug the ribbon at the back of my head and tear my mask free, knowing that it's pointless anyway. I'm not a seductress with five men wrapped around her finger on the dance floor, having the night of her life—I'm something *less*. Something broken and bitter and *hurt*.

Everything *hurts*.

The woman beside me rummages through her clutch and hands me a travel size mouth wash, placing it directly in my palm and wrapping my fingers around it. She squeezes my closed fist. "You did good for your first time." The smile she offers is warm, and I realize that it's genuine. "Not all of the men here are that rough, though. If you find a suitable partner, it can be fun for both of you." When I stare blankly at her, she nods. "I promise."

I scrub my hand down my face and shake my head. "Somehow, I doubt things will ever be fun with them."

She tilts her head. "You mean the men? You can play for the other team here. No one will judge. It's a safe space. Lots of us are bi or bi-curious." Her eyes twinkle as she winks. "Among other things."

My smile is small, but it perks her right up. "I appreciate that, but it's not what I meant." I take a minute to gargle the mouth wash and try not to get self conscious about the fact that she's watching me do it. I don't know how to unload my situation to anyone, let alone a stranger, so I settle for half-truths. After rinsing my mouth, I continue, "there are three of them, actually, and I'm only used to one at a time." She tears open a paper square from her purse and hands me a makeup wipe. I remove the dark smudges on my face while she waits for me to continue. "It's not just the sex, although that's intimidating in itself."

Will they try to fuck me at the same time? Valentina's told me stories about her men—and although I'm not keen on picturing Mikhail naked, I've always been curious about how she makes it work. *Three* men. I shake my head and sigh. "It's how they treat me like I'm—" I crumple the wipe in my hand—"like I'm nothing but a tool to get them off."

"Oh, honey." The woman wraps her arm around my shoulder. Her perfume is crisp like apples in autumn, her blonde hair frizzed at the edges like she's been working up a sweat. But she's pretty, I realize, even with the glittered mask on her face. The warm gold swirls match the color of her hair. "If it bothers you, then you have to do something about it. Have you tried talking to them?"

Someone behind us scoffs. "That one didn't look like the talking type."

The blonde woman looks over her shoulder while I check the mirror. Although the carousel of ladies continues to filter in and out of the bathroom, one woman lingers near the wall. Her hair is bright red, and I don't know how I never noticed her before. Green eyes pierce mine as she joins us at the mirror. She pats her tit through her dress until she finds what she's looking for and reaches into her cleavage to to produce a tube of lipstick. She grabs my wrist and drags me closer, popping off the top of the tube to apply a coat to my lips. "You need to fight back," she says simply, "in a language he'll understand."

"I've been fighting," I say.

She smacks my boob. "Hold still or you'll look like the Joker." Once she's done applying a layer, she pops her lips to indicate I should do the same. "Wrap your lips around your finger so it doesn't get on your teeth."

Once she's satisfied, I continue. "I've tried," I grumble, "fighting back only makes him fight harder. He doesn't take no for an answer."

"Then stop saying no." Rolling her eyes, she sticks the lipstick back inside her bra. "If he's gonna hold you down and fuck you, you've gotta do the same."

The blonde nods enthusiastically. "Yeah, tie the

fucker down. Then he can't grab you too tight. You'll be in control of what happens—"

"—or doesn't," the redhead says. Her gaze softens and she takes my hand in hers. "I saw the way he was looking at you near the end. You have a lot of power over him, babe. You've gotta use it."

"On all of them." The blonde takes my other hand. "There's more than one, right? If they all want you like that, then you're sitting on a goldmine. They'll be eating out of the palm of your hand."

I wither under their hopeful stares. "I don't know how to do that. I don't feel like I have any power."

And a woman without power will *never* take back control over her life.

They share a look between themselves. "Trust us, you do." The blonde fixes my lace mask back on my face and ties it tight behind my head. "You've just gotta figure out how it works with them." She grazes her lips over my cheek in a parting kiss before heading to the door.

"And if I can't figure it out?" I ask, already dreading the inevitable reality where these two are wrong. I'll be locked in a cage for the rest of my life, forced to succumb to whatever twisted fantasy the brothers conjure up.

Shrugging, the redhead holds the door as the blonde walks past. She keeps it open for me, jerking her head to suggest we leave together. "Then I guess you'll have to kill them."

Chapter 8

Rage

Celia and I dance around one another for the better part of an hour. I don't know what passed between her and the other women in the restroom, but the two regulars—a fiery redhead who goes by the code name Fox and a preppy blonde we dubbed Angel the minute her photo landed on our desk—keep their eyes on Celia the entire time.

It's *annoying*.

Sure, Celia has caught the eye of many of our male clientele after getting on her knees for me, but they know to keep their distance. Women, though? They don't like to play by the rules on account of *girl code* or what-the-fuck-ever they call the weird bonding thing they do. In the short six minute and forty two second blip when Celia was out of sight, they bonded over something.

I want to know what it is.

I want to know *everything* involving my woman.

So when she lingers near Fox's little threesome and

starts to get friendly, I cut my conversation with the new mayor short and join them. Sliding up behind Celia and wrapping my arms around her waist, I tug her back against my chest, enjoying her warmth. She stiffens immediately, her breath catching as she stares straight ahead and ignores me as best she can.

That shit annoys me even more.

My smile is too sharp at the edges as I nod toward Fox and her followers, two men who haven't been here nearly as long as she has. Fox has this routine of stringing people along until the new crop comes in; then she pits the old and the new against each other to see who *really* wants to stick around when there's competition for her attention.

Oftentimes, she loses out on lovers before she's even broken them in. These two men will likely be the same. I don't care to learn their names.

"I see you've been making friends," I murmur, brushing my lips against Celia's cheek. She flinches away from me, and my blood boils. "Introduce me, Beauty."

She huffs, gripping my forearms as tight as she can. Her nails dig into my flesh, and a wave of satisfaction radiates through my chest. Those little divots will last for hours. *Days*, maybe, if I piss her off enough. I wonder if she'd make me bleed.

Her voice is tight. "They know who you are."

I hum low in my throat. "You're being rude."

"*You're* an asshole."

I lift my palm to her neck and wrap my fingers around her throat, squeezing gently. She swallows, and a flash of heat rolls through me at the memory of her swallowing my cum down her pretty little throat. I should have asked her to open her mouth and show it to me first.

Next time.

I draw a ragged breath and lower my lips to her ear. "Play nice, *krosotka*, or your friends will see how perfectly your ass fits in my hand. I bet it gets red after only one spanking." I lick my lips at the mental image. There are so many things I want to do to this girl. "Should we find out?"

Fox gives Celia a look, the two of them having a silent conversation I can't fucking interpret. It *annoys* me. I grit my teeth and try to keep my cool. Despite how often our clientele rotates out, Fox has been a steady presence since the club's inception. The boss will be royally pissed if I fuck with our best donors.

Still, she better keep her fucking ideas to herself.

Celia can make her own damn decisions without some bitch poisoning them first.

Tilting her head back, Celia glares up at me. "Fox," she begins, "this is Rage. He's been stalking me for weeks."

One of Fox's men clears his throat and looks away.

I grin down at my little spitfire. "Don't be shy, Beauty. Tell them about how you come in my mouth every morning." I lace my fingers together across her neck, remembering the taste of her. It gets my dick hard.

Her teeth left their mark, though. Pinpricks of pain settle across my shaft. I suffer in silence as my dick gets harder at the spark of defiance in my girl's eyes. She's hurting too, nursing a slight limp that I know Ruin and I put there. Probably banged up her knees earlier.

But that's not the pain I see reflecting back at me—it's something deeper, locked away inside her chest. Her warm brown eyes narrow as I stare into her face and search for the key. Will she melt if I kiss her? If I tell her how every man in the room is jealous of me right now? Will she finally let go of that pride she clutches way too damned tightly and let me in?

What Rebel said earlier tonight is only halfway true. If things were different between us—*better*—I wouldn't want to cause her any pain. But if she's too goddamn stubborn to accept my pleasure, if pain is all I'm able to provide, if it's the one thing she'll relent in our endless game of tug of war... I'll take it.

Her pain will become my promise.

Celia holds my stare. "The only thing he's good for is his mouth."

Fire burns through my veins. She's trying to hurt me back, *and it's working*. I hiss through my teeth, "Guess we're a perfect match, then. Your mouth is—"

Mine.

I switch from using the word *perfect* at the last second. "—good enough."

Her nostrils flare and satisfaction curls in my chest. That's right, give it to me. Everything you're feeling. Eyes on me. I want to watch you unravel and taste the bitterness on your tongue. I barely hold back the rumble in my chest as I drag her away from the group.

Enough socializing.

"What are you doing? Let me go!" Celia trips over her feet, so I quickly toss her over my shoulder, smacking her perfect ass once it's high in the air. The sound ricochets across the room, drawing attention again. There's something about Celia and me that makes our collision messy—it's loud and painful, all long limbs and sharp teeth—bleeding out from the two of us and infecting the room. People get handsy on the dance floor. Mouths meet. Skirts lift. It's a chaotic frizzle of energy that makes me want to smack her ass again to hear that *pop* of sound, the delicious gasp on her lips.

But the difference between what's going on everywhere else in the room and what's going on with the woman I've chosen is simple: they all give their enthusiastic consent to be touched, fucked, *desired*.

Celia hasn't given me that permission, not explicitly. It's pretty clear that aside from my vigorous clit-licking, she doesn't want anything to do with me—and it makes absolutely no fucking sense.

"We're going home." I carry her across the ballroom to the foyer. The grand staircase is stupidly elaborate—something Celia's brother Mikhail insisted on when we built the place, actually—flaring out at both the bottom and the top with a curve that mirrors a woman's waistline. A lush burgundy carpet drapes down the center, widening along with the stairs at the base. It belongs in a mansion, not an underground swingers club, but Mikhail paid for the building, so he got the final say in the blueprints.

All I remember about the reasoning for the staircase

is some bullshit about allowing a woman her *moment*. Whatever the fuck that means.

The one I'm with would probably shove me over the railing in one of her *moments*.

I grab Celia's supple ass as I take her up the stairs to the second floor. Guests aren't allowed up here, which is perfect because it means that it's quiet. The bass from the main floor doesn't permeate the upper floor or its walls, so the only sounds are my footfalls and Celia's yelps as she tries to steady herself across my back. I get elbowed in the spine more than once, but I grit my teeth and carry on.

If I let her go, she'll bolt.

"This isn't how tonight was supposed to go." My chest heaves as I slam my palm on the scanner to open the private suite in the west wing. *My* suite. *Ours.* Fuck.

"I'm sorry, does sexual assault offend you?" The venom in Celia's voice slips into my veins, toxic and unwelcome. "You do a pretty good job of hiding it."

"I'm not hiding anything, Celia." Once we're inside the steel outer door, I charge for my bedroom, the air around us pulsing. My skin's hot. My body's tight. I can't take a full breath without smelling her pussy. I'm not sure if it's because my face is near her thighs or I'm that goddamn horny, but *fuck*.

She makes me want to tear out of my skin and bury myself in hers.

I toss her onto the bed and can't bring myself to look at her. Staring at the wall over the headboard, I clench my jaw so tightly that I feel it behind my eyes. "You're sleeping here in my bed. I don't want a single fucking complaint or your ass will be darker than your knees." It's a threat that feels like a twisted, gnarled thing inside my chest. I don't like it, but I don't know how else to get through to this woman.

If I held her face in my hands and kissed her, begged her to stay the night, she'd spit in my face.

She reacts like I expect, kicking her leg out at me.

I grab her ankle before she connects and glare at the bottom of her shoe. Red soles, black straps, bright buckles. I bought these for her a week ago but never actually gave them to her. "Where did you get these?" She tries to retrieve her foot, but I hold on tighter. "Where did you get these?" I ask again, growing impatient.

Did Rebel give them to her? Take credit for *my* gift? I wouldn't put it past him—the man loves to steal whatever's shiny enough to catch his interest and isn't bolted down—but I'd been planning on surprising her. New shoes. New dress. Dinner out on the water. A smile that's more breathtaking than the setting sun.

A real fucking kiss, given willingly, *gratefully*, a soft sigh on her lips as I pour myself into her.

That plan's already gone to shit and I haven't even made the fucking reservation yet.

"Who cares where they're from!" She jabs her heel into my thigh while I'm glaring at the wall and imagining my brother's cocky fucking smirk staring back at me. "Get the fuck off of me! I'm not sleeping with you!"

I release her ankle like it's an iron-hot brand, hissing through my teeth. "*Fine*, then don't sleep." Slamming the bathroom door in her face is a weak victory that rings as hollow as it sounds. I wince in the bright light and turn on the faucet to drown out her screeching. She's obviously tried to open the door to the den—but it locked the moment it shut behind us. We're trapped in here together, for better or worse, until I choose to unlock the door.

Or one of my idiot brothers meddles again.

Or she kills me in my sleep and figures out how to undo the locks.

I'll have to sleep with one eye open tonight.

"Are you *kidding* me? Is it Fort Knox in here?" She bangs on the door, then lets out a sharp cry. Yeah, that shit's gonna hurt no matter how tiny your fists are.

I could tell her to stop. She's going to hurt herself if she rams against the door.

But I don't.

I listen to her heavy breathing, the way she paces the room like a cat in a cage, grumbling the entire time. She picks things up. Puts them back down. Opens the closet door and rummages through the racks. Tears open drawers and slams them back shut.

I wasn't kidding earlier—I have nothing to hide.

The dull drag of metal on metal catches my attention. She huffs, clicks her heels toward the door, and slams something heavy against it. Wood splinters and cracks, and she laughs in triumph.

My fucking dumbbells.

Snarling, I tear open the bathroom door and bear down on her. She lifts the dumbbell again, a ten pound weight that shouldn't do much damage, and rams it back into the center of the door. A tiny hole materializes, letting a sliver of light in from outside.

"What are you *doing?*" I growl, snatching the weight from her hands and tossing it behind me. It *thuds* like a boulder, but I don't give a shit about the floor.

Her wild grin takes my breath away.

It breaks as soon as she realizes I'm crowding her in, giving her zero chance of escape. Her hazelnut eyes widen as I back her against the splintered wood and slam my fist beside her head. The wood groans beneath my throbbing knuckles.

"You can't escape me. You can't escape *this.*" Exhaling hotly across her face, I grab her throat and kiss her hard on the lips. Her body goes rigid, the instinct to fight coursing through her veins. I growl against her mouth, slamming my fist into the door, and feed her my anger.

I'm so goddamn *furious* with her all the time.

"Why can't you stay?" I lower the hand gripping her neck to her chest, feeling her heart beat wildly inside her ribcage. A heart that's *mine.* I stop myself from saying what I really want to know—

Why can't she *want* to stay with me?

"It's one night. *One* night. With me." A shudder rolls through me and I kiss her again, moving my lips over hers even though she's frozen solid.

This is worse than when she's mad at me. It's nothing at all. A blank expanse of body heat without any emotion attached. But I know she's in there, and it kills me to have her so close but utterly *vacant.*

I dig deeper, sliding my tongue between her lips, groaning at how she lets me in. I bury myself inside her warmth, searching for any piece of her she'll allow me to find. When I come up empty, a shudder courses through me.

If I go any deeper and tear out what I want—her pleasure, her pain, her fear—she'll hate me for eternity for taking it by force.

But I'm starting to believe that's the only way I'll ever truly have her.

Finally, she lifts her hand and touches me, placing it on my chest. But she doesn't push me away—she slides her palm up to my shoulder, across the back of my neck, and into my hair. Grabbing a fistful and *pulling*, she rips my head back and glowers up at me, lips pulled back, teeth bared. "Because it's not one night! Nothing with you is one night! I learned that the last time I was in your secret fucking club!"

Heat sears across my scalp, but I take it. I'll take anything I can get from this woman.

Even if it's not the things I'd dared to hope for.

Love feels impossibly out of reach.

"Give me tonight." It won't be enough, but it will give me time to think. To plan. I've been anticipating that Celia would give in to me eventually, but it's becoming increasingly clear that her aversion to me is bordering on permanent. It's something I'm doing wrong with pursuing her—like there's a secret thread holding all the answers that I have yet to unveil. Pull the right thread, and she'll unravel in my hands like the most beautiful flower, blossoming for *me*.

I just have to find the right one...before my brothers do.

While she processes my request—as if she has a choice in where she sleeps tonight—I take my fill of her body. Her chest rises and falls with every breath in her lungs, the flush across her cheeks trailing down her neck. It lingers near the topmost edge of the deep V cutting between her breasts, but the milky skin of them peeks out on either side, untouched by the sun. Her complexion is warm despite the coming winter, meaning that she either tans topless at the spa, or she never bothered tanning to begin with and she's naturally honey-toned.

I've never seen any bikini lines across her hips or thighs.

The urge to *touch* roars in my ears, but I clench my fist beside her head and take a deep breath. The hand on her chest, however, stays right where it is.

Her heartbeat keeps me steady and solid while I wait for her reply.

"One night and you'll let me go? I won't be trapped here?"

I measure my words carefully. "One night in my bed, *tonight*, with me, and I'll take you home in the morning." I can't promise anything after.

She bites her bottom lip, and my cock twitches. I stare at her mouth for a long moment, swallowing hard.

I want to kiss her again. I want to *make* her mine. Throw her onto the bed and climb on top, taste every inch of her skin, and make her *scream* my name as she comes on my fingers, my tongue, my cock, all of it, all night, all at once. Can I fill all of her holes at the same time?

Mmm. I know I can.

"One night," Celia murmurs, flicking her gaze away from mine. "Then I go home in the morning, and you walk away."

My voice rumbles deep in my chest. I don't miss the way her body shivers or her nipples harden. *Fuck.* "A full eight hours minimum, *krosotka*."

"You can't fuck me."

I lick my lips. She's going to make this difficult. "Define *fuck*."

Her face flames. "I don't want your dick anywhere near me!"

I laugh before I can stop myself. "A little hard to manage, given how it's fucking attached."

She glares and pulls my hair again, arcing my neck back. A wave of pleasure licks down my spine, making my balls ache. "I won't put my dick inside you, or between your tits, or between your thighs, or anywhere else." There's a lot of places I could slip inside or between to get off, or get *her* off. I uncurl my fist and lift my hand from her chest to hold them both out in front of me. "But my dick *will* touch you, because it's fucking massive." To emphasize my point, I grind my cock into her hip, enjoying the little gasping sound she makes.

"And you're welcome to touch it with any part of your body, any time."

Her upper lip curls in disgust, but it rings false against the backdrop of her eyes, blown wide open for me.

I didn't make her come at all today, and it shows. Her body misses me.

"I won't," she snaps, "so keep it to your fucking self!"

Ah, my little spitfire.

Im-fucking-possible.

I lift my hand to her chin and tilt her head back as much as the door will allow. "Kiss me," I murmur, leaning in until our noses brush, "and you've got a deal." Her hand lingers in my hair but she doesn't pull me back. Then her tongue darts out to wet her lips, flicking over mine in the process, and *fuck*, my cock tries to tear through the zipper, throbbing painfully. It will be sore for a few days, maybe even bruised, but if she lets me put it inside her, or against her soft skin, or pillowed between her ass cheeks or her goddamn armpit at this point, I'll fucking do it.

And I'll come for *days.*

Celia's hand trembles as she touches my cheek.

She closes the distance between our lips.

I swallow her soft sigh like it's my final breath, holding it deep inside my chest so long that it burns. A single word ricochets around my skull like a bullet in my brain.

Mine.

Chapter 9

Celia

"Do I at least get to change clothes?" I rub the sheer fabric of my skirt between my fingers. "I'm gonna freeze in this."

It takes Rage a few seconds to respond, like he's barely processing what I'm saying. "You won't freeze," he says gruffly, unbuttoning his dress shirt. "Not with me beside you."

My face flames, and I scowl at his dresser. "I'd still like something else to wear. A t-shirt? Sweatpants?" When he doesn't make a move to get me anything, I take initiative and practically sprint to the other side of the room.

Anything to stop me from seeing his bare chest.

It's one thing to know he's hot on a fundamental level. All three brothers are ridiculously sculpted, each of them embodying different aspects that make men attractive. Rebel has this devil-may-care smirk and lean physique, Ruin has the whole mystery man thing going for him, and Rage...

He's got *alpha male* written all over his huge, muscled body.

I tug open the top drawer. My eyes widen at the expanse of handguns and knives carefully tucked inside, each one pressed into foam to keep them from shifting around. Rage's hand brushes over mine as he shuts the drawer.

"I don't own any t-shirts." He reaches for the second drawer and pulls out a pair of boxers and black socks. "You can wear these."

I pull a face as he drops them into my arms. "I'm not sleeping topless."

He stares at me, the hard line of his mouth unforgiving. "You'll be more comfortable that way."

Rolling my eyes, I dig through the second drawer, then the third. He was serious about not owning t-shirts. I don't even find a pair of sweatpants or shorts. "What do you work out in?" I turn to stare at the benchpress and weights along the far wall. "I'll wear that."

His lips quirk into a smirk as he shrugs off his shirt and reveals the wide expanse of his torso. I've never seen it before, and my eyes rove the contours of his muscles, the well-defined ridges along his hips, the start of the deep V leading straight to what lies hidden beneath his slacks. A trail of dark hair starts at his belly button and dips lower, also hidden, until he undoes his belt and drops his pants.

The thick outline of his cock juts out, stretching his black boxers.

I swallow hard and avert my gaze. I don't care if he

sleeps in his boxers. Per our agreement, he's not allowed to touch me with his dick tonight.

But then he drops those, too, and I catch the bob of his cock in the mirror overlooking his weightlifting station. My body ignites, and I squirm in place as I try not to look.

I fail miserably.

His voice rumbles over my shoulder. "I workout in my boxers, *krosotka,* but I sleep nude."

Of course he does.

He chuckles, grazing my forearm with his knuckles. The rough bandage around his fingers scratches my skin, and he suddenly flinches away.

"What's wrong?"

Ignoring me, he pulls open another drawer and retrieves something from inside. I barely catch a glimpse of silver before he spins me around, snatches both of my wrists, and holds them behind my back. Something stiff locks them into place, and he grunts in satisfaction.

I try to pull my hands back to the front and find that I can't. They're locked together at the wrist, the clink of a metal chain keeping them secured against my back. "Did you just handcuff me?" Spinning around, I check my reflection in the mirror, straining to see what he's done. Leather cuffs connected by a silver chain are cinched around my wrists. "What the hell, Rage!" They jangle behind my back the more I struggle. I twist my wrists and pull, but they don't budge and my hands won't fit between the cuffs.

Something in his expression closes off, creating a wall

I have little hope of penetrating. "I won't fuck you tonight, but I can't have you running loose, either." He runs a hand through his hair, mussing it up as he averts his gaze. A muscle in his jaw tics. "Or killing me in my sleep."

Grabbing onto the cuffs, he pulls me into the bathroom and closes the door behind us. Walking backwards usually sucks, but walking backward in heels *double* sucks. I grit my teeth as he picks me up and plops me onto the bathroom counter, hooking my cuffs over something behind me. The faucet, if I had to guess, from the awkward angle it forces me into. The edge of my butt dips into the rounded sink.

"Wait here while I shower." He barely looks at me as he spins around and starts the water, stepping inside before it's even warmed up. I watch him through the glass as he steps under the rainfall and drenches himself, rivulets of water following the hard lines of his body.

It's impossible not to stare at the appendage jutting out from his hips.

He exhales slowly, tilting his head back and closing his eyes.

I could have used a shower after the blow job earlier, but the last thing I want is to get naked with Rage in the vicinity.

I'm grateful he hasn't forced me in there with him.

While he lathers up, I scour the contents of the counter, looking for antiseptic cream or lidocaine. I can handle bruised knees better than my bruised ego, but that doesn't mean I should *have* to. The man's loaded, not to mention responsible for my discomfort, so the least he could do is spring for some pain meds or creams.

The heady scent of amber soap fills the air. I give up on my search and close my eyes, content with a few minutes of relative silence. If I can't find painkillers on my own, then I'm shit out of luck. There's no way in hell I'm asking this man for anything.

It gets uncomfortably hot and humid after a few minutes of steam pouring from the shower. Rage must have the water turned up to *hellfire*. Likely attempting to scour the sin from his skin.

I roll my eyes. Not fucking possible.

I shift my weight and lift one of my legs onto the counter, leaving the other to dangle over the edge. Warm, moist air greets my inner thighs, and I try not to imagine it as anything other than *air*.

Innocent, comfortable air, unlike the heavy exhales and groans Rage makes when his face is buried between my thighs.

My thigh twitches, and I bite my bottom lip to fight the ache of desire deep in my belly.

Damn him and his raging-fucking-hormones getting me all riled up. Sweat slicks my skin. I'll need a shower after this, or my makeup will clog my pores. While I'm mentally tallying all of the nighttime routines I'm going to miss—face wash, floss, hair brush, toothbrush—I hear a rush of water spilling to the shower floor, followed by a groan that rumbles across the room.

I know that sound.

I know that sound *very* well.

My nipples harden. Heat pools between my thighs. If I listen closely enough, I can hear Rage's movements from behind the shower door, the steady, quick tug of skin and the deep *growls* that spill past his lips.

Fuck. Me.

My *asshole-not-boyfriend* is jerking off six feet away.

I bite my lip and clench my eyes shut tighter.

I *can't* enjoy this.

He's a horrible person. The last man on the planet that I want to be around, let alone stuck with for eight hours tonight. *Sleeping next to.* I should file a police report. Stalking, breaking and entering, assault. I'm sure the cops could come up with more charges than that for all three of them. I could use my brother's name for even more leverage—*hell*, I could use *my* last name for leverage.

Rage might be powerful underground, but I'm powerful *above* it.

Another groan spills past his lips, and all of that alleged power feels oceans away as he drags me under with him. My body tingles and my pulse races, the ache between my thighs roaring to life.

I'm used to the way he sounds when he's hot and bothered, but it's different this time. We're not rushing through an orgasm before the next work rush. This is oddly... intimate. *Close.* Even when I sucked him off earlier, it wasn't about *us* then. It was a show of force to prove to me—and the entire room—who I belonged to.

But right here and now, I'm the only one listening. He isn't putting on a show for the masses.

He's putting on a show for me.

I open my eyes and search for him through the haze of steam in the air and streaks of water on the glass. Although the image isn't perfect, I can clearly see his profile and the hard strokes of his hand on his shaft. He isn't facing the wall like he was earlier.

He's facing *me*.

His liquid gaze burns into mine, lips parted, jet black hair slicked back, one hand on his cock while the other presses against the glass separating us. Once he notices me watching, he swipes his hand through the condensation and clears the view so I can watch unobstructed. A smirk catches on his lips. He leans toward me, his shoulders pitched forward, his hips rocking in time with every stoke.

My whole body shivers. I press my thighs together and wiggle on the countertop, seeking friction but finding none. *Dammit*. I tug on my bindings, but they don't budge, the leather digging into my wrists and the chain clinking against the faucet.

Rage's smirk is blazing hot, his breathing ragged as he notices my struggle. "Say you want me," he rumbles deep in his chest, "and I'll make you come. Isn't that what you want? My mouth on your pussy? My tongue flicking your clit?" He shudders, gripping his cock tight, stroking harder, slower. "I can make you feel good. You *know* I can."

Hatred burns through me. I detest everything about this man, from his wicked mouth to his unrivaled confidence. The way he jerks me around, cuffing me, slapping my ass, *turning me on.*

I'm burning alive from the inside-out, and it's all his damned fault.

I keep my mouth shut.

Rage stops jerking off.

He turns off the water and steps out of the shower, not bothering to dry off, and slinks closer to me. He takes a deep breath and pinches his bottom lip between his teeth, groaning as his eyes rove my body. "You're fucking gorgeous, Celia." He drags in a shaky breath, reaching out to drag his fingertips down the front of my dress and across the generous side boob peeking out the front, all the way to the bottom of the V sitting over my sternum. He presses his palm flat against my ribs, his expression serious as he feels my heartbeat.

It skips beneath his touch.

He smiles, and it's a beautiful, broken thing that takes my breath away. Slowly, he pulls my breast free from my dress, then does the same for the other side. Palming my tit, he massages it in his warm hand. "Don't you want me, Celia?" Lowering his head, he sucks my nipple into his mouth, sending shockwaves of pleasure through my body. My back arches and I choke on a whine that never quite breaks free. He groans, the vibration of it making my toes curl.

"Your body says yes, but your mouth keeps saying no. Why is that?" Rage doesn't look up at my face. He plays with my breasts, sucking and plucking my nipples into sensitive peaks between his lips, his teeth, his fingers, driving me into a frenzy.

I grind my hips against the counter, whimpering as desire slicks between my thighs. *God*, he's insufferable.

Without waiting for an answer, he runs his palms up my outer thighs, lifting my skirt with ease. Kissing down my chest and stomach, not caring for the fabric in the way, he sighs. "Are you scared, *krosotka*? Scared of *me*?" The bandages on his hands are gone, revealing raw, aching flesh from his knuckles to his fingertips. The bruises are mottled purple and red, the skin swollen and hot to the touch. The color matches my knees, both of us aching from what we've done to each other.

He beat a man unconscious because I crossed a line.

I got on my knees as punishment for it.

Fox's lilting voice lashes across my mind.

You need to fight back in a language he'll understand.

I still don't know what that means.

"I'm n—"

Rage digs his fingers into my hips.

"—not scared of you." A delicious shiver rolls down my spine as he spreads hot, open-mouthed kisses down my thighs. It isn't a complete lie. I'm *not* scared of him like normal people probably are. They're worried he'll mug them on the street or marry their daughters for inheritance money.

I'm worried that I'll lose pieces of myself that I'll never get back.

His lips brush over my knees, kissing the tender skin

there. "I hurt you." It isn't a question, but a statement. An admittance of guilt, perhaps.

Except when he looks up at me, there isn't a shred of guilt in his eyes. "I'll hurt you again."

Still not a question.

I tilt my hips up, snaring his attention between my thighs. His nostrils flare and he spreads my legs wider, dipping between them to kiss even higher along my inner thighs. My body flushes hotter, my legs twitching as he gets closer to where I want him most. I bite my lip and nudge his collarbone with my knee to get his attention. When he looks back up at me, my voice comes out as a whisper. "Do you want to?"

There's a moment of silence as he considers his answer. "If that's the only way I can touch you, then..." His fingers tighten around my hip, his nails digging into my flesh. "...yes."

It's not a good answer. How can someone saying they want to hurt you *ever* be a good thing? My ex-husband wanted to hurt me after I couldn't give him what he wanted, and he cut me deep enough to leave scars. If Rage hurts me, I have a feeling that he won't just cut deep, he'll *shatter* me.

Then he'll pick up every single piece and lock it away to keep for himself.

Nothing about Rage will be half-measures. It's all or nothing.

But maybe that extends beyond *hurt*.

Can a man who wants to own you understand what it means to love you?

I shimmy my hips closer to the edge of the counter. "I want you to touch me." The angle pulls my back muscles and digs my shoulders into the mirror, but I'm resigning myself to it as a fact of our relationship. Nothing with Rage will ever be *painless.*

I'm starting to learn that.

"You want my touch, but do you want *me*?" he asks, jaw clenched tight. He drags my panties down my hips, the fabric chafing my thighs. "Say you want me, and I'll —" his voice cracks at the edges—"I'll make you feel good this time. I promise." The heat in his eyes blazes, flickering in their depths like embers in the night. He exhales harshly as he pushes my right leg up to remove my panties, his eyes lingering on my heels. A muscle in his jaw tics, and when he returns his gaze to mine, those embers have ignited.

All I see is fire, threatening to consume him from within.

"Who gave you these?"

The sudden change of subject throws me off balance. I stumble around the word *what?*

He growls, grabbing my ankle hard enough to dig the buckle into the bone. I flinch, but he's staring at the shoe, not at me. He flicks his thumb over one of the straps.

I wish he were flicking my clit instead.

"The—"

His eyes ping to mine, searing straight to my core.

"The, um, guy gave them to me." My cheeks are already flushed, so they burn crimson as embarrassment floods through me. My answer feels lame, but it's all I have. "The guy in the limo. He picked me up tonight. I don't know his name."

Why the hell does Rage care about my shoes when my pussy is wet and waiting for him? I try to close my thighs, but Rage holds them open, his lips curving into a malicious smile.

"You mean Thanatos." He shakes his head, chuckling deeply. "*Thanatos.* The fucker's gone for five years, and he comes back to give *my* woman gifts." Licking his lips, Rage grabs my hips and pulls me to the furthest edge of the counter. I scramble for purchase, my heels sliding on the granite countertop as I try not to fall off, but Rage sets my thighs over his shoulders and *growls.*

"This is *my* fucking pussy," he roars, spitting on my clit. Saliva drips down my slit and over my crack to pool on the countertop. "*My fucking woman.*" Sliding a thick finger inside my heat, he inhales deeply, his pupils dilating. "Fuck, you're soaked." His body goes rigid for a split second before he slides a second finger inside. "Wet for *me*, or wet for *him*?"

I'm barely breathing, too strung out on the feel of something *finally* inside of me to process his questions. "W-what?"

He drags his fingers out before pushing them back in. "It's a simple question, Celia. Are you wet for *me*, or are you wet for *Thanatos?*"

"I—I don't even know who he is!"

Rage flicks his gaze up to mine. An inferno of fury roars in his eyes. "He's my brother," he snaps, pressing his thumb against my clit. My hips buck up to meet him, and he punches his fingers inside of me faster, grunting as the scent of *pussy* fills the air. The sounds of my body taking him in are *loud*—so much louder than when he stoked himself in the shower. The wet squelch makes my body shiver, a low-pitched *keen* catching in my throat.

"My *half*-brother," he unnecessarily self-corrects, spitting the words out. Rage suddenly stands, bending me in half as he crowds closer, burying *three* fingers inside of me and panting over the top of my head. He lowers his face mere inches from mine, drinking in the lost haze in my eyes, the way I search his face, unfocused and untethered, as he finger-fucks me.

Maybe that goes against the rules for tonight, but it's hard to care when I'm *this close* to coming.

"Tell me who you want, Celia. Me or Thanatos?" Rage's lip curls on his half-brother's name, like it disgusts him. Maybe it does. I'm not sure how they're related or what the history is between them, but it screams *bad blood*.

"I want you!" I cry, writhing my hips, trying to ride Rage's fingers. How could I want a man I've never properly met? Just because he gave me some shoes to wear?

Rage is fucking *crazy*.

He shudders, burying his fingers all the way, grunting as he grinds his palm against my clit. "That's right, you fucking want me," he snarls, scraping his teeth across my temple. "I'm the only one who makes you feel this good. The—" he curls his fingers inside me—"*only*—" grabs my throat and squeezes—"one." He crashes into me, barreling his chest into mine and swallowing my scream as I come undone. He groans into my mouth. "So goddamn beautiful," he murmurs, kissing me again, sweeping his tongue between my lips. "Of course you want me. Of course you do."

Even strung-out and trembling, I recognize his words for what they are—something to soothe the ache inside his heart. The kind of self-soothing lies we tell ourselves until they come true...

Or until we believe they do.

Chapter 10

CELIA

Not only do I convince Rage to find me one of Rebel's t-shirts to wear to bed, but he dresses me in it, too. He takes his time pulling it over my chest, enjoying the sight of my naked tits too much to rush the process, but he does as I ask, even pulling a pair of his boxers up my thighs and over my hips before laying me down in his bed. He stares at me with a frown on his face before joining me and wrapping a heavy arm around my waist to pull me close.

Removing the leather cuffs for the brief moment he slipped off my gown and redressed me in my makeshift pajamas was a tease, making me forget that we *aren't* simply a man and woman going to bed together.

I'm still his prisoner. Every clink of metal behind my back solidifies that reality.

Idly, Rage strokes the tiny gap between where the leather touches my skin with his fingertip. "What would you do--" he plucks the cuff—"for me to take these off?"

I pinch my lips together, trying to ignore the way he smells. Something manly, like cedar or sandalwood, deep and woodsy. It must be his soap. I hold my breath as best I can, shutting my eyes to block as much of him out as I can. But between the body heat radiating off of him and the weight of his arm draped over my waist, it's impossible to ignore him.

Then there's the featherlight brush of his fingers on my wrist.

Another tease.

I squirm, uncomfortable with this entire situation. "*Nothing.* Because even if I *did* believe you, which I don't, you wouldn't take them off."

Rage hums softly. "I would for the right reward."

"Oh, so this is—what, a gift? An act of kindness?" I scoff. "You don't get rewards for doing things for the sake of others. It's called being a good fucking person. And for the record, you wouldn't have to take them off if you hadn't put them on in the first place!"

Ignoring my tirade, he simply says, "So you don't want them off?"

"Of course I do!" I snap. "But not if it means giving you something in return, asshole!"

He presses his lips to my jaw and hums again, like he's enjoying his little mind game. "Wake me up when you change your mind." He drops back onto the pillow and stretches, getting comfortable. My limbs ache, my muscles coiled tight simply because I can't unwind them. Even though Rage's bed is wide enough to fit three people, he stays close, taking up the middle of the bed like he owns it and keeping his arm around my waist like he owns *me*.

I guess, technically, he does.

For the next eight hours, at least.

I listen to his breathing, waiting for the moment it slows. Time passes in blind increments. I search the room for a clock, but there is none. Although I feel Rage's limbs twitch as his body tries to succumb to sleep, he never fully relaxes. Is that his normal, or is he waiting for me to take him up on his offer? Is that why he can't sleep?

What the hell would I even give him for it?

All the possibilities that come to mind are of me on my knees choking on his cock again or of me spreading my legs for him to shove it as deep inside as he can while he relentlessly fucks me for the remainder of our eight hours together.

Neither of which are fucking happening.

But still, the idea settles somewhere in the vulnerable part of my mind between waking and dreaming, hooking its claws in so that I'll think of it not only when I'm asleep, but also when I'm wide fucking awake.

Like right now. I am *wide* awake.

I replay the events of the night in my head, going over everything with a fine-toothed comb. What could I have done differently? Would it have made a difference, or would I still be here in Rage's bed, cuffed like a prisoner... or a plaything.

The neon pink sign for *The Playroom* flashes through my mind. Then the blinding white sign for *restrooms* follows. The two women who helped me in the restroom—Fox the redhead and the blonde nicknamed Angel. I chew on their advice as the silence between me and Rage stretches on.

If he's gonna hold you down and fuck you, you've gotta do the same.

You'll be in control of what happens—or doesn't.

Is that what I need to do to take Rage's power away? Fuck him first?

I don't think I'm understanding their advice correctly. That *can't* be the answer. Then I'm giving him exactly what he wants—my body, my attention, my *everything*. Giving in feels a lot like losing.

But so does lying in the dark for the next eight hours, unable to move beyond what Rage allows.

Tentatively, I twist my body toward him. What do I even say? *Hi, I've changed my mind, can I fuck you?*

Yeah, that's *really* gonna show him who's boss.

I need to act first, ask for permission *never*. It's what Rage would do. It's how he keeps his power. He *takes*.

Steeling the nerves fluttering in my gut, I press my body into Rage's, smashing my tits against his arm and laying my thigh across his. I can't push myself up and into his lap without the use of my hands, so I use what I can to get Rage's attention.

I rub my pussy on his thigh and press my knee into his crotch, feeling his cock swell from the pressure. If he wasn't awake before, he is now, the harsh inhale giving him away. I keep moving my hips, hitching my clit on his muscled thigh, rubbing his cock with my knee.

It can't be comfortable or anything close to soft, but within seconds, his cock has sprung back to life.

Pleasure skates up my spine as I use Rage's body for my own benefit. This is new for me. I don't dry hump people. Or pillows. Or dildos. Or *anything*. But Rage's body is so *warm*, the hard muscle of his thigh flexing as I rub against him as best I can from this angle. I pant these tiny, hot puffs of air near Rage's ear, and finally, he moves.

Gripping my leg, he drags my thigh further over his hips, trapping his cock in the crevice where my calf meets the back of my knee, and shifting my body so that I can better grind against him. I whimper as he thrusts, rubbing his dick against my leg while I do the same with my pussy and grind my hips to increase the friction.

We both pant these hushed, heated breaths, neither of us speaking, both of us seeking our own pleasure.

It isn't until I bite his shoulder on a particularly magnificent swivel of my hips that he groans and reaches for me. Gravity tilts as he drags my body on top of him and forces my legs apart, making me straddle his hips.

The head of his cock presses insistently against my clit, the long length of him slotted against my core, the soaked crotch of my boxers molding to our bodies. I drag in a needy lungful of air while he palms my thighs, running the rough pads of his hands up and down in these slow, long drags of skin-on-skin.

"What are you doing, *krosotka?*"

I shudder from the rumble in his voice, followed by an impatient twitch of his cock. I've given him a way to break his word. He could spear me on top of his cock and force me to take his length, his girth, all the way to the hilt. It would be *easy*. For him to take, and for me to let it happen.

But that's not what this exercise is about.

"I'll give you *this*—" I roll my hips and moan, grateful for Rage's punishing grip on my thighs or else I might fall off of him. "—when you take the cuffs off."

He thrusts, pinning me in place as his dick rubs against my overheated core. Despite the thin barrier between us, I can feel him pulse with need as his desire roars between us.

I came on his fingers on the bathroom counter.

He didn't come at all.

"I'll make you come," I clarify, "but we're not having sex."

Rage huffs. "I want to fuck you, Celia, not dry hump you. It won't work. I can't come like this. Nice try."

"You *will* come," I insist, grinding my hips and gasping at how fucking *good* it feels, "because I will."

He doesn't sound convinced. "You'll ride my cock until you come?"

I nod before I realize he can't see me in the dark. "Yes. But with my underwear on."

"That's *dry* humping, Celia—it'll chafe more than anything, and I'll have blue balls for the rest of the night. The answer is no."

"You can suck my tits while I do it."

"Lights on," he counters, "with kissing."

"No kissing."

"It's *my* reward for removing the cuffs. Kiss me while you ride me, or there's no deal."

I should have known this wouldn't be as simple as helping him bust a nut before bed. *So much for all that power I supposedly have.* But for one, it'll get the cuffs off. For another, I'll get to come again, which means I might actually get some sleep. Maybe Rage will, too, if he comes hard enough.

I better put on a damn good show.

"Fine," I bitterly agree.

While he reaches behind me and undoes the cuffs, he buries his face in my tits and mouths a nipple through my t-shirt. I gasp, my hips jerking, and he groans. "Take this off," he orders, turning on the bedside lamp in the next instant, "and ride me, beautiful."

My shoulders scream when I pull my arms back to the front, but I don't linger on the pain. I lift my shirt over my head and toss it to the floor, rolling my hips once to test our connection.

Rage palms my bare tit but keeps his eyes on my face. I know what he wants, and it kills me to give it to him. I delay the inevitable, building into a rhythm that makes my breath catch and my body flush *hot*. Unbearably hot. Our desire flows like water between the two of us, drenching us both where our bodies meet.

As my pleasure mounts, I imagine what if would feel like to sink on top of him. How full I would be. How hot and slick and *perfect* it could be. I grip Rage's shoulders tightly, using him as an anchor. I'm so turned on that it *hurts*. It shouldn't feel this way—*he* shouldn't make me feel this way.

I can't want to fuck the man I hate.

When I make no move to kiss him, Rage takes over, growling as he drags my face down to meet his. Our lips crash in a tangle of teeth and tongue, both of us moaning and thrusting in time with each other. Rage's tongue slips inside my mouth as he punches his hips up, slamming the tip of his cock against my clit and making me see stars. I drag in a lungful of air and he groans, nipping my earlobe. "I can feel you, *krosotka*, so fucking wet, drenching my cock in your sweetness." He attacks my mouth again, biting my lip, seeking dominance.

The pain mixes with the pleasure. I'm too far gone to care, digging my nails into his skin, jerking my hips in tiny, short bursts to maximize the pressure and heat on my clit.

Sex would be better, but this is pretty fucking close.

"I'm gonna—I'm gonna—" I clench my eyes shut as I explode, crying out as both pleasure and pain ricochet through my body. Rage grabs my hips and slams me down, shoving an inch of his cock between my lips, forcing his way inside. His cock pulses, each hot burst filling my underwear with nowhere else to go. I feel the wet heat as if it were my own, already soaking between my thighs. Trembling, I hold onto Rage until my orgasm wanes, barely registering that I'm still twitching my hips in time with his thrusts.

He lays back onto the mattress and drags me with

him, burying his hand in my hair and holding me tight against his chest. I can feel his hammering heart, then the laugh rumbling around his ribs. "You proved me wrong," he murmurs, gently scratching my scalp. "Feel free to do that again. I could go for another round."

Somehow, I think he still came out on top, in the end. It rattles my confidence, crashing my high. I let him caress my sides, my hips, and my back for a few moments before rolling off of him and hopping out of the bed to search for a fresh pair of boxers. I change in record time, finding the t-shirt on the floor and whipping it over my head. The boxers make me wish for a shower for the second time tonight.

Rage watches me the entire time. His smile is cat-like, wicked and triumphant. "You should sleep naked."

I scoff. There's no way in hell that's happening.

Unless...

"What are you willing to do—" I lift the hem of my shirt high enough to flash the underside of my boobs— "for me to take these off?"

Swallowing hard, Rage sits up against the headboard. Red scratches tear across his shoulders, much like how I'm sure his fingerprints are pressed into my hips. His dark eyes glitter with a thousand possibilities. I have no clue what he's willing to give me in return for a naked night between his sheets, but I need to play this smart.

He is ruled by his desires. I can use that to my advantage.

A shower would be heavenly, but this is a long game

we're playing. I need to think beyond tonight. What do I need to be the one on top?

Before Rage can offer me something, I jump ahead of him. "If you answer all of my questions, I'll sleep naked tonight."

"Three questions." His lips curve into a sinful smirk. "Unless you wanna fuck. Then I'll answer anything you want."

I gape at him. "How can you still want sex? We just—we basically had sex!"

"Not the same." He pats his thick thighs, and I catch a glimpse of his glistening cock. It isn't hard, but it *could* be very soon if I don't shut this down. "Come sit on my lap and I'll answer your questions."

"Three questions, and I'm not sitting in your lap. Keep that thing away from me."

He clicks his tongue. "You *like* my thing."

My face flames. I undress without addressing his *thing*. I don't even look at it, focusing instead on the empty space on the bed beside Rage. I slip between the sheets and keep the blankets between us, determined not to touch him. "Okay, first question." I pick the first one that comes to mind, knowing that I can ease into the tougher ones. "Why did you hurt that man?"

It's not the question I'm expecting to ask, and clearly Rage isn't expecting it, either. He stares at me for a long moment, scanning my face. Slowly, his smile fades. "Because he doesn't deserve you. Is that what you want to hear?"

I fiddle with the comforter. "I don't want you to tell me what I want to hear. I want you to tell me the truth."

"That is the truth." Rage sighs, rubbing his jaw. "Seriously. He *doesn't* deserve you, Celia. None of us do." He blows out a breath.

This is a new revelation. Rage, showing self-doubt? "You can't honestly believe that," I chuff, rolling my eyes. "You're the most self-absorbed person I know."

Rage's throat clicks on a swallow. "You asked for honesty. I'm being honest."

I purse my lips, not believing it for a second. Is he saying that he's not a good guy? "Well. I guess we can agree on that, at least." I level him with a look. "You *don't* deserve me."

The statement rings as hollow as Rage's subsequent laugh. "You think I don't know that?" Shaking his head, he tumbles to the mattress and climbs on top of me, the comforter the only thing between us. "It's impossible to fucking miss with how often you've been throwing it in my face. That's what you've been trying to tell me this entire time, right? With all your fighting and your pushing and your flinty fucking gazes." He growls, tearing at the blankets to get to me. We wrestle over the comforter, but he's stronger, pulling it from my grasp in no time. Once my body is bared to him, he spreads his palm over the bottom rungs of my ribcage, like he's searching for the heart tucked safely inside. "You fight so hard, Celia, *so fucking hard*. But I won't take no for an answer. You even tried to spend your evening with someone else tonight—" he snarls, the hurt in his eyes crackling like lightning—"and I nearly killed him for it."

Then Rage kisses me, crushing my body beneath his own. He leans on his forearms and cradles my head in his hands, bringing my mouth closer to his, like he can't get enough of the taste of me. With a groan, he releases my lips and leans his forehead against mine. "A better man would let you go. I know that. But I *can't*. Ever since I laid eyes on you, I *knew* you were mine. *Ours*," he corrects, chuckling in that bitter, humorless way again. "But *mine* more than anything. I can feel it in my bones, Celia. You were made to be mine. And no matter how much you resist me, I can't let go."

My heart flutters like a wild bird caught in a cage. People don't talk like this about others. About *anything*. This level of desire isn't normal. "I don't understand," I murmur, touching Rage's face. There's a tiny indent over his cheekbone—a scar, if I had to guess. "Why me?"

There are any number of reasons why someone might want to sleep with me, but Rage doesn't want *just* sex. That's abundantly clear by how he sticks around during the daytime and agrees to me sleeping in his bed at night without actually *sleeping with* him. It's not like we're friends—I don't know him from within the fashion industry—and I can't recall ever having met any men named Rage, Rebel, or Ruin when I cavorted within the bratva's circles. I don't even know why they invited me to *Midnight* in the first place.

I don't know why they chose *me*.

I take a shallow breath, a new question on the tip of

my tongue. It might be my last one, I'm not sure—"Have we met before, Rage? Before *Midnight*."

Rage unfurls his hands from my hair to fist the sheets beside my head. The sound he makes is agonizing. "*Yes.*"

My heart is already racing, but it jumps a beat. "When?"

"That doesn't matter." He shuts the question down immediately, nipping my jawline. "You asked me why I need you." He moves to my neck and swipes his tongue along my pulse point, humming in satisfaction as it jumps. He pushes himself up to stare into my eyes. Even in the lamplight, his eyes are endless pools of black, consuming everything they meet. The flush on my cheeks. The sheen of sweat across my brow. The way there's not a sliver of distance between us, our heartbeats warring against each other's. When his gaze pings back to my face, he draws a deep breath and releases it nice and slow. "I *need* you, Celia. Body. Mind. Soul. All of you. Because you're perfect. I know you don't believe me, but I promise, you are. For me, for my brothers, for the bratva. *Perfect.*"

I shake my head in quick, successive bursts. "No, you're lying—"

He pitches his hips forward, punching the air from my lungs with a heavy drag of his cock against my stomach. "Say that again," he warns, "and I'm shoving it in your mouth."

"You can't!"

"I can," he counters, clenching his teeth, "because your dis-fucking-belief supersedes everything else. I'm not lying to you, Celia, I'll *never* lie to you. So if I need to shove my cock down your throat so that you'll listen without interrupting, I fucking will."

I snap my mouth shut and glare at him.

He actually *smiles,* and it softens his features. There's a sparkle in his eye and a gentleness to his lips that makes him even more handsome than when he's acting all macho and possessive. It punches me in the gut so strongly that I have to gasp to catch enough oxygen for my brain to catch up.

"I need you," he begins again, "because you are fierce. You value life so much that you'll fight for it, even when it's not your own, which is fucking insane." His eyes narrow, but there's no heat behind it. "Don't do that again, by the way. No sacrificing yourself for strangers."

I don't know what he's talking about, but the threat of cock-suffocation is enough to keep me silent. When have I ever tried to save a stranger?

He continues, "you have a gentle heart. You don't like bloodshed. You're all sappy and in love with love—"

This part *can't* be true. I'm a wrecking ball when it comes to love.

"—and it makes me—" Rage shakes his head, his shoulders bouncing with a warm chuckle. "It gives me hope that you could ever love a man as dark and twisted as me. As my *brothers.* You may have rejected the bratva, but it runs through your veins stronger than you realize. Otherwise, you would have crumbled by now." He wedges himself between my thighs and lifts up onto his knees, dropping the bedsheet behind him. The cool night air makes me shiver, but then Rage is pressing his scorching hot erection against my pussy, and I choke as heat engulfs me, spreading from the apex of my thighs to every square inch of my body. He doesn't thrust, sitting perfectly still as his eyes rake over my naked body.

"You're still here because you can handle it." He cups my knees gently, brushing his thumbs over the bruises. "Because as much as you claim otherwise, you *want* to be here." Licking his lips, he draws another breath. "I know that scares you, but think about it. You could have run over to that drawer—" He nods toward his dresser— "and plunged a knife into my heart or put a bullet in my brain, but you didn't. You *could have*, but you chose not to."

I pinch the inside of my cheeks between my teeth, unable to look away from him. The hard planes of his torso aren't smooth like I had thought; rough patches of mottled skin stripe across his chest and one of his shoulders. I think of the scar on his cheekbone—the tiny, inconsequential indentation—and realize that whatever caused *this* covered a much larger area and took a longer time to heal than what punctured his cheek. I lift my hand and trace one of the streaks with my fingertips, feeling its rough, bumpy texture.

Rage's abdominal muscles tense as I skirt around his belly button.

It's easier to focus on Rage's body than what he's saying. Part of me knows that he's right—I could have run over there, grabbed any one of those handguns, and shot him dead. If I *really* hated him, I would have.

But I didn't.

And that makes everything more complicated than I'm willing to admit.

"Maybe I should have." I pinch my lips together, knowing that it's a shitty thing to say. It's also another lie, and I shut my eyes to avoid looking at Rage and his gorgeous fucking body. "But that would make a mess."

"You didn't let your brother kill me, either."

"It would have ruined half my inventory."

He grunts in a noncommittal answer.

I crack open one eye. He's still staring at me and rubbing these tiny, little circles over my kneecaps. Gently, he says, "you said I could have you."

My exhale is little more than a puff of exasperation. "You are *not* having sex with me right now—"

Rage clenches his jaw. "That's not what I mean." His hand slides over my knee to the front of my thigh. "When you came to *Midnight* the first time, you said that you were ours. That was a promise, Celia, whether you intended it to be or not."

I purse my lips. "That's not fair. I was coerced." I distinctly remember both Rebel and Rage kissing and touching all over my body that night.

"You wanted us then. You still want us now." Rage reaches over and turns out the light with a *click*, shrouding us in darkness. His hand travels higher, tickling my inner thigh. "Stop breaking your promise, *krosotka*, or I'll break mine. You won't leave this bed without my cum buried so deep in your pussy, you'll reek of it for days." He pushes my thigh up, bending my knee toward my chest and making me hiss from the ache. "Then when your belly is round and swollen with *my* child—"

My back arches on a moan as he aligns our hips and grinds against my pussy. *Fuck.* Fuckfuckfuck. Not this again. Any mention of having a child makes my hormones rage. My body throbs hot with need, the mental image of me being pregnant and glowing with happiness cutting deep inside my chest, pouring out of me in a strangled cry.

I want that more than anything.

As Rage rotates his hips, I grind right back, unable to stop myself. Panting, I reach for him, blindly hoping that maybe it won't be so bad, having Rage as the father. Maybe he'll be good to me, then, and good to our baby.

Maybe he really means it when he says I'm perfect for him.

He hisses and pulls away, extricating himself from the bed, from my limbs, tearing away any hope that I have.

"—then, you won't be able to deny that you're *mine.*"

I've pissed him off, but I'm not sure how. He paces the room in the dark for a few minutes before climbing back into the bed, as far away from me as possible. He doesn't even grab the sheets, leaving them all for me.

"Rage?" I brush my hand across his shoulder, feeling stupid for even that small of a gesture. I hate going to sleep without resolving an argument, though. After a year of cold, sleepless nights with my ex, the last thing I want is another one. I never used to know how to appease my ex-husband, but with Rage, I have a feeling that bridging the divide is the first step. When he doesn't answer me, I slide up behind him and wrap my arm around his middle. Part of me is terrified that he'll suddenly decide to say *fuck this* to our little negotiations, flip me onto my stomach, and have his way with me, but another part of me is terrified that I might *want* him to.

If he can give me a baby...

I shut down the thought, unwilling to entertain it for another second. Getting my hopes up will only lead to a crash so massive, I won't be able to recover.

I might actually kill myself this time.

Admitting my fears to Rage feels like swallowing a mountain, so I start small, with the tiniest one I can.

"I don't know if I—" I take a quick breath—"if I would make a good partner." I hug Rage tighter to ground myself in my body instead of allowing my mind to drift out into a sea of sorrow. "I wasn't exactly..." I wince. "...wife of the year, in my last marriage. Not that we're getting married!" I resist the urge to *run far away* and bury my face in Rage's back instead. Breathing in his scent, I refocus. "I, um, don't know if I'll ever be ready for that. Again, I mean. *Ever* again."

Rage laces our fingers together and lifts my hand to his lips. Softly, he murmurs, "if I do my job right, you'll *want* to marry me." He draws a deep breath and lets it out slowly, clutching my hand tightly in his. "Not because I force you to, but because... you want to."

We fall into silence, with Rage pressing a kiss to my palm every few minutes. As we lie in the dark and breathe in the stillness together, I imagine a golden thread looping around us, tying our aching hearts together.

Because as much as I've wanted to be desired since the brutal heartbreak of my divorce, I realize that Rage might have been looking for that, too.

Desire.

Need.

Love.

Chapter 11

Ruin

There's a hole in Rage's bedroom door. It's too small for my hand to fit through, but large enough that I can see shadows of Rage and Celia within, two shapes created out of darkness, unmoving.

They're sleeping—or pretending to.

That's their first mistake.

What's the point of being *with* someone and not learning how they breathe? The little twitches of their muscles as they fall asleep—or the way they lift their leg or roll onto their stomach in the middle of the night. There are thousands of things to catalogue about Celia at night, and Rage is wasting his opportunity to learn every single one of them.

She's wasting hers to learn more about him, too.

I pick at the hole in the door, prying off splinters of wood and flinging them to the floor. I don't realize that I'm doing it at first, but once I recognize the steady pull of my fingertips and snap of wood, I can't stop. I pick and pick and *pick*, harder, longer, peeling away the layers between us, digging my way inside.

As the hole expands, it's tempting to slip my hand inside, but even after an hour, I can only manage up to my wrist. My arm won't fit. I can't unlock the door from this side—not without Rage's handprint. But from the inside, with the right amount of leverage, the lock will pop and the door will swing open.

Rebel chooses this precise moment to wander in from the club well past five AM, wandering to the connected kitchen to chug a bottle of water. I remain still as he shuffles through the motions of undressing, dropping his clothes where he stands. It drives Rage crazy when the house is untidy, so he'll pick them up before leaving in the morning and throw them at Rebel's closed door.

I know all of this, because I watch it unfold.

Just like how I know that Rage thinks he loves Celia, because I watch him struggle with it every day. He isn't used to loving things. With us, it's easy—we are a constant in his life, always present, never changing. Sure, we argue with him when we don't like a call he makes, but we don't throw it back in his face, because we know that he's usually right when it comes to making decisions for our best interests.

Celia doesn't understand that yet.

She keeps fighting him.

I don't think Rage likes it as much as he claims he does.

I think he's so desperate for another point of stability

in our lives that he's clinging too tightly to the possibility of one—and pushing her away in the process.

Celia isn't like Rebel or me. She doesn't *have* to be here. She doesn't *have* to accept us as we are.

He keeps forgetting that.

She keeps trying to remind him.

Rebel walks past me on the way to his bedroom, pausing when he notices me lingering in Rage's doorway. "What are you doing?" Not only is he shirtless, but he's stripped completely bare, uncaring about the chill in the air. He brushes his hair out of his eyes and walks closer. "Is that a *hole?* Rage is gonna flip his shit."

"She's in there." I press my body flat against the door, staring through the hole. Celia and Rage haven't moved, but they must hear us, because they're not really asleep. They're still pretending, with Celia wrapped around Rage's back like she's holding him.

I wonder what that feels like.

"Are they fucking?" Rebel shoulders me, but I don't budge. "Hey, let me see."

"They are not."

"I want to *see.*"

I take a step to the right and Rebel takes my place at the door. Cursing at what he finds within, he screws his eyes shut and rubs the back of his eyelids. "They should be fucking. They need to get it out of their system before they explode all over the fucking place. The club went crazy after they left." He tears himself away and goes back to the kitchen for another bottle of water. Chugging half of it, he huffs out an exhale. "I had to break up three fights *and* revoke someone's membership. Then, my clients were—" his face scrunches up—"more handsy than usual. I barely got away without someone tearing my dick off."

We stare at each other for a heartbeat.

"Which ones?"

Shrugging one shoulder, he tosses his half-empty water bottle to the couch. "Too many to name, man."

I catalogue this info for later.

"Don't worry about it." Rebel's eyes search mine, his fingers twitching by his sides. "Seriously. We can't have another incident."

I disagree, but I don't tell him that.

Rage will be waking soon. Even without an alarm, his body works off of a routine he's spent years perfecting. Event nights don't interrupt his body's internal rhythm.

My shift is ending, too, so I stare through the hole again as my skin starts to itch. "I haven't seen her today." Or yesterday. Although Rage and Liara handle the logistics of the club and its events and Rebel slips between roles to fill in any gaps in the line, my work never stops.

Last night's shift began before I was ready. I got caught up the job and wasn't able to visit Celia at all while she slept... which means that, aside from holding her steady for Rage earlier, I haven't touched her in over twenty-four hours.

That little stunt in the ballroom earlier tonight doesn't count. I barely remember the feel of her beneath my fingers. The sounds of her breathing. The scent of her desire. All of the things I crave about Celia were lost in a sea of red, so I've missed the pieces that matter most.

Now is the time to rectify that.

Reaching my hand inside the hole in the door, I tear through as far as my body will allow, pulling past the wooden splinters to grab the handle. My fingertips graze it, slipping over the tip, my arm on fire as my skin peels back in jagged grooves. The metallic scent of my blood fills the air. A dull sense of pain radiates up my arm.

I couldn't care less.

I try for the handle again, grunting when my fingers slip over the metal, both slick with blood.

"Ruin," Rebel hisses, smacking my shoulder. "I wanna see her, too, but you don't see me tearing my fucking arm off to get in there." He frowns at me before turning around. "I have the key." Leaping for his clothes, he pats his pockets before running back to me with his cell phone. The screen lights up the room as he clicks open our security app.

Out of paranoia, Rage keeps the apartment off limits for the security system. If anyone were to hack into our system, they could run through the club and all of our adjoining properties with relative ease until the system automatically resets. I watch with little interest as Rebel taps a few buttons on his screen. It's not surprising that he found a rule to break, but it's surprising that Rage hasn't caught it yet.

What's even more surprising is that when Rebel unlocks the door and I peel my arm back, Rage doesn't move.

Maybe he *is* sleeping.

We swing open Rage's bedroom door, both of us hovering on the other side. The room stands still like it's holding its breath, waiting. Neither of us speaks.

Neither of them moves.

Blood drips down my arm, the subtle *tap tap* on the hardwood barely audible over the deep breathing inside the room. Rebel's breathing quickens, his leg jerking forward. I doubt he's seen this side of Celia before. It's the one I usually keep for myself, tucked away beneath the sheets.

She looks different here, in another room, with another man.

Different, but no less appetizing.

Rebel and I step into the room in unison, hovering at the end of the bed. This is usually when a sleeping person stirs, their body sensing something amiss, a presence that lingers where it shouldn't. I usually have tools to combat the twitching limbs, the flicker of eyelids, the panicked whimpering. But just how Rage's work shift is beginning soon, mine is ending.

I don't have my tools with me.

But I don't need them with Celia.

Unlike my usual marks, Celia doesn't wake in a panic at being watched. She's slow to rouse, like I'm dredging her body out of a pit of sand, each falling grain bringing us closer together. Her wavelength meets mine somewhere between waking and dreaming, hovering in that precipice between life and death like it finds comfort there, in the in-between.

I understand it all too well.

Rebel, however, has too little patience and too much energy. It frizzles around him in every move he makes, fraying at the edge of his consciousness. Event nights always string him out, affecting his rhythm more than the rest of us. He sweeps his hand over Celia's bare calf, hovering over her knee.

Even in the relative darkness, I can picture the bruises on her skin.

A shiver rolls down my spine, making my balls tingle. I lick my lips and watch as Rebel climbs into the bed, slipping beneath the blankets to spoon Celia from behind. He fits like a missing piece, easily contorting his body to hers, sighing into her hair as he nuzzles close.

I don't care to join them, so I watch instead.

Then, I reach out and touch her.

I start with her foot, brushing my bloodied fingers over the top, waiting for her twitch. Then I press the pad of my thumb into her arch and sweep up, massaging the knot that keeps coming back. I play like this for a while, dirtying her skin, trailing my hand higher, palming the curve of her calf, the thick expanse of her milky thigh.

There is no window in Rage's room, but I imagine the sun rising. The black blood would warm in the light, revealing streaks of crimson across Celia's skin. Another shiver rolls down my spine and blood flows to my thickening cock. My body warms, making my skin tight. There's never enough room when I'm trying to fit Celia inside, too, like she's too much for me to hold.

All my broken pieces beside all of her whole ones.

I wonder if snapping and cracking bits of her will make room for shards of me in between.

Rage wakes first, his body's natural rhythm winning over the need for sleep. The transformation is immediate—all of the tension in his body snaps back into place, his voice a low, warning rumble once he realizes we're here. "Get out."

Neither Rebel or I move.

He clutches Celia to his chest tightly, like he's trying to convince himself that she's here for only his pleasure.

But we agreed before this ever began.

She doesn't belong to him.

She belongs to *us*.

I stare at my palm pressed to Celia's thigh. When I lift it, a bloodied handprint stains her skin. Her leg slides an inch higher on the mattress, like she's expecting me to bend her knee and spread her thighs.

I could.

I *should*.

But I don't.

I stare at the three of them in bed. "What does she feel like?"

Rebel's the one to answer, a pleased sigh on his lips. "Warm. Soft." He wedges his knee between her legs and hugs her body to his chest. "Perfect."

Celia sighs and rolls onto her back.

The three of us go still.

"You two aren't welcome," Rage grumbles, scrubbing a hand down his face. "I have eight hours with her. It's only been two."

"It's been three," I point out, tapping my fingertips on my thigh. "You left the party at three AM. It's six."

"*Two*," he insists, "because the clock didn't start until later." He rolls onto his other side, facing Celia, and unabashedly palms her tit. "We made a deal."

"*We* made a deal, or have you already forgotten?" Rebel wraps an arm around Celia's waist and pulls her closer to him. My brothers glare at each other over her naked chest. "You can't hog her all to yourself."

"The fuck I can't. She's in *my* bed."

"You locked her in here! If she had a choice, she sure as hell wouldn't be sleeping next to *you*."

"What, you think she'd choose you?" Rage's laugh is bitter. "Because you kiss her on the mouth instead of her pussy?" He growls. "I know what she needs, and it sure as hell isn't some high school boyfriend bullshit."

"The fuck did you just say?"

Celia's eyes snap open. "Will you both *shut the fuck up*?" She smacks Rage's hand off her boob and tears Rebel's arm from around her waist. Snagging the bundle of blankets, she pulls them as high up as she can, huffing when they get stuck under Rage's muscled thighs. She manhandles him until she can tug them free, wrapping the bedsheet, then the comforter, securely around her body.

It's wrapped tight enough to rival a straightjacket.

The two men by her sides look like they want to murder each other on top of it.

"Boys," she snaps, "I'm *tired*. I don't know what godforsaken time it is, but you've stolen enough of my night. Either go to sleep, or get the hell out so I can get mine."

Rage grabs her chin and turns her face toward him. "Our deal was eight hours." Brushing his lips over hers, he rumbles, "I never promised sleep."

"I never promised anything," Rebel murmurs, purring into her ear.

"You're not a part of this!" She blindly reaches behind her and smacks Rebel across the hip, eliciting the faintest chuckle past his lips.

Their banter shows familiarity with each other, a certain degree of comfort. Rebel blows air across the back of Celia's neck, and she *barely* seems annoyed.

Rage notices this, too. Any lingering serenity from waking up beside his woman disintegrates in an instant. "Rebel, get the fuck out of my bed."

Rebel stretches languidly, humming softly in the back of his throat. "I don't think I will."

I cross to the floor lamp near the bench press and pull the chain. Harsh LED light floods the room, but Celia's the only one who flinches. Rage is glaring daggers at our brother while Rebel simply flexes his thighs, poking Celia in the hip with his cock.

She freezes, eyes widening a single notch. Her lips part in this pretty little *O* and her breath hitches.

Then she surprises all of us by wrapping her arms around Rage's shoulders and pulling herself closer. "You *promised*," she murmurs, wide eyes pleading with him.

Though I'm not sure *for what.*

A muscle in his jaw tics, his eyes pinging between her and Rebel. He cups the back of her head and kisses her slowly, coaxing her to relax. Once she releases the breath she's holding, he brushes his knuckles across her jawline and stares into her eyes.

I feel it then—that something has changed. There's a missing piece between what I knew when I found them lying in the dark together and what I know now from seeing them lying together in the light.

There are hints. The hole in the door. The clothes on the floor. The way Rage's hair is still damp—but hers is bone dry.

The way they look at each other, the weight of this unknown promise settling between them.

Separating the two of them from the two of us.

The three short hours between when they left the party until now should have been as insignificant as the last twenty-four spent without her, but it's clear that something has changed. It's small, like a single drop of rain falling into the vast expanse of a turbulent ocean. It won't ripple or cause a surge when there is already chaos erupting around it.

And yet.

Rage and Celia's chaos has shifted from a roar to a rumble in those three, short, inconsequential hours.

I don't want to leave them alone anymore.

Unlacing my boots, I step out of them and place them near the door, then I close and lock it. Tiny shreds of my skin stick to the wood, and I glance down at my arm.

The cuts aren't deep and the blood is already coagulating, so I'm not concerned with it. Rage, on the other hand, grows incised when he realizes what's happening. Not only is Rebel refusing to leave, but so am I, *and* I'm bleeding all over his belongings.

"Goddammit," he curses, screwing his eyes shut. "God *dammit.*" Kissing Celia hastily—not savoring her *at all*—he growls into her mouth before letting her go. "The med kit's under the sink. Fucking hell. Clean yourself up." He grimaces when he notices the stains I've left on his comforter, his teeth clenching once he peels it back to find Celia's legs marked with it, too.

I hesitate in the bathroom doorway, admiring the sticky handprint on her thigh.

Crimson, just like I'd imagined.

Celia gasps, flailing to disentangle herself from the blankets, from the men, from the situation. "What the hell is that? Oh god, is that *blood*?" She makes this high-pitched *squealing* sound and climbs over Rebel to get to the bathroom.

I follow her inside.

She strips from head to toe and jumps in the shower before the water is even turned on. "Gross, gross, *gross,*" I hear her muttering, then the flick of a cap, the slosh of suds lathering on skin.

Walking to the shower, I pull open the door and watch her scrub her leg clean, then her foot, her little fingers digging between her toes to ensure every drop of blood vanishes. It washes down the drain in a swirl of pink foam.

Once she's satisfied with her work, she finally looks up and notices me. Her pretty pink lips part to say something, but she stops herself, shaking her head. "Are you okay?" Frowning, she rinses off her hands and takes a step closer. "Those look new."

I nod. "They are."

Sighing, she turns off the water and grabs the towel slung over the shower door. Wrapping it around her body, she sidesteps around me and takes a closer look at my wounds. "I'm not scared of blood," she clarifies unnecessarily.

I grunt, not really caring if she's scared of it or not. She'll see much more blood the longer she's with us.

"I just don't like it on me." Her lips pinch together. "Did you do that? The blood and the, um, handprint?"

I lick my lips. She might not be scared, but it's close enough to tickle my nervous system. "I like it on you. The red." I scrape my nails down her cheek, enjoying the flush of pink, the three stripes blooming on her skin.

She blinks up at me with wide, owl eyes. "Why?"

My relationship with *red* is complicated, all crossed wires and broken things. But I *like* broken things. They're easier to play with.

I watch Celia shift her weight from foot to foot while she waits for my answer. Her gaze flicks to my fingertips and she swallows. "Ruin? Did you hear me?"

Taking a breath, I press my index finger into the

pillow of her cheek, making her flinch. "Yeah. I heard you."

When it's clear I'm not going to answer, she bites her bottom lip and tears her gaze away. "Let's patch you up, okay?"

I'm much more interested in her reaction to my fingertips, but I follow her to the sink. She rummages in the bottom cabinet for a minute before retrieving the first aid kit. It's a large zipper pouch with everything from burn cream to a suture kit. We each have one in our rooms, courtesy of Rage's over-preparedness. He uses his kit for patching up his knuckles more than anything, so most of the items within are unused.

Mine is nearly empty.

Celia clears her throat and sets the kit on the counter, eying my arm with unease. "You can't do this yourself, can you?"

I'm too busy watching a bead of water travel down a lock of her hair to answer.

"Hurry up," Rebel whines from the bedroom. "Patch him up and get your sweet ass back here, baby."

Rage huffs and clicks off the light. "The bed isn't big enough for four people."

"Ruin can sleep on the floor, then."

"*You* can sleep outside."

They bicker amongst themselves while Celia gently washes my arm in the sink, wiping away the dried blood and examining the cuts. "I don't think you need stitches, but I'm not exactly an expert..." She unwraps gauze and winds it around my forearm, taping it down once two layers are in place. "I've only done this a few times."

Hm. A few times. "For yourself?" I can't imagine Celia getting into catfights with other women or full-on brawls with men.

She shakes her head. "For my dad. He used to come home with these scratches all over his arms..." Her nose crinkles. "They weren't like yours though." She exhales slowly and returns the supplies to the kit. "Anyway, after he started coming home with new ones every few days, my mother refused to help anymore. Said it was his fault he got them in the first place."

I don't know much about Monrovia senior. Rage keeps tabs on the bratva as part of everyday responsibilities, but Rebel and I aren't main players within the organization. We're sideliners, called in for specific jobs for specific purposes. I never crossed paths with Monrovia or his son Mikhail... and especially not his daughter Celia.

If Rage hadn't brought her to my attention, I'm not sure I would have ever noticed her at all.

Rebel and Rage are eagerly waiting when we return to the bedroom, both of their gazes snapping to her the moment she steps back into the room. She wrapped her body in a towel and dried her hair with another. Crossing her arms, she levels each of us with a stern look. "No one is allowed to fuck me tonight. I have a few more hours of *peace*, and I intend to make the most of them. Which means sleeping, in case that wasn't clear."

Smiling at her, Rebel crosses his arms behind his head and spreads his thighs, his flaccid cock flopping to the mattress. It twitches when Celia makes eye contact with it, and she flushes a bright shade of pink.

Will she blush like that when she sees my dick for the first time, or will she bite her lip—like she's doing now—and blush deeper for me?

"You both need to put clothes on."

Rage grumbles. "No."

Rebel sucks his snakebite into his mouth and runs a hand through his hair. "No can do, baby. I'm all natural, all the time." His eyes light up with mischief. "Are you nervous that you'll wake up with one of us inside you?" He groans, his cock swelling. "That is *so* fucking hot—"

"That is *not* happening," Rage hisses, glaring at Rebel. "If you so much as *think* about it, I'll hand her a knife and hold you down for castration." He pats the space beside him at the edge of the bed. "Come to bed, Celia. No more delays. It's fucking sunrise already."

Celia hesitates.

I press my hand into the small of her back and guide her to the middle of the bed. "I can lay on top of you," I offer, breathing hard against my mask. It'll be different than when I'm grinding the heel of my palm into her clit and watching her drift off to sleep after she comes, but I'm twitching at the prospect of six more hours with Celia.

Different bedroom. No clothes. Three men.

Everything about this situation is new, and it's *exciting*.

As she crawls onto the bed and settles in the middle between Rebel and Rage, she peeks up at me from beneath her long lashes, the faintest dusting of pink on her cheeks. Then, she reaches her hand out to invite me in.

"I... I'd like that. Thank you."

Unlike my brothers, I know how to listen.

I keep my clothes on.

Chapter 12

Rebel

I always imagined that the first time Celia saw me naked, we would be outside. Running from the cops. Caught in a rainstorm. Skinny dipping. The possibilities were endless little temptations that I rewrote in my head over and over again, anticipating that the real thing would be sort of... magical.

My brothers would give me *shit* for saying that.

But after spending a few weeks in her home, feeding her snacks, watching her offload from a day spent on her feet or surrounded by sketchbooks, listening to her chat about everything and nothing at all... I wanted something special for us.

Something that we could share without my brothers getting in the way.

A secret between the two of us.

Nothing about lounging on Rage's bed while he pops a rage-boner—no fucking pun intended—and

Ruin fantasizes about bleeding all over our girl screams *special* or *secret*.

It cries out with a wail of *fucking pathetic*.

That's what I've been reduced to: *patheticism*. The middle brother isn't expected to amount to much—that's usually what I like about being a few years younger than Rage and a few years older than Ruin. Shit flies under the radar. I can get away with murder.

Literally.

But when it comes to Celia...

I stare up at the ceiling with this huge, heavy frown on my fucking face, because the *last* thing I want is for her to think that I meet the standard of middle-child-mediocrity out of necessity.

I only meet it out of *convenience*.

There's a huge fucking difference.

Rage has his arms locked around Celia's body like a cage. I couldn't break her out if I tried. The man has at least fifty pounds of muscle on me and a whole lot more of that obsessive factor that tips people over the threshold of normal and into the *insane* category.

Pissing him off when he's running on two hours of sleep, *if that*, will lead to something breaking, and I sure as hell don't want my manhood on display when he starts swinging.

Which leaves me little choice but to lie in the dark and wait.

Six hours is a bitch of a time for waiting, though, and I'm not much use for being idle. I tap my fingers for a few minutes before that gets boring. Then I tug on my cock for a little while, but although it's filled to bursting, I can't bust a nut to save my life. Rage is awake, and although he should have his nose buried in Celia's hair, he's determined to make this situation miserable for all of us.

He's fucking glaring at me, even while I've got my dick in my hand.

"*Bro,*" I deadpan, rolling my eyes. "Get a fucking grip." There's a joke in there somewhere about how hard I'm choking my chicken, but it's lost on Rage's humorless ass. He keeps on glaring.

I stroke my cock a little slower, hoping he enjoys the show.

"Put that fucking thing away," Rage growls, somehow managing to pull Celia's body another inch away from mine, "before I have Ruin cut it off."

I glance at our younger brother sitting in an armchair in front of the door. Once Celia fell asleep, he dragged the chair in from the living room and plopped down for our six hour hold. "He wouldn't," I say dryly. "He actually likes me."

Ruin plays with the edge of his mask, like he's itching to take it off. The man never leaves the house without it, but sometimes when it's just us, he takes it off for a breather. I bet he's tempted right now.

"She's asleep," I offer, gesturing toward Ruin's face. "You could..." I mime pulling the mask off. "...you know."

He stares at Celia for a long, silent moment, before grunting in response.

The mask stays in place.

I give up on my cock and cross my arms behind my head, sighing. I should be sleeping right now, but I'm too wired. *Celia* is here. In our apartment! In Rage's bed! Next to me!

It's a fucking crime that Rage is keeping her all to himself.

Rolling onto my side, I watch as he idly strokes her back. In another life, maybe it would be me holding her instead. Maybe Celia and I would have been high school sweethearts. Laughing and cutting class and shit. Getting caught kissing beneath the bleachers or going to second base in the back of the theater. I never had a girlfriend in grade school, and I lost my virginity to a junior sometime during the ninth grade. But she wasn't my girlfriend—she was just a girl looking for some trouble when she found me.

I had trouble written all over me, even back then.

I fiddle with my snakebite, rolling it between my teeth. Does Celia like bad boys, or is she only with us because Rage is shoving his cock down her throat?

"Maybe we need new rules." I cringe from the way that sounds, but now that I've said it, I can't take it back. Rage's hand stills near Celia's shoulder blade. The fucker loves rules just as much as he knows I love to break them.

"What do you have in mind?"

My eye twitches. "For starters, how about actually sharing her like we'd said we would?"

"You get her in the evenings," Rage grunts, "that *is* sharing."

I shake my head. "No, man, it's not. We shouldn't take shifts. Besides, by that logic, you took her during Ruin's night. That's not fair, and you know it."

Ruin nods from across the room. At least he's paying attention.

"Then what do you suggest, brother?" Rage's smile is full of sharp teeth. "Letting *her* decide who she sleeps with?"

That's actually not a bad idea.

Rage catches the look on my face and hisses.

"She won't know where to find us." Ruin props his foot up on the bench press. "Unless we leave her breadcrumbs."

"You'll probably leave her a blood trail and scare her half to death."

He inclines his head. "She is not scared of blood."

I lift an eyebrow. "Could've fooled me." The bloodied comforter's been tossed to the floor and a new one brought in from the linen closet.

"She will *not* decide on her own," Rage grumbles, "because she'll choose wrong."

Ruin and I stare at each other, then at our brother. Rage always thinks he knows best. Or, at least, he refuses to be wrong and manipulates the situation until he's proven right about whatever's got him bent. It's usually something to do with the bratva, or the club, or all of the boring meetings he has to attend as an honorary city board member. He likes to be right.

But this isn't something I can let him bulldoze his

way through. I won't let him lock Celia in a cage—the metaphor will turn real if we let it slide now.

"You don't trust her?" I ask gently.

Rage's face contorts into something pained. He glances down at Celia, shifts her weight in his arms so that she's leaning more on the pillow than his chest, and presses his forehead to hers. Then he murmurs something too soft for me to hear, presses a tender kiss to her lips, and lets her go.

He *actually* releases his death grip.

A muscle in his jaw tics as he peels himself away from her, careful not to jostle her as he gets up from the bed. He crosses to the bench press and sits beside Ruin's foot, then picks up one of the heavier dumbbells.

Then the fucker starts to pump iron.

I get it—he's stressed.

At least it gives me room to slide up next to Celia and curl into her warmth. That's the thing about her that's different from most women—she's *warm*. In all the evenings we've shared, I'm the one shivering once the sun goes down. She's the one stripping into a tank top in the middle of winter. I get cold just *looking* at her.

Rage exhales slowly, pausing with the weight draped across his bare thigh. "I don't know." His gaze flicks toward Celia, and thankfully, he doesn't flip his shit that I'm touching her. "She hasn't done much to prove that she's..." He presses his lips into a thin line. "*Happy* about it. About *us*."

Despite how old Rage is—somewhere over the cusp of thirty and inching closer to forty every day—sometimes I think he has a lot of growing up to do. Like I'm one to talk—*shit*, our whole family's kind of fucked in that department.

Our parents weren't exactly role models.

"She won't be happy if you keep suffocating her." I level him with a stern look. "With your fist *or* your cock."

"Or both," Ruin murmurs, still keeping up with the conversation. "She only wants *gentle* suffocation." He flexes his fingers, like he has experience with this.

I mean, *strangulation*, yeah, he does. But with Celia?

My eyes narrow as he idly reaches toward her and mimes grabbing her. I'm not sure what he's imagining—his hand around her wrist or around her neck?

Either way, I'm not sure I like it.

Rage clearly feels the same.

"Hey. Look at me." He snaps his fingers to get Ruin's attention. "You can play with her, but you can't suffocate her."

"And no knives." I slide my fingers into Celia's hair. It's soft as fuck, and I cradle her head against my chest. Warmth spreads from her body to mine, sending a shockwave of something heavy through my bloodstream. I lick my lips, enjoying the way she wiggles to get comfier. She's passed out cold despite the conversation happening around her. *About* her.

The tiniest smile curves on her lips.

I find myself smiling, too.

It's what makes Ruin's interest that much harder to swallow. When he finds something he likes...

He breaks it.

"No knives," I repeat, closing my eyes. They're starting to ache from how long I've been awake today. *Yesterday.* Jesus, what day is it? "And she's not allowed in your room."

Rage nods in agreement. "Definitely not."

Ruin leans back in his chair and doesn't argue. That doesn't mean he'll listen, though. It just means he won't put everything on display.

We'll have to keep an eye on him.

"Anyway," I sigh, "new rules. She gets to pick who she sees."

"Or does not see." Ruin tilts his head to the side and cracks his neck. "I like this."

Rage puts the dumbbell back on the rack and picks up a lost one from the floor. Once it's back in its proper place, he frowns at Celia's reflection in the mirror. He clearly doesn't like it, but it's two against one.

"Meeting adjourned." I bury my face in Celia's hair and take a deep breath, ready for the next six—five —*whatever* hours left to be over. Once she wakes up, everything will be different.

Excitement *zings* up my spine and crackles through my bloodstream, better than any drug.

Maybe the next time Celia goes to bed, she'll take me with her. We can burrow under the sheets in the middle of the afternoon, hide from the daylight, and pretend that at least for a moment, we've only ever been *ours.*

Chapter 13

Celia

Rage is moody all afternoon. Even something as simple as brushing his teeth becomes a battle with his toothbrush, the short, jerky movements so violent that it's clearly self-mutilation. When he spits out blood, I'm not surprised.

But I *am* confused.

"What's going on?" All three brothers have been twitchy the entire morning. "Did I talk in my sleep, or something? Kick someone in the balls?" I slept like the dead, which would have been *wonderful* were it not for the circumstances surrounding it. I should have never let my guard down like that around three ridiculously horny men.

As it stands, it's *mortifying*.

If I kept them up all night snoring—or worse, *sleeptalking*—I'll never live it down. The humiliation alone is enough to ensure I never fall asleep around them again. Not to mention, I might as well revoke my woman card for trusting them to keep their word about not fucking me. If I was knocked out cold, they could have done *anything* to me.

It was reckless and stupid and *I can't believe I actually fell asleep with three crazy men in bed with me.*

Rebel's gray eyes light up from across the kitchen island. If he lost any sleep last night, he doesn't show it. He's been bouncing around the apartment ever since we stepped outside of Rage's room, like a golden retriever let loose after a night locked inside a cage. "You talk in your sleep?" He pours me a glass of orange juice and slides it across the countertop. Lifting an eyebrow in Ruin's direction, he asks, "why didn't you say something sooner? I bet she's spilled all kinds of secrets by now."

Thankfully, Ruin isn't much for conversation. He slips a piece of buttered toast beneath his mask and munches in silence.

"We need to talk," Rage interrupts, stabbing an egg like it's next in line for murder. He glares at the dripping yolk before shoving the plate away from him. "It's important."

I blink owlishly at Rage, unsure about this new development. "Um. Okay."

He grinds his teeth for a full ten seconds. "Pick someone."

I take a slow sip of my juice. "You'll have to be more specific." He could be asking me who his next target should be.

If that's the case, the obvious choice should be himself.

"Pick someone for what?" I ask.

Rage looks like he's swallowing battery acid, the heavy bob of his Adam's apple somehow painful to watch. "You get to go home, *krosotka*." He goes back to glaring at his untouched breakfast plate. "Only one of us can take you."

"The rest of us have to *wooork*," Rebel whines, spinning on his barstool. "So you should definitely pick me. I'll make the drive fun." He grabs the edge of the island and steadies himself, then tosses a wink my direction.

I still don't understand. "Aren't you taking me home?" I ask, peering up at Rage. That was our deal: I spend the night with him, and he takes me home once it's over.

He won't return my gaze. "You get to choose." Rage's frown twitches at the corners. "Hurry up."

I look between the three of them for a long moment. "Is this some kind of trick question?"

"For fuck's sake," Rage snaps, slamming his fist on the counter. His fork clatters against the edge of the plate and tumbles to the floor. With a growl, he tosses his full plate into the sink with a *crash* and storms off. "Forget it. I'm late enough as it is."

I watch as he storms out of the apartment and slams the door shut behind him. The walls rattle from the force of it, and Rebel lets out a low whistle. "Man needs to get laid," he murmurs, scratching the stubble on his chin.

"He's all wound up all the time." His eyes slide from the front door to *me*, a slow smile curving on his lips. "You know... if anyone can calm him down—"

My jaw drops. "*Me?* He just stormed off because of me!" I cross my arms over my chest and glare at Rebel. "*You* sleep with him!"

"That's called incest, baby." His eyes glimmer with mirth. "Plus he's not my type." He licks a stripe across his front teeth. "You, on the other hand—"

The front door suddenly blows open and slams against the wall. I shriek and jump out of my seat, heart pounding, as Rage blitzes back into the room. His muscles are coiled tight, the white shirtsleeves shoved up his forearms wrinkled to hell and back, like he's been tugging them up and down for the past thirty seconds since he walked out. Jaw clenched, eyes tight, he crosses the room and stands in front of me. A vein in his neck throbs.

I gape up at him. "Um. Welcome back."

"Can I—" He winces, clearing his throat with a hard cough. His fists clench and unclench by his sides. Swallowing, he tries again. "Can I... take you home?"

Twelve hours ago, I would have spat in his face. Called him a bastard. Stormed out the door without looking back.

Of course, he would have followed me and dragged me back inside.

But that was twelve hours ago. This is *now*.

And for some reason...

I bite my lip and meet his eyes, wondering how long

he waited outside before coming back in. *Why* he returned in the first place. If he wanted to, he could have picked me up, tossed me over his shoulder, and carried me out the door an hour ago.

It's not like his brothers can beat him in a fist fight. If they challenge him physically, they'll lose. So will I, for that matter. I can do little more than kick and scream in the face of his determination.

My stomach churns at the memory of last night. The blood on the ballroom floor. The salt of sweat and tang of metal on my tongue. The way Rage decimated Goliath with only his fists.

The way he targeted *me* next.

If I close my eyes, I can still feel the weight of him on my tongue. My knees ache like I'm still kneeling in front of him with an unforgiving fist wrapped around my hair, my jaw unhinged as I swallow every last drop of his fury.

But then the memory shifts to soft sheets and decadent down pillows. Warmth spilling from one body to the next. These quiet little breaths. The brush of a hand across my back. Lips caressing the curve of my neck.

Gentle whispers murmured in my ear.

Telling me that I'm beautiful.

That I'm treasured.

That I'm *his*.

Two sides of the same man, constantly warring with each other. Briefly, I wonder if I'm the problem. Maybe if he were with someone else, he could handle his emotions better. Be nurturing instead of nuclear.

I picture another woman on her knees as he gently

glides his cock between her lips, Rage murmuring praise as she swallows him down easily, *eagerly*, aiming to please and be pleasured in return.

But something soft like that isn't in the cards for us. Even now, for him to ask to take me home instead of demanding it, feels like a small step in the right direction, but I know better. He shouldn't even *ask*. I'm the one who's supposed to be able to make the decision. Giving over control to someone else, even with something as simple as a decision like this, is impossible for him.

It's why I shake my head and tell him *no*.

"No?" He grits his teeth, skin flushing red. "How could you say *no?*" Glaring first at me, then at his brothers, he chuffs. "Right. You already chose one of them. Well which one is it, then? Rebel is the obvious choice. You clearly *like* him." He drags his sleeves back up his arms, bunching them at his elbows. "Unless you want a little pain instead of pleasure. Then Ruin's the one you want. But me?" A bitter laugh rattles in his chest. "No, you can't pick me. I might get the wrong idea and think you actually *like* me."

I shove him on impulse, and he tips back slowly like a tree swaying in the wind, snapping back only once the surprise clears. Grabbing my wrist, he holds my hand to his chest, turning his glare on me. "Touch me again—"

"Show me something to like!" I scrape my nails against his shirt as I drag my fingers into a fist. "No, I'm not choosing you, because you're just so—" I cry out in frustration. "You're so fucking *suffocating!* Give me some space, Rage. Treat me like a person instead of a possession, and maybe I'll actually *want* to kiss you."

He closes the distance between us in a single, hard step. "Oh, you want to kiss me." Gaze burning into mine, he dips his head and exhales hotly across my cheek. "Just like I want to kiss you. This thing we have—" he grabs my hip and pulls me into him—"this hot, tight feeling in my chest—" he pants, crushing my hand over his heart. Its beat is a wild, frantic thing, as loud as my own. "It's magnetic. Fucking *impossible* to ignore."

Our lips brush, and we both shiver on impact.

"I'm not fighting it," he rasps, eyes fluttering shut, "so why are you?"

My throat closes, making it impossible to answer. But I know the reason—it's clear as fucking day.

Rage is the kind of man who only knows how to break hearts. He doesn't know how to fix them.

Mine can't break anymore. It's already shattered.

When Rage doesn't get a response, he tears himself away from me and pries my fist from his shirt. "Yeah. I know." Dragging a hand through his hair, he avoids my gaze. "I'm a bastard, right?"

This time when the front door closes behind him, it barely locks into place, swinging shut in slow motion. But it might as well *bang* for how loudly it ricochets through my body, tearing through muscle and bone, breaking me down into even tinier, sharper pieces than I thought was possible.

Rebel whistles again and taps his fingernails on the countertop. "Man, you two need therapy." Shaking his head, he chuckles. "I thought Ruin was the crazy one, but put you and Rage together in a room, and he starts to look pretty fucking normal."

Pain lances through my chest. I turn my glare on Rebel next. If all he's gonna do is laugh at my expense, then that makes everything ten times easier. Walking over to the only masked man in the room, the one who hasn't said a single *word* since I rolled out of bed an hour ago, I lace my fingers through his.

The flash of hurt across Rebel's face makes me hold on tighter.

"I choose Ruin. You ready, big guy?"

Ruin doesn't hesitate. He pulls me away from the kitchen and grabs a jacket slung over the back of the couch. It's huge, heavy, and warm, smelling like cedar and smoke. He wraps it around my shoulders and zips it in front, locking my arms against my chest.

At this point, I don't care about being restrained as long as I get the fuck out of here.

"Seriously?" Rebel hops off his bar stool and blocks the path to the exit. "You're gonna let *him* take you home? He looks like Jason! You know, the murderer!" His face falls. Quieter, he says, "you're wearing *my* shirt."

It takes some twisting and turning, but I manage to pull my arms free from the t-shirt and pull it down my body, even with Ruin's winter coat in the way. I shimmy out of it and let it drop to the floor in a puddle around my feet. "There, now you're free of me, too."

"I don't want to be!" Rebel growls, sounding more

like his older brother by the second. "Goddammit, Celia, this doesn't have to be hard! You can choose all of us!"

I shake my head and wander toward the door. "That's not how the world works."

Rebel grabs the bottom edge of my jacket to stop me from leaving. "It's how *our* world works, baby." Sighing, he grabs my clutch purse sitting on the back of the couch and slides it into my jacket pocket. "When you're ready for that, call me. I saved my number in your phone." He pulls me in and presses a kiss to my lips, soft and slow, and it actually makes me feel a little better. Some of my anger dissolves, and all that's left is a void of uncertainty.

"Okay?"

I nod. "Okay."

Tension in Rebel's body relaxes. "Can I come see you tonight?"

I look between him and his brother. "You mean I have a choice?"

Rebel flinches. "You get to choose who you want to see. For now."

Ruin grunts like he's in agreement. Or growing impatient. I'm not sure which.

"So I can choose none of you?"

There's a beat of silence. "I wouldn't do that."

I want to ask why not, but I think I already know the answer.

Rage won't allow it.

I'm starting to understand that none of them will.

"I'll let you know if I feel like having company," I answer lamely, knowing that in the end, it won't matter.

They'll always find a way to infiltrate my life, even if I don't invite them in.

"*When* you feel like having company," Rebel gently corrects.

"Yeah. Of course."

Walking away after the last twenty-four hours should be easy, but for some reason, walking away is even harder than standing still.

Chapter 14

Celia

I DON'T SEE the brothers for the next three days. At first, I think they're avoiding me, but then I realize that they're just good at hiding.

It's on the third day that Rage's patience wears out. A shadow falls across my desk at the boutique, and I look up from my sketch to find his massive frame blocking the light. Every muscle in his body is clenched tight. "Celia," he rumbles, "you haven't called."

"I know." I go back to my drawing, but my hand shakes. I barely scratch a single line before looking up again.

He's still in my office. *Waiting.*

"You could text me." He places his palms flat across my desk and leans closer. "Tell me about your day. Or night." A thick vein in his forearm pulses in time with his heartbeat. His sleeves are rolled up, and I get a flashback to our last moments together.

This thing we have—fucking impossible to ignore.

I take a deep breath. "I don't want to text you."

He chews on his response for a minute. "Why not?"

Sighing, I set my colored pencil down and lean back in my chair. This is the same room where, less than a week ago, he'd pick me up, sit my ass on the edge of the desk, and eat me out until I couldn't see straight. If I let my mind wander, I can still smell my desire and feel the rough pads of his fingers gripping my thighs.

But all that wandering will lead me right back into his grasp.

That's not where I want to be.

I study Rage's face. "Because you haven't shown me someone worth my time."

That pisses him off. He bares his teeth, looking every bit as menacing as I know he can be. I've witnessed the brutality of his fists—I know he could hurt me if he wanted to.

Our conversation from the other night echoes in my mind. I asked if he wanted to hurt me. Normal men would have said, "the last thing I want to do is hurt you."

But Rage isn't a normal man.

If that's the only way I can touch you, then... yes.

I press my lips firmly together. I refuse to give in to his desires out of fear. If I let him touch me for any reason, he'll interpret it as me giving in because I *want* to. He'll think that I might actually *want* to be with him.

Something twinges inside my chest. I clench my teeth to block it out. I *don't* want to be with him. Or any of them. Not when they're only pretending to care about what I want.

This sudden "freedom of choice" they've given me? It's an illusion.

But I'll ride it out as long as I can.

My words are clipped. "Are we done, yet? You're blocking the light." I grip my pencil harder to hide my shaking hand. "I'm on a deadline. I can't have any distractions."

That part is true, at least.

"We are *never* done, *krosotka*." Rage reaches over the desk and pinches my chin, forcing me to meet his eyes. "But I'll let you pretend for a little longer. That's how generous I am."

"Great. Thanks for stopping by."

As he's leaving the boutique, my employee Sara walks in for the start of her shift. "Oh, hey!" She smiles, but Rage ignores her. What an *asshole*.

Sara laughs awkwardly, the bells over the door chiming along with her. They both dwindle out at the same time. Once she's sure no one else is around, she joins me in the back. "Are you guys fighting?"

I swallow my sigh. I'm never going to finish any of my custom designs at this rate. The charity gala is in a few weeks, and I've agreed to designing not just one, but three elaborate evening gowns *and* fulfilling them with enough time for alterations. It was already a rush job when I accepted, but I took the job before three stubborn men decided that my life was more interesting with them in it. I am *terribly* behind schedule.

I drop my pencil, close my eyes, and rub my temples. Sara asked me a question. What was it again? Something about Rage? "I guess we're fighting, yeah."

"Aw, that's too bad. I think he really likes you."

I try not to roll my eyes. Despite how often she calls out lately, Sara has been a blessing ever since she joined my staff. She doesn't deserve my shitty attitude. "What gave you that idea?"

"He used to visit you every day!"

Choking on my own saliva, I try not to spontaneously combust. Sara should have been nowhere *near* the vicinity when Rage came around in the mornings. If she knows he was here, then she might know what exactly he was doing *while* he was here... I clear my throat and glance over at the thermostat. It's a breezy seventy degrees, exactly how I like it.

I'm not sweating from the temperature.

"My boyfriend really likes me," Sara continues, turning the spotlight from me onto her. "He sends me flowers and asks me all kinds of questions!"

Normally, I'd be annoyed at the incoming lovesick ramble, but today I'm grateful. I feed into her fantasy about her new lover. It's the first one she's had in a year. "That's sweet of him." Maybe Rage could take a page out of his book. "How long have you been together?"

"Oh, I don't know," Sara laughs. "A week or two, I think? He just moved into town for work."

I don't warn her that men who travel for work don't usually stick around or take their new girlfriends with them across the country once their current assignment ends. "You're moving pretty fast," is as close as I get to a warning.

She waves off what little concern I have. "Love should be like that, though, right? Fast and messy and—" she takes a quick breath, bright eyed with lovestruck wonder—"overwhelming, don't you think?"

I grunt, neither agreeing nor disagreeing, and she continues talking without me. My gaze wanders the room, from Sara's blushing cheeks, to the thermostat stuck on seventy degrees, to the wide window separating my office from the shop floor. Across the building, I look even further out, past the front windows and onto the street. People wander in clusters of two or three, chatting with each other, staring at their phones, huddling together to ward off the winter chill in the air. I watch them for a while, wondering if any of them have obsessive not-boyfriends, too, and how they handle it.

Probably better than I do.

Once Sara's ramble slides past the thirty minute mark, I glimpse a shadowed figure in the courtyard past the street. They're standing beneath a huge oak tree, barely hidden from view.

A white mask covers their face. Their *entire* face.

He looks like Jason! You know, the murderer!

Shaking my head, I stand from my chair. The last thing I need is Ruin stalking me in broad daylight. Interrupting Sara feels shitty, but she doesn't seem to mind, smiling broadly at me even as I pack up my things. "Can you lock up on your own? I'm gonna head home." I leave out the back door, avoiding Ruin completely.

I half expect Rebel to be waiting for me at home, but he's good at hiding, too. *Sort of.* The only evidence he was here at all is the half-empty bottle of vodka on my kitchen counter, the china cabinet drawer that's askew, and the hint of cigarette smoke hanging in the air.

I try not to miss him, but the house echoes without his laughter filling the empty spaces. My bed feels like a vast ocean without Ruin standing over it, my body a ship lost at sea.

And my chest—too hot, too tight.

Almost like a magnet missing its mate.

~

"Why didn't you tell me you have a boyfriend? I have to hear from Mikhail that you're dating again?" My mom *tsks* across the line. "You should tell your mother these things, Celia. After everything I've done for you, honey, the least you can do is keep me informed." She takes a breath, her chair creaking as she shifts her weight. "Really, Celia. Think of your poor mother. It's dreadful to learn these things secondhand."

"I'm not dating anyone." My nose twitches. Fucking *Mikhail*, meddling where he doesn't belong. He's still pissed that I'm avoiding his calls. I have nothing to say to him—other than a big, fat *fuck you.*

My blood boils, but not toward my mother. I rein it in, taking a deep breath before continuing. "Mikhail's the one you should be worrying about."

Humming to herself, my mother tactfully avoids the

subject. Like always. Heaven forbid that the favorite twin do something wrong.

Like murdering dozens of people at his own fucking wedding.

My head throbs. I don't know that I'll ever forgive him. The longer I hold onto my disgust, the harder it is to remember anything else about that day. About *him.* The brother I used to know fades in the memory of blood on the chapel walls and screams reverberating in the rafters.

My mother conveniently forgets that part of the day's events.

"At least he's married," she says with a sniff.

Here we go.

"Maybe this one will stick, honey. The boyfriend. Have you talked about marriage at all?"

"I'm not dating anyone," I reiterate, grinding my teeth. "I already told you that, Mom."

"Mikhail says you're dating again. He wouldn't lie to me. He knows how important it is for you to settle down. You're almost thirty, Celia." The chastisement stings a little less than it did the last time she reminded me of my status as a single—no, *divorced*—woman.

In my mother's eyes, I may as well have had the affair myself and ended my marriage. She blames me for it more than she blames Ted.

"What are you doing for your birthday? You should throw a party. You were always so good at throwing parties. Invite your new boyfriend. I want to meet him. Does he want kids?"

This time when I sigh, I'm not nearly as good at hiding it.

My mother goes silent across the line. "If you do that while on the phone with your boyfriend, he's going to take it the wrong way. I know you don't mean to offend me, honey, but it's rude to make that sound when someone is talking to you. I'm sure Ted told you that, too."

My heart beats a little faster as the urge to *flee* slams into me. "I've got to go, Mom. I'm getting another call."

"Tell your boyfriend that I want to meet him. Goodbye, dear."

I hang up and stare at the *call ended* screen. A minute goes by. Then two. I take a deep breath and pour another glass of my favorite sparkling wine, all the way to the rim. Maybe I'll finish the bottle, too. It's the weekend. I'm allowed to indulge.

Gulping a mouthful, I try to decide what to do next. The house is eerily silent, like it's mocking me for being alone. In the first few months after the divorce, I let it creak and moan without much thought. We were doing it together—*falling apart*. Only after I heard that Ted was dating again—from my mother, of course—did I pick myself up and get back to business. Mikhail happily invested in my clothing line, and getting the proper licenses for the shop was a cinch with all of our connections within the city. The process was expedited at every level, the universe likely hearing of my downfall and deciding to throw me a bone.

I thought the sudden invitation to *Midnight* was

another one of those gifts from the universe. A chance to start over. To reclaim something I'd lost.

It sure as hell feels more like a curse than a blessing.

Cell phone in hand, I open my contact list and scroll down to the *R's*. There are only three names listed—Rage, Rebel, and Ruin—in alphabetical order. Possibly chronological order, now that I think about it. How much older is Rage than the others? Is Ruin the middle brother or the youngest?

Where does that other guy, the half brother, fit into the mix?

It's probably a good thing that I don't know more.

I might think that I *care*.

I put all three *R's* into a group message, but once my thumbs hover over the keyboard, I'm not sure what to say. *Thanks for making my mom think I'm a shit daughter for not telling her about my nonexistent boyfriend?* I can't truly blame them for my mother's low opinion of me. I've been a cyclical disappointment to her my entire life.

When Ted and I announced that we were trying for a baby, she was elated. But the longer it took to conceive, the more critical she became. What positions are you trying? Are you temping yourself? Tracking your ovulation? You know, your father and I had to pray every Sunday for three months before we got pregnant—why don't you speak with the pastor? Or better yet, why don't you speak with God?

Sometimes I think that the reason my marriage fell apart isn't because Ted had an affair—it's because I didn't have Faith—the one with a capital F. If I believed in God, he'd bestow gifts upon his humble follower, wouldn't he?

A happy marriage?

A healthy baby?

A womb that works?

I swallow two more hearty mouthfuls of wine and type out a message for the group.

> Do any of you want children? Answer honestly.

I hit send before I lose my nerve. If they say no, then I know that the universe—or God—is still punishing me for my lack of Faith.

If they say yes, it might be an even greater punishment...

Having a baby with a Russian criminal is probably on a list of sins somewhere. People are born with sin—isn't that something I've heard from a Sunday sermon? Does that mean that the child inherits the sins of the parents?

My stomach churns.

If that's true, then no matter what I do, I'll always be a bad mother. I'll have doomed my child before they even take their first breath. My chest constricts as the idea settles deep inside, weighing me down. I sink further into my chair, no longer battling the depression looming in the back of my brain.

I let it wash over me in full force.

My phone chimes loudly in the empty room. It takes me a minute to muster the strength to move. When I do, it's in slow motion. I set my wine glass down on the coffee table and take several deep breaths, each one longer than the last. Then, I wrap my favorite throw blanket—the fuzzy one with silver hearts—around my shoulders and pluck my phone out of my lap.

The text message is from Rage.

Of course it is.

I have to read it a few times before my brain processes what it actually says. I'd forgotten the question already.

> RAGE:
> I only want children with you.

My breath hitches as I imagine the timbre of his voice rumbling in my ear. Hasn't he said that before? I sift through all of our conversations, but before I can come up with the answer, my phone chimes again.

> REBEL:
> i want 6 kids minimum
>
> so I can chase them around the house
>
> it'll be fun
>
> (thumbs up emoji)
>
> RAGE:
> How many children do you want, Celia?

He isn't asking *if* I want children, only *how many*. Shit, didn't I tell him once that I didn't want kids? Is it too late to shut this conversation down? I clench my eyes shut and take another breath, unable to block out the ache thrumming through my body. I want my own kids.

Desperately. My heart flutters inside my chest as I imagine a house full of them, all different ages, like we're on the set of *Cheaper by the Dozen*. Up until recently, I've always been close to my brother, and I'd want my children to have siblings they can rely on.

> Six might be too many. Maybe four. A girl and three boys. Or two girls and two boys. But I'd be happy with only one.

> okay, two

> siblings are important

RUIN:
> (smiley face emoji) ☺

The irony of Ruin's text isn't lost on me. I've never seen the man's smile, let alone his face.

REBEL:
> miss u baby

I type back *miss you too* but catch myself before hitting send. I *can't* miss Rebel… or any of them. Locking my phone and shoving it under a throw pillow, I pick myself up from the barrel chair in my living room and leave my wine glass on the table. It's empty, but I'll clean it up tomorrow. Same with the blanket I leave piled on the chair.

Tomorrow, I'll put everything back to normal.

For tonight, I want to lie in bed and imagine how many children can fit under one roof. Which ones have dimples when they smile. Dark, unkempt hair no matter how often they brush it. Deep ocean eyes, capable of taking in an entire room with one glance.

And a mother who loves them all, no matter the sins of their mother... or their father.

Chapter 15

Celia

I TOSS and turn all night long, my body fluctuating between too hot and too cold at the flip of a coin. I picture a golden dollar spinning on its edge, flicking between the two opposites in flashes of muted gold. I count its rotations, thinking it will help me sleep. Hot. Cold. One. Two. Three. Four. Hot again. Shivering. Sweating.

With a groan, I switch on my bedside lamp and sit up against the padded headboard. If I stare long enough at the doorway, the shadows bleed into shapes. I picture someone walking through, stepping into the light and taking true form.

But I can't tell who it is. Huge and muscled like Rage? Lean and long like Rebel? Or a bit of both, striding into the room with the grace of a panther, the eyes of a predator glowing behind his mask.

I don't know which is worse: knowing that I keep thinking about them, or wondering if I *want* to.

Even their ghosts help block out the hollowed loneliness rattling through the house. It's a skeleton of my former marriage—and all the promises that came with it.

We were supposed to have children within our first year of marriage. Ted promised me that if I quit working, he would provide all I needed to be happy. The money came easily. The friends flowed like wine. But family? The one thing I really wanted?

It never came.

I wrap my arms around myself and stare into the darkened hallway until the sun begins to rise. The shadows lift from the deepest blacks to midnight blues, the promise of tomorrow turning everything into a fuzzy gray.

Even the daylight looks depressed today.

Skipping my morning shower, I shove my feet into my slippers and pad down the stairs. My eyes catch on the empty wine glass in the living room. The throw blanket still piled on the swivel chair. The sunlight suddenly shifting to a harsh pink, painting the room in an eerie, blood-red glow. I stare at the pillows hiding my phone.

Did they text me all night?

Were they annoyed that I didn't answer?

Biting my lip, I drift from the living room to the kitchen. The bottle of vodka on the counter absorbs the rusted sunlight, turning its contents a bitter orange. I unscrew the top and pour what little remains down the sink, crinkling my nose at the sudden waft of alcohol this early in the morning.

I think I'll skip breakfast.

My gaze lingers on the empty bottle, the white label peeling at its edge. How many of these have I seen? Just as empty. Just as bitter. Without thinking, I snatch the bottle by its neck and fling it to the ground, shrieking as it shatters. Shards of glass skitter past my feet, but I'm already climbing onto the countertop and reaching for the cabinet over the fridge.

Rebel has raided this cabinet numerous times, but there are still bottles shoved all the way to the back. All of them are open, their labels peeling from age. I have to stand on my tiptoes to reach the furthest one, but I drag them all out and toss them to the floor.

The *crash* echoes through the empty house. Goosebumps rush down my arms. The vodka spills across the tile floor from one square to the next, flowing like rivers of rust, turning yellow with the sunrise.

Once morning breaks, everything turns clear again. The broken bottles sparkle. The trickle of spilt alcohol slows to a stop, looking as innocent as water. The light loses its color, fading back to its normal, crisp white.

I feel like I can breathe again.

Careful to avoid stepping on glass, I swing into the pantry to grab the broom and start sweeping. Then comes the mop. I lose myself in cleaning, the first hour of the day slipping past. Then the second. There's a familiarity to it that's comforting. Cleaning up after parties became a chore I enjoyed. It kept my hands busy and my mind occupied.

Most of all, it kept my husband locked in his office all morning. He offered to hire someone to handle it, but never followed though. Truthfully, I'm grateful. It kept me distracted enough to ignore how often his secretary came by to *review the week's progress.*

As I carry the bag of broken things to the trash can by the street, something red in the front window catches my eye. At first, I think that Rebel left one of his beanies in the house, but as I walk back up the driveway, something glitters in the light beneath it.

I walk up to the window and stare into my dining room. Sitting in the center of the table is the largest bundle of red roses I've ever seen, arranged inside a spiraling crystal vase.

Not a forgotten hat.

A *gift.*

I look around my front yard, half expecting one of the brothers to be standing behind me. That would be just like them—watching me work all morning without lifting a finger to help, all because they're itching for me to notice the *real* gift they've left out for me.

Rolling my eyes, I walk through the kitchen to the dining room. The scent of roses hits me like a freight train. I'm surprised I didn't notice it when I first came downstairs, but after trashing those bottles in the kitchen, the harsh burn of alcohol in my nose could have blocked out everything else. When did they drop this off?

Was it after our group text?

Nerves skitter down my arms, but I lift my hand to

rub a soft petal between my fingers. It comes loose, floating down to the table.

Flowers are supposed to be romantic, but it's the vase that *really* piques my interest. It's clearly antique, *heavy*, with a solid base and a wide lip. The spirals are short and jagged, each one only an inch or two long, like the artist wanted to create something for flair instead of function. The points dig into my palms as I lift the vase and carry it into my office. Once I've arranged both the vase and its bouquet perfectly, I step back to admire them.

Two dozen roses, *at least*. I stop counting after the first sixteen. "Who dropped you off, hm?" The better question is *why*.

They don't answer, of course, but I talk to them anyway. It fills the silence and drowns out the numbness creeping in.

My ex-husband used to bring me flowers like these after he'd thrown a fit the night before. It was a stupid gesture—flowers can't fix a failing marriage—but they made pretending easier. People used to comment on how pretty they were. I'd smile and say, *Ted got them for me!*

I don't think I actually like flowers anymore.

A card sticks out from the back of the bouquet. I stare at it for an entire minute before tearing it open, ripping the crease on accident.

for a special girl

I purse my lips and tap the card against my palm. "Well, that could be anyone." I open the card again and notice black smudges around the corners—*fingerprints*. Mine? Frowning, I drop the card and turn over my hands to inspect my palms. Soot stains my fingers and dusts my hands. I *just* cleaned, too. Was there dirt on the trash can? The door handle? I stare at the card, then at the ash powdering the table around it.

No, around the *vase*.

Lifting my hand to my nose, I smell smoke. Running my finger along the edge of the vase, black powder appears. It's stuck in the grooves, like whoever cleaned the crystal didn't actually bother *cleaning* it properly.

Fucking weird.

"Has to be from Ruin." Who knows what kind of freaky shit he gets up to. He probably stole the vase from someone's garage. I bet the roses were Rage's idea. Maybe Rebel dropped it off while I was sleeping.

A true joint effort between them.

The mental image of three walking disasters planning a romantic gesture is funny enough that I laugh. It spills from my chest so brightly that I jump in surprise.

My phone chimes from the other room, and I wipe my hands on my pajamas as I go after it.

I've missed seven text messages and two calls. Most are from Mikhail—he probably heard from our mother again—which I promptly ignore, but three are from the group chat.

REBEL:

want breakfast?

RAGE:

Invite me over.

REBEL:

i asked 1st dipshit

My stomach flips with butterflies. It feels silly. I know what these men are capable of. And yet...

They got me flowers.

> Meet me at 75th? I need a shower.
>
> *and coffee*

REBEL:

i got u baby

RAGE:

she asked me

REBEL:

your 2 busy

im on the way

RAGE:

I'll pick you up, Celia. Don't leave.

REBEL:

send us a pic. I bet ur soaking wet

(wink emoji) 😉

The flowers *definitely* weren't Rebel's idea. I'm smiling as I temp the water and get undressed. My phone pings while I scrub my hair, and I reach outside the shower door to grab it.

Rebel sent me a picture in a private chat. I nearly drop my damn phone. "Shit. *Holy* shit." He's lounging in bed shirtless, the colorful tattoos inked across his chest on full display. There are no words, only thick outlines filled with deep greens and blues and reds. I can't make out the design, so I refocus on his face.

He's ridiculously handsome when he smiles.

Staring directly at the camera, he takes my breath away. The snakebite in his bottom lip catches the flash from when he took the photo. His hair is messier than usual, both falling into his eyes and sticking out at the same time. From up close, I realize that his irises aren't gray—they're hazel, with deep, dark brown roots near the center.

> REBEL:
> ready 2 see me?

I blush furiously, feeling younger than I have in years. I don't text people often, and I never, *ever* send photos unless it's for a client.

But this time, I make an exception. Snapping a selfie, I giggle as it sends. Three bubbles pulse while Rebel types his reply.

> REBEL:
> damn baby

> gonna give me a (heart emoji) 🖤 attack with that smile
>
> show me more?

He knows I'm in the shower. I didn't exactly try to hide it.

REBEL:
> ive got more for u 2

Another picture pops into our chat, and this time, I *do* drop my phone. "Ah!" It lands on the top of my foot, making me hiss. "Shit! Fuck!" I scramble for my phone, but it's sitting at the bottom of the shower, soaking wet, just like me. The screen is dark. The buttons won't work. Those texts and pictures are gone forever.

But the sight of Rebel's dick, flushed red at the tip, his hand gripping the thick shaft, with not one piercing but *three* glinting in the light, is burned into my mind.

My flush deepens and I swallow hard. I bet a picture doesn't do him justice. I bet his cock is just as pretty as he is.

And now, he probably thinks I'm ghosting him after seeing his dick.

"Fuck. Me."

I rush through the rest of my shower, anxious for whatever comes next. Because if I'm being honest with myself...

A breakfast date and a little flirting doesn't sound bad at all.

It actually sounds *good*.

Really good.

I get dressed in record time, putting on a racy red pair of panties, a pleated cotton skirt, thick thigh high socks, black leather boots, and a creamy cashmere sweater. I blow dry my hair and throw it into a messy bun on top of my head, framing my face with a few loose waves. My makeup is light, but I'm rushed, and this is *breakfast.*

It's not like it's a *real* date. Just a casual one.

But if things go well, I might return the favor and show Rebel a little more of myself, too.

A knock echoes down the hall from the front door, and I shove my broken phone into my purse and practically run down the hall. I'm breathless when I pull the door open, a carefree smile on my face, my keys in hand. "I'm ready for that coffee—" The winter chill hits me square in the chest, my smile freezing in place.

Rebel didn't say he would pick me up.

Rage did.

Our eyes meet and he sucks in a breath, eyes widening. When my smile fades, Rage's expression goes from pleasantly surprised to closed off in a heartbeat. "Don't look so excited to see me." His voice is as gruff as his demeanor as he takes my arm and leads me down the front porch steps.

For the first time since I met the man, he avoids looking at me.

My heart flip-flops between relief and disappointment, each one so startling that I gasp for air. It chills me to the bone, and I wish I'd worn sweatpants and slippers instead. Or a Snuggie. And a hat with those little ear flaps.

Something big enough to swallow me whole so that I disappear altogether.

Because when Rage first laid eyes on me today, he actually looked *happy*—and I snuffed it out so fast that I don't even think he realizes he was smiling at all.

Chapter 16

Rage

75TH AND MAIN is one of the most well-known cafes in the upper half of the city. It's boujee, made for girls having peppermint lattes and dainty little breakfast sandwiches before they walk the Avenue to window shop—or in Celia's case, where she has the most unfulfilling breakfast of her life.

Not only does she keep looking over my shoulder to check the door every minute, but she won't speak more than three words to me.

How's your toast?

Fine.

Are you cold?

No.

Do you want another coffee?

I'll get it.

No, *thank you for taking me to breakfast* or *thanks for picking me up despite your busy schedule*. I glare at her plate, the slice of bread with green mush spread on top a fucking *offense.* "You can order anything you want," I repeat, grinding my molars. It's becoming a habit the longer I spend with Celia. It's like she's always looking for ways to upset me, and my body handles it the only way it knows how: by grinding the feeling into dust until it disappears altogether.

She takes another bite of avocado toast and shrugs one shoulder. "This is good. Really."

Four words. An improvement.

"How's your coffee?" I ask, spreading my arms across the back of our booth. The movement catches her eyes, the lightest dusting of pink on her cheeks. She likes how I look. I *know* she does.

So why is she acting like she's embarrassed to be seen with me?

I look good. I smell even better. I've got more money than I could ever spend, and I'm willing to throw it all at her feet. If she told me to take her down the Avenue for a shopping spree, I'd cancel all of my meetings and spend the day following her around.

Happily.

Because she *chose me.*

Her outfit is cute, the skirt high enough to show a solid two or three inches of warm skin where her stockings end halfway up her thighs. The sweater hugs her tits. Her boots are worn but clearly well-loved, the soles scuffed but not torn apart. She put effort into her appearance this morning, spending what little time she had between our messages and my arrival to put together an outfit that I would enjoy.

No, not *me*.

Rebel.

The fucker.

"Where is he, anyway?" Celia picks at the flaking crust of her toast, trying to look casual. But there's a tension in her shoulders that gives her away. The way she wrings her hands together when they're not clutching her mug. Her knee bouncing up and down.

"Who?" I lift an eyebrow, knowing damn well who she's talking about. I want to hear her say his name.

Meeting my eyes, she straightens her spine, her mouth twitching as she wrestles with how to respond. We're in public, so I doubt she would make a scene. Her upbringing would have conditioned her to be polite when out in the city. Really, it should have conditioned her to be polite all the time, no matter what I do or say to her.

Apparently she trained herself out of that.

"The better brother." She traces a manicured nail along the edge of her cheek as she brushes a lock of hair behind her ear. "Obviously."

I lean across the table toward her, crowding close enough that I can smell her perfume. She holds her ground, looking up at me from beneath her long lashes with a wide-eyed innocence that I *know* is as fake as my smile. "I assure you..." Brushing my knuckles up the back of her forearm, I bring my lips to her cheek. "Whatever fantasies he's put in your head won't live up to the real thing, *krosotka*." I press a gentle kiss to her skin, holding her jaw to keep her from moving away. My mouth lingers long enough that I'm tempted to claim her lips, too.

But I don't.

I release her, enjoying the simmering outrage sparking in her amber eyes as I go back to lounging on my side of the booth.

"You're full of shit," she says casually, like this is just another conversation. I suppose that's a skill she perfected, too. Despite the fire in her eyes, she's no longer nervous or twitchy at being alone with me. She's in control, putting on a perfect show for anyone foolish enough to eavesdrop.

"I will never lie to you, Celia."

"You're so threatened by your own brothers—" her smile is fucking *dazzling*—"that you can't let them win, can you? Not even for a moment. I bet they're suffocating, living with you. Under your rule." She takes a slow sip of her coffee, letting her words sink in. "How does it feel to be the reason your family is so fucked up?"

I let her think that she's right for a full minute. She preens like a bird ruffling its feathers, a cat-like glow to her eyes. She's fighting back—not with her fists, but with her words.

I fucking *love* this side of her.

"We look out for each other. We always have. That's why I agreed to share you with them. Not because I *want* to—" I hook my foot around her ankle and pull her leg closer to mine—"but because I *have* to."

All three of us need her, but I still don't think she understands that.

She tries to pull her leg back, but I trap her thigh between my knees and squeeze. If my hand were under the table, I'd slide it up her stockings and beneath the cheeky ruffle of her skirt.

Those red fucking panties are a *tease.*

I know she wore them for Rebel, but I'm the one who's going to enjoy them while he's locked away in his room, unable to get out. Ruin will return home eventually and shove the furniture I used to barricade his door out of the way, but until then... Celia is all mine.

The flash of anger in her eyes turns me on.

"You're so full of yourself! Like you're God's greatest gift to the world." She laughs loud enough to turn a few heads, but they see the same thing I do: a diamond sparkling in the sunlight. Warm rays bathe her honeyed skin, highlighting auburn streaks in her hair. I wonder if they're natural or if she goes to the salon. Her nails are perfectly manicured, too, but she could do them herself. I could see her being picky enough that anything less than perfect isn't acceptable.

Will she turn that perfectionism onto our children, or will she love them in spite of their flaws?

Oh yes, I remember our little texts from last night. I'll never forget them. She let a secret slip—revealing the lie she told the other night.

She *definitely* wants children.

And I'm going to give them to her.

Celia is still on a verbal rampage, though, so that conversation will have to wait. "They don't need you to take care of them—"

A woman wearing the most obnoxiously loud perfume and white platform boots interrupts Celia with a shriek, running from the front end of the cafe to our table in the back. "Oh my stars! Is that really you, darling? It's been ages! Oh, you look stunning!" She leans over the table and forces Celia into a tight hug, wrapping her arms around Celia's shoulders and squeezing. "When I heard about the divorce, why, I just knew you'd be a wreck. But look at you now! You'd never know that snake of a man ever bit you."

I catch Celia's frozen smile and wide eyes before she corrects herself. "Heather Hanson, you are too much!" Her expression warms as she looks the older woman over. "What are you doing here? I thought you moved east."

Heather waves her hand. "East side can't handle me, darling. I was only there for two months before I moved right back. But that's old news—what's this I hear about you designing again? Janette Fowler will not *stop* talking about these dresses you're making for the upcoming charity gala. You have to show me the sketches! Janette's keeping them close to her chest, and you know how much I love to come out on top. I can't be outstaged, darling." She laughs, but there's not a joking bone in this woman's body. Her gaudy rings catch on Celia's sweater as she tightens her grip. *A threat.* Celia better not design something *too* pretty for this Janette Fowler, or Heather will retaliate.

Blood rushes to my head, pulsing hot in my ears. I glare at Heather's hand, her skinny little arms, her fake fucking tits.

No one threatens *my* woman.

Before I can react, however, Celia has a business card in one hand and a sketchpad in the other. "Tell me what look you're going for this year, and I'll draft something up for you." She slides the business card into Heather's purse. "At a discount, for a friend." When she smiles, it draws Heather in, and the older woman suddenly slips into our booth and hurriedly whispers in Celia's ear. Nodding while she draws a preliminary sketch, Celia must capture the essence of Heather's vision, because Heather's already pulling out her checkbook.

I count the zeros in her deposit and can't keep a smirk off my lips.

This cafe isn't just a trendy place to show off your haul from the day's shopping spree. It's a *networking* opportunity.

"I'll call you once I have the initial mock-up ready," Celia promises, tucking the sketch into Heather's hand and curling her fingers around it. "Expect to hear from me by the end of the week."

Heather thanks Celia excitedly before strutting across the room to her own table, immediately nodding toward us the moment she sits down with another two ladies. Their eyes ping between me and Celia, curiosity in their gaze.

"You didn't introduce us." I rap my knuckles on the table. "Worried she might like me?"

Even my presence can't pop Celia's bubble. She wraps up the remnants of her toast in a napkin and shoves it aside. Shaking her head, she exhales, yet even that is brimming with excitement. "Worried you might ruin the sale. I saw that look." She stares across the table at me, a coy smile on her lips. "You wanted to eat her alive."

"Never," I murmur, reaching across the table to take Celia's hand. There's only one woman I'd like to devour. I link our fingers together and squeeze. "But dismemberment? That's still on the table."

She laughs, the sound rich and full of life. "If she stiffs me, I'll be sure to let you know."

I neglect to inform Celia that if either Heather Hanson or Janette Fowler dare insult my woman's work or skill by shorting her money or praise, they'll be screaming it from the rooftops while I peel off their eyelids.

Either way, it's a win.

I get to hold Celia's hand, and she gets to sit across from me looking just and pretty and perfect and *happy* as she deserves.

∽

Once Celia has a to-go latte in hand and we step outside the cafe into the late morning chill, she pulls us to a stop on the sidewalk, clears her throat, and straightens her spine, like all of a sudden, walking down the street by my side is more serious than sitting with me in a cafe. She looks up at me with a tiny divot between her eyebrows.

I don't care what it is she has to say, as long as she keeps letting me hold her hand. It's a funny thing. We're barely touching, yet my entire body's on fire. My cock could cut glass, and I'm sweating beneath my suit jacket. She fidgets with her purse strap while she stalls for time.

"What is it?" I ask, trying not to laugh. She was perfectly in control of herself inside the cafe, but now that we're out of familiar bounds, she's twitchy again.

I long to kiss the nerves right out of her system.

So that's exactly what I do.

Pulling her into my chest, I cradle the back of her head and cover her mouth with mine, humming at how sweet she tastes, like cinnamon. The tension in her shoulders eases, and she leans into the kiss.

My heart damn near beats out of my chest. This is different from all of our other kisses—I'm not forcing it on her because I can't stand the distance between us, I'm doing this as much for her as for me.

She *melts*.

It's satisfying as *fuck*.

When she looks up into my eyes, I can finally see it —*gratitude*.

"Thank you," she murmurs, her cheeks turning pink. "That was, um, okay. The breakfast. Not the kiss. That was—" her breath hitches—"fine."

"We can do better than *fine*," I promise, slanting my lips over hers. She lets me in for the briefest moment, her dainty hands clutching my shirt as she just... *lets me*. Taste her. Hold her. *Fuck*. It's everything I've wanted, yet nowhere close to complete. It's a glimpse of what our future could be like—these small, soft moments. Then it's over too soon, somehow turning my body into fucking lava despite how brief it was—but also *so* fucking worth it. There's this dazed look in her eyes, and the little dimple on her forehead is erased.

She *likes* gentle kisses.

Maybe that's why Rebel's so fucking whipped for them.

"I, uh..." She licks her lips. "I need a new phone."

"Mmm." Maybe I'm a little dazed, too. I inhale her scent and try to wrap myself in her presence. My lips ghost over hers.

"Rage," she murmurs, peeling herself from my arms. She stands a few feet away, catching her breath. "Did you hear me? My phone broke this morning. I need a new one."

I drag my hand across my jaw. She was texting us just fine two hours ago. "What's wrong with it?"

She shakes her head. "It got wet. I dropped it."

I blink at her. "In the toilet?"

"In the *shower!*" Her mouth gapes. "I need a new one, okay? Please take me to the phone store."

What was she doing in the shower with her phone? I narrow my eyes at her skirt, imagining the smooth, creamy velvet of her thighs hiding beneath, a hand sliding between them and white, frothy suds dripping from her fingers. "Why did you have it with you?"

Her cheeks burn. "I was texting."

She sure as shit wasn't texting me.

Sighing, I nod. "We'll get you a new phone. I know a guy."

Celia follows me back to the car. "I don't want *a guy*,

Rage, I want a phone store. You know, how normal people fix their phones."

"We're not fixing it, we're getting you a new one. Isn't that what you said you wanted?"

She purses her lips. "I want a phone that works. It doesn't have to be new." This woman gives me whiplash. It's like she goes out of her way to disagree with me.

While she buckles, I call my guy and put in the order. Extra-wide screen. Amazing speakers. The best tracking device in the country, linked directly to my phone, laptop, and car.

Only the best for my girl.

～

"It's so big!" Celia fiddles with her new phone while I handle payment.

"I know you like them big," I rumble, smirking at her.

She inhales sharply, that spark of defiance in her eyes. I turn back to Terrance and hand him her old phone. "Upload the data to our server." I'm going to find out what was so distracting that Celia gave her phone an unexpected bath. "And text me once it's done."

"You got it."

My phone rings in my pocket as Celia walks back over to me. She chats idly with Terrance, thanking him for helping on such short notice and promising to send more customers his way.

"He doesn't need references," I inform her, checking

my phone screen. *Ezra.* My boss. I have to take this call. "I keep him busy enough." Really, the entire bratva keeps Terrance busy, but she doesn't need to know whose money paid for her phone.

If she finds out it's blood money, she might throw the fucking phone in my face.

"Does he handle your security at the club?" Celia wanders the room, idly checking the dozens of monitors, hard drives, and technological baubles lining the walls. She's probably referencing all of the security panels within our apartment. There's one on the outside wall, then one more for each bedroom door within. An armory has two separate scanners, one for hands and the other for eyes, and the escape hatch hidden beneath the floor is connected to a completely different system.

She doesn't need all of that information. "Something like that." Terrance doesn't have access to any of the security feed or systems within the apartment, but he monitors the club. It's close enough that I don't have to bend the truth too much.

The call goes to voicemail, and I immediately call back. While it rings, I keep my eye on Celia. Thankfully, she notices a picture frame on Terrance's desk and strikes up a conversation with him about his kids, giving me time to step into the hallway and greet my boss. "Ezra."

He grunts across the line. "You missed meeting this morning." His Russian accent is thick today, meaning that he's likely been up most of the night. "Have you found Jimmy?"

The only good reason to miss a weapons trade with a

rival bratva is finding one of our missing men, apparently. I know it's been bothering Ezra, that one of our own would disappear into thin air. He takes the family aspect of being a member of the bratva seriously. As the head enforcer-turned-bodyguard to the bratva, all men, women, and children are under his protection. "Haven't seen him." The lie flows easily. If Ezra finds out that Ruin killed him on *my* orders, we'll both be punished for acting without permission. It's okay to kill an enemy at our own discretion, but killing one of our members, even someone as two-faced as Jimmy, is bad for our reputation.

But Jimmy was fucking shit up left and right. I don't have proof, but I know he was intentionally missing drops and pocketing something in return. Until I have the proof, though, it's my word against a dead guy's. The odds would be unfairly stacked in my favor, and it would look suspicious.

Best that Ezra thinks Jimmy ran off on his own—

"There is killer on loose," Ezra murmurs, sounding displeased. "You know this."

—or that Jimmy died to some stranger with a death fetish.

Catching killers is only my forte when there's money involved or the boss puts in the hit. We don't know who this new player is, and until bodies start dropping on my doorstep, I'm not too concerned. "I've heard the rumors. Only women are being targeted. Jimmy might be ugly, but he's not the guy's type."

Ezra grunts. "Jimmy could be practice dummy. We

need to find body. Confirm death. See if there is connection between victims."

I stay silent. Technically, he hasn't given me an order. We don't really play detective in the bratva—we shoot first and ask questions later. Or, we *used* to. Having a new Queen could change things, but those decisions are above my pay grade.

Apparently, they're above Ezra's too. Once I don't supply him with any new details, he moves on from the serial killer topic and goes back to Jimmy. "We need to tell family. Mother is nice woman. Go see her today. And call the Kolzovs to reschedule meeting. They will not be patient." A woman's voice in the background says something about *flowers*. Ezra grunts again. "Bring flowers to family. Put on best face."

I glance across the room at Celia. "I'll go tonight." I hate dropping her off back home so suddenly, but visiting a bereaved family member sounds like a shit job. Dragging her with me won't exactly endear her to me. I'd rather she sit at home alone than watch me pat some old woman's back in fake concern for her missing son.

"You will go *now*. I have canceled other meetings. This is most important. Kolzovs will wait until tomorrow, but not after."

Shit. It will take me at least thirty minutes to get to Celia's house, then another thirty to wind my way through the streets to Jimmy's. The fucker still lived with his mom. She should be *grateful* that he's no longer around to leech from her saggy tit like overgrown devil spawn.

There's no way I can take Celia home without Ezra finding out about it. "I don't know shit about flowers, Ezra."

A pause, then, "ask your woman."

Fuck. Of course he knows about Celia.

"Yes, sir."

Ezra hangs up the call, and I watch *my woman* fawn over a bundle of pictures dangling accordion-style from Terrance's wallet. The man must have a dozen kids. She smiles and compliments each one, her laugh bubbly and bright, her enthusiasm genuine.

If that's how much she likes a stranger's kids, I can't wait to find out how much she's going to love our own. My heartbeat trips as I imagine Celia sitting in a rocking chair with one toddler bouncing on each of her knees, while I hold up a picture book for her to read aloud. Or the opposite. Maybe I'm the one with two kids in my lap, and Celia is sitting across from us near the fireplace, rocking a baby in her arms, the most beautiful smile on her face as she pours her love into something we've created.

That's what I'll give Celia.

The family she's always wanted.

I picture her with a rounded stomach, our hands meeting over the swell of her belly, and everything in my body feels *fuzzy.*

"Are you ready?" I ask, taking her by the hand. She's still smiling when she turns to me, but there's a shine in her eyes that wasn't there before. She hastily looks away, thanking Terrance again before slipping her hand from mine.

"Yeah, I'm ready." Her voice catches, and I follow her out the door and onto the street. She's walking fast enough that I have to jog to catch up.

"Celia."

She ignores me.

"*Celia.*" I grab her arm and spin her around.

Tears track down her cheeks, and she chokes on a strangled sob. "D-don't get mad," she squeaks, patting both of her cheeks. "I'm sorry, they'll stop soon, I'm so sorry—"

I pull her into my arms and mentally curse Terrance to every single level of hell there is. "What did he say to you?" Cupping her face, I search her eyes. "Did he hurt you? *Touch* you?" My voice clips, a rumble vibrating through my chest. "I'll *kill* him."

"No!" Celia clutches my neck, pulling my face down to hers. Our foreheads meet and she clenches her eyes shut. "No, he didn't do anything! This is my fault! I'm just—I'm a mess, okay? Just take me home." There's a pleading whine in her voice.

Whatever is going on in her head must be serious if she's turning to *me* for comfort. She doesn't even *like* me. I'm not flirtatious Rebel or mysterious Ruin.

I'm the man who keeps hurting her because as much as I can get off on her pleasure, I also enjoy her pain.

But apparently even that has its limits, because seeing Celia like this when it *isn't* my fault, when I'm not the one who is causing her pain, makes my world go haywire.

I keep my voice as steady as possible. "What's wrong, Celia?"

"It's nothing!"

We're close to one of our safe houses. I can take her there until she calms down. I don't want to drag her to Jimmy's house for her to start crying all over again. Then I'll have *two* hysterical women on my hands. Besides—"I can't fix it if you don't tell me what's wrong." I brush my thumbs over her cheeks. "Tell me what's wrong, *krosotka.*"

She shakes her head in refusal, making my next decision easy. I lift her into my arms and carry her back to the car, buckle her in, and speed down the road. The safe house is in one of the grimier parts of the city. We call this area *The Backyard*, because it's only a few streets away from the influential, high-end storefronts like *75th and Main*. As we pass by run down alleys and boarded windows, Celia starts to pay attention.

"This isn't the way to my house," she murmurs, rubbing her eyes.

"We're not going to your house."

Her eyes shine with unshed tears as she glares at me. "Take me home."

"No."

She raises her voice. "Take me home, Rage! I'm fine."

"You're not fine." Something about Terrance, the phone, the store? That can't be it. The pictures? The children? I keep an eye on Celia as we close in on the safe house, its location only a few minutes away from the Avenue. Something set her off. Something sharp, digging into her chest, making it hard for her to breathe. I can see it in the way her hands shake. How her eyes keep glazing over, unfocused, as she loses herself in an internal fog.

Ignoring the problem isn't going to fix it. She's probably been doing that for months. *Years.* That woman from earlier, Heather, hadn't seen Celia in *ages.* If I had to guess, Celia's been hiding ever since her divorce. Ignoring her problems. Ignoring her *pain*.

There's only one way I know how to handle something this deep—by burning straight through it.

Chapter 17

Celia

Rage takes me to an unmarked hole in the wall and expects me to be *happy* about it. Although the outside walls are cracking and there's a hint of urine in the air —*gross*—once we're inside, modern appliances make the six hundred square foot room look more like a studio apartment. A *clean* one. There's a stainless steel fridge and microwave set into a faux granite countertop, an open-shelf used as a basic pantry, and an entire wall taken up by a desk with various medical equipment, bandages, pill bottles and syringes, and a floor to ceiling gun safe. There's a single door on the far wall, leading to what I can only assume is a bathroom. Whether or not it has a shower is up for debate.

"This is a safe house," I say numbly, rubbing my arms. I'm not surprised that the bratva has them all over the city, but I'm not sure what Rage and I are doing in one. I glance at the double bed, but the last thing I want to do is lie down.

"Yes, it is." Rage stands in front of the door, arms crossed, watching me. "You're safe here."

I snort. "I wasn't questioning my safety, thanks."

His eyebrows pull together. "You're upset." A muscle in his jaw tics. "I wanted to get you off the street."

"Don't want to be seen with a crying woman?" I shake my head, exhaling hotly. "We could have stayed in your car. You could have taken me *home.*"

It takes Rage two long strides to reach me. He cups my face in his warm, calloused hands. I've seen these hands break a man's body. The bruising along Rage's knuckles has lessened, but the evidence of his power resides in not only the discoloration, but the scars. One jagged cut has scabbed over, more recent than the others, but there are bumps and ridges across his knuckles that show the passage of time, countless beatings recorded only in memory. Were Rage a professional boxer, he'd wrap his hands before every fight. Even MMA fighters, despite a lack of a padded boxing glove, still wrap their hands to protect from fractures and sprains.

Rage uses his body as a weapon—without any thought of protection or longevity. Maybe the fights are always spur-of-the-moment, but I have a feeling that he has plenty of time to choose his targets. Hell, he could fight with guns, knives, any number of weapons—but instead, he uses his fists.

Without a barrier between him and the pain he inflicts, some of it is bound to recoil back into his body. He could be holding countless scars—both on his flesh and within it.

Maybe *that's* why he's so quick to anger. He's always fighting.

"If I took you home," he says slowly, midnight eyes searching mine, "you would have been alone until Rebel or Ruin could get to you. I never want you to be alone when you're like this, Celia."

Tears sting my eyes. "I'm fine." The words are tight, high-pitched lies, but I desperately want them to be true. I *should* be fine. It's not like I've lost a child—Ted and I never conceived. I should be happy to celebrate others' families.

But there's this jagged, twisted knot inside my chest that writhes with jealousy any time I see others experiencing the life I want. It's a cruel twist of fate to be simultaneously overjoyed for someone and drowning in envy every time they walk in the room with their family. Married, unmarried, one child or five—the variances don't matter. It's the love I see in the parents' eyes as they talk about their children, or the way the younger ones rush into their arms after an hour apart.

I want that.

So badly.

Rage can't possibly understand.

He closes the distance between us and falls into me like we're sinking in quicksand—slow, deliberate, every ounce of his attention on the spaces where our bodies meet. He tangles a hand in my hair and slants his lips over mine with such tenderness that it tugs on something inside my chest. I fall to pieces in slow motion, the hitch of breath caught in my throat, the silent tears that overflow, the way my body unravels beneath Rage's touch. There's no anger in how he undresses me, all of the impatience and greed to claim my body disappearing as quickly as it comes. I watch him battle with it—the need to *take* washing away beneath the need to *feel*.

Goosebumps trail down my arms once he lifts my sweater over my head. His hands follow their path, his lips scorching against the column of my throat. I stumble out of my boots while he unzips my skirt, pulling it over my hips with a kiss to my stomach, then to each hip bone. "You are breathtaking," he rasps, gazing up at me with pure, overwhelming awe. My body flushes with heat that settles deep in my belly, and I gasp as he lifts me easily and lays me down on the mattress.

I don't feel breathtaking.

I feel exposed at my core, aching to the depths of my soul. Rage isn't doing this to me—it's impossible for one person to tear me open so deeply—but I lay bare for him all the same, my worst fears on display. "I can't do this," I gasp, pushing myself up onto my elbows. "*We* can't, Rage—I, I *can't*." Tears threaten to spill, and a sob catches in my chest. "I don't want to have sex if we can't have a baby."

His eyes find mine, their depths molten pools of black. I once imagined that they were twin black holes—all-consuming, terrifying, unending. The way he looks at me makes me believe it, like he wants nothing more than to swallow me whole and trap me in an abyss that only he can reach. A master of his domain, with me as his eternal muse.

He doesn't speak, pulling at the buttons on his shirt and exposing his chest, his throat bobbing with a swallow. "Eyes on me, *krosotka*." Slowly, he pulls the shirt off his back, exposing black and grey tattoos along the edges of his ribs, down the sides of his torso. Among them are patches of rough skin, some stretched pink, others matching his natural skin tone but mottled with definitive scarring. His jaw clenches as he undoes his belt and strips out of his pants, allowing me to see even more scars across the tips of his shoulders as he bends to remove his shoes. Once standing, he climbs onto the bed and nudges my thighs apart to make room for his hips.

We aren't fully naked, both of us still in our undergarments.

Rage brushes the tears from my cheeks with a sigh that settles into my bones, like he's the one falling apart. "Everything that I am," he murmurs against my lips, "is yours." He grabs my hand and holds it tight against his chest, the beat of his heart strong and steady. "Everything that I *can be* is already yours." Rocking his hips into mine, he grinds the hot length of his cock against my center, his eyes burning with a fire that's immeasurable. "Take it. Take *me. Use* me. I will give you everything you've ever wanted, everything you've ever dreamed." Melting into me, he groans against my lips, one hand cupping my throat while the other hitches my leg over his hips. He grinds deeper, rotating his hips. "Let me give you what you need, *krosotka*."

The ache in my chest fizzles like a fire being doused with rain. At first, each of Rage's kisses—on my lips, down the side of my neck, across every inch of my collarbone—makes the pain hiss and snap as it lashes out to stay alive. When Rage cups my breasts and takes my nipple into his mouth, the fire screams as he douses it with soothing licks of his tongue, the heat still burning but tolerable. He slides my panties down my thighs and nestles between them, glancing up at me before pressing a hot, open-mouthed kiss to my slit.

The moan that tears from my chest makes him growl, and he dives in, licking and sucking my clit with a fervor that's unmatched. No one has ever eaten my pussy like this—not even *him*. His eyes spark with that all-knowing confidence that drives me crazy, but I can't hate him for it, not when he's washing away the gnarled thorns in my chest, breaking them down until the ache subsides.

We could do this.

We could *actually* have a baby.

Rage smiles up at me while he hooks two fingers inside, rubbing the spot that always makes me come undone. Pleasure zings up my spine, and I clutch the bedsheets as a tremor wracks my body. "That's it, *krosotka*, that's my beautiful girl. You want to come, don't you?"

I keen in response, grinding my hips onto his fingers.

"I'll always give you what you want," Rage groans, mouthing my clit, flicking it with the tip of his tongue.

My body seizes as I come, the room fading into white noise, bright light, and the weight of Rage settling over me. I open my eyes and he's smiling at me, so beautiful that it hurts. Seeing him so open, every single one of his scars on display, unlocks my heart.

He may be a monster, but he's the monster promising me every dark part from his world—and all of the light from mine.

"I want a baby," I plead, nodding my head. "I want a baby, Rage."

"You want *my* baby," he corrects, pulling free from his boxers. His cock bounces against his abdomen before setting over mine. "Say that you want my baby, Celia."

My heart skips, but it's beating too fast for my mind to catch up. "I want your baby."

Rage slots his cock against my entrance and thrusts, sliding it through my lips without entering, the tip pushing against my clit. My breath hitches as he does this again, one hand wrapped in my hair, the other searing against my hip as he holds me steady. I squirm, knowing exactly where I want him, but he pants hotly in my ear and keeps rubbing me, coating his length in my desire.

"Say it again," he rumbles, nipping my earlobe. "Tell me that you want my baby."

"I want your baby."

"Louder."

"I want your baby!"

"Fucking *promise me*," he hisses, gripping my hair so tightly that it stings. He leans on his forearm and gazes into my eyes, his own narrowed into slits. "Promise that you want my baby, that you'll *have* my baby, that you'll fucking *love* my baby."

"I will!" I cry, wrapping my arms around his neck

and pulling him closer, crashing our lips together. When I break for air, I hold him close, panting into his mouth. "I'll have your baby, Rage. I'll love them, keep them, treasure them."

Until my dying day.

He punches his hips and slams inside of me, growling as he claims my mouth. "Oh, *krosotka*, my beautiful girl. So ready to be a mother."

I cry out, but he swallows the sound, groaning as he buries himself to the hilt and grinds his pelvis into mine, the pressure causing pain, but the heat and swell of his cock fucking *magnificent*. I keen as he pulls out only to slam back in, hitting the deepest parts of me.

"I'm going to pump you so full of my cum," he moans, "so fucking full of me." His cock twitches and he pants. "*Fuck*, mama, I'm already gonna bust. Take my seed. That's it. *That's it*." He bursts deep inside, his cock pulsing as it fills me. The hot, wet sensation between my legs makes me wrap them tighter around his waist, keeping him inside. I don't want a single drop wasted.

Rage groans. "Oh, I've got more. Don't worry." He chuckles deep in his chest and kisses me hard, sliding his tongue between my lips. Grabbing my breast, he massages it roughly, pinching my nipple between his knuckles. "You're gonna take three loads, aren't you, mama? Three thick, fat loads. I've been saving them for you." He shudders, pulling his dick a few inches out before sliding it back in. He rocks into me with hard, steady thrusts, notching his teeth on my neck and sucking a bruise into my skin. "Gonna mark you up so good, too. The whole world will know you're mine. Say it. Say that you're mine." He punches his hips, making me gasp.

"I-I'm yours."

I don't even know if I mean it. Having his baby is one thing, but giving myself completely to this man?

What more could he want from me?

What more is there to give?

It doesn't matter if I'm sure or not, because Rage comes with his teeth clamped on my neck, groaning as he fills me up a second time. Pain mixes with pleasure and I writhe beneath him, so close to coming that I feel it in every square inch of my body. "*Rage*," I whine, digging my nails into his shoulders. "I can't—I'm gonna—" His fingers find my clit and he presses hard, pushing me over the edge.

I'm expecting him to pull out, but he sits up on his knees and grabs my hips, slamming me onto his length while he thrusts faster, sweat dripping down his forehead. My pussy clenches, and I feel the slick heat of Rage's cum and my own slipping down my body, coating my thighs and sliding between my cheeks. Rage grinds his teeth and slams me onto his cock, growling like an animal. "Get ready, *krosotka*, so fucking wet, so fucking good for me, gonna fill you up so good—" Everything blurs together, from Rage's nonsensical words to the pounding of my heartbeat and the sensation that I'm falling—further and further into this man, seeing the deepest parts of him that he promised were mine.

Everything that I am is yours.

Heat builds in the deepest parts of my body, where Rage and I are joined, where my heart bursts into flames, where my soul resides. Rage is giving me the very essence of his life to create a new one, and I don't know what to do with that.

How can I take him into my body without at least respecting the man willing to give me the one thing I've wanted most in my entire life?

He comes a third time as promised, flooding me with his seed, and collapses on top of me. The weight of him drowns out the frantic beat of my heart with his own. He keeps his cock nestled inside of me, but I can feel his cum leaking out as he finally softens. With a groan, he slants his lips over mine and kisses me. It's sloppy and wet, but no less enthusiastic as he sucks my bottom lip between his. "Lie still," he instructs. "I'll make sure it takes."

Before I can question what that means, he's pulling out and leaning back to grab my knees. Lifting them high into the air, he bends me in half so that my pussy is lifted toward the sky.

"Hey!" I smack my hands against his thick thighs. "It doesn't need to be that high! A pillow works!"

Rage grins at me, then looks fondly at my leaking pussy. "I like the view from here." He spreads my thighs, and I can feel my lips separating, the thick cream sticking to my swollen skin. Gently, he gathers the cum spilling down my thighs and pushes it back inside, slicking his finger and groaning. "So full of my cream. Gonna knock you up, *krosotka*. Then everyone will know who you belong to." He plays with my soaking wet pussy, a satisfied smile on his lips. "Here, taste how good we are together."

He holds his glistening finger up to my lips, nudging them with the tip. "Open up, mama."

I part my lips and he slides his finger inside up to the first knuckle.

"Lick it clean."

I swirl my tongue around his finger, tasting our desire. Then I moan as the taste spills into my mouth, my pussy throbbing, pulse soaring. I whimper, and Rage lowers my thighs down to the mattress.

Replacing his finger with his lips, he kisses me like it's our first time, taking it slow, savoring the moment. Relief washes over me as I realize that this could be the beginning of a new chapter—something beautiful and bright, precious and perfect.

"I'm all yours," Rage promises, wrapping his fist in my hair, "you're all mine," he presses the flat of his palm over my stomach, pressing firmly, "and *this* is all ours."

In that moment, I believe that even if Rage isn't perfect, he's at least right.

Whatever bonds we've made today don't only belong to me or to him—they're ours.

And *that* might be what makes them perfect after all.

Chapter 18

Celia

The safe house *does* have a shower, but Rage denies both of us the pleasure.

"We are *not* going shopping like this!" I gape at him while he redresses, moving swiftly through the motions like we're on a deadline. "You have got to be kidding me!"

He grabs my arm and pulls me into his chest, kissing the next protest from my lips. "We're not going shopping. I have business to attend to. It can't wait, and I'm not leaving you here without me."

I'm wearing panties, but a thin strip of cotton is no match for the flood between my thighs. "I can't go out there like this! I'm in a *skirt*, Rage! People will be able to —" my face flushes—"smell me!" I tug my skirt lower, but it's no use. It's a *mini* skirt, so named because of how little coverage it provides. "I wasn't planning on having sex when I put this on!"

"You should *always* plan for sex with that on."

Rage's smile turns wolfish. "In fact, we'll keep it on next time."

My face flushes crimson. I want to tell him that there won't be a next time, but—didn't I promise something like, oh, I don't know, having his baby? I press my hand to my stomach, butterflies fluttering rapidly within. I can't be held responsible for decisions made under duress. Surely, Rage will understand if I tell him that I didn't mean it—

He catches what I'm doing and a sunny smile breaks across his face.

Shit. Maybe not.

The door suddenly opens, and I shriek in surprise and cover my chest with my sweater. My bra is still lost to the floor somewhere.

Ducking through the doorway, the limo guy from the last club event at *Midnight* enters the room. What was his name? Thanos? His gaze flicks between Rage and me, disinterest quickly turning into something sour. Lip curling, he shoulders the duffel bag slung across his back before dropping it to the ground. "Did you just have sex? *Here?*"

"Thanatos," Rage greets, ignoring the question while he buckles his belt. "This is good. We need to talk. Have a seat. No, actually, grab your things. We've got a job."

"*You* have a job. I just got back." There are dark circles under his eyes that weren't there the last time we met, his hair unkempt and dirty. He drags his bag across the floor to the bed, frowns at the messy sheets, then drags it over to the desk. Unzipping it, he pulls out a handful of weapons of all sizes. Knives. Pistols. A semi-auto rifle and multiple ammo cartridges. Once he's rummaged around for all the loose bits, he kicks the bag back toward the bed. "I'm not due in for another six hours."

Six hours. What a shit schedule.

Rage bends, plucking my bra from beneath a small accent table, and tosses it toward me. "Get dressed, Celia."

"I need to shower!"

"No, you don't." Even Rage looks freshly-fucked, a sheen of sweat still sticking to his skin. He wears the sexed-up look well, dripping with confidence that makes my pussy flutter. *God,* I shouldn't want to have sex with him again so soon.

But me, on the other hand—I bet I look like a drowned rat that barely made it out of the river alive.

The other guy's gaze flicks toward me once he's seated in a flimsy metal chair that looks like it'll snap under his weight. His eyes narrow as he looks me up and down, clearly disliking everything about me.

The feeling's mutual, asshole. The buzz from life-altering sex is officially killed.

"Yeah, she does. She smells like a whore."

I choke on saliva.

"But not here. I'm staying here, Rage," he sighs, running a hand over his close-cropped hair. "Get the fuck out with your—" he *laughs,* throaty and deep, cutting himself off before he can finish his thought. "God, I need some sleep."

"Celia. Bra. Sweater. Boots." Rage fixes me with a stern look before walking over to his half-brother. He grabs the gun Thanatos is trying to clean, impeding his progress. "That *whore*," he rumbles, "is *mine.* She has a fucking name. Use it."

Thanatos glares at Rage, then at me. "You need a goddamned shower, *princess.* There, happy?"

A frustrated cry catches in my throat. "I'm not a princess!"

"You're not anything!" he snaps back, standing so fast that his chair crashes to the floor. "You're not a part of this fucking family *or* this bratva. What the hell is she doing here, Rage? If she's just a hole for you to fill—"

I gasp aloud.

"—do it in your fucking club! Not in my bed!"

"She is my *woman*," Rage seethes, clenching his fists. "I'll fill her up as much as I fucking please, wherever I please. You'll be happy about it when you're jerking off to our cum on your sheets."

Thanatos's jaw clenches, a muscle in his neck pulsing. "I will *not* jerk off to some prima donna bitch."

I shove my arms through my sweater and tug it over my head. Screw the bra.

"*Excuse me*, I'm right here!" I storm over to both men and plant my hands on my hips. "An actual human being, not a cum dumpster, or a prima donna princess, or whatever stupid title you're gonna throw at me next." I glare at Thanatos. "I didn't know you were living here, so I'm sorry. I'd hate if someone else had sex in my bed, too—" I wince at the memory of that *exact* thing happening to me—"but I genuinely had no idea. You don't have to be a dick about it. And *you*," I hiss, jabbing Rage's chest with my fingertip, "stop being so vulgar and maybe someone will actually like me! It's like none of you grew up with a sister or a mother or anyone other than yourselves. Our image matters! How people perceive us *matters*. We can't go around swinging our fists every time someone insults us." I roll my eyes.

"That's all you princesses know, isn't it?" Thanatos crosses his arms over his chest. "Petty bullshit about makeup and parties and fancy red heels. Fake smiles and faker tits." He glares at me. "There are *real* threats out there, ones that you can't fuck into submission." He turns his glare onto Rage. "I never expected to come back and find you pussy-whipped. You've even talked the others into it! All three of you are obsessing over this girl like she's some God-given miracle, when all she is, is leftover trash her husband threw out."

It's like a punch to the gut.

Thanatos isn't finished yet, his face burning red as he rages. "Your daddy couldn't stand having such a weak daughter, could he? Had to kill himself just to get away from you. You weren't even chosen as our interim Queen when Valentina left, because you were too scared to marry one of our own, running off to some white collared bastard—"

"*Shut up*," Rage roars, jamming the barrel of a Glock under Thanatos's chin. "Shut up, *shut up!* You have no idea what any of us have been through, because *you* left! Five years, Thanatos! Who do you think kept Rebel from snorting himself into an early grave? And Ruin—he needs an outlet for all the fucked-up shit he's been through, so who do you think gave him one? Because it sure as shit wasn't our older brother. Off chasing ghosts —" He growls, cocking the gun back. "There's nothing out there but shadows, Than, because we killed our demons. Don't go looking for them here, too."

My heart races. I don't really like the guy at this point, but Thanatos is Rage's *brother*. "You can't kill him," I stammer. "Rage, that's your—he's *family*."

"Family doesn't walk away," Rage retorts, glaring. "But maybe a *half*-brother does. God, you sound just like Dad. He pulled the same bullshit, and look how that ended up." Rage shakes his head. "That grudge you've got, Than, it's real fucking ugly. It'll get someone killed." He lowers the gun and shoves it into his waistband behind his back. Then he pulls his arm back and swings, connecting with Thanatos's jaw with a sickening *crack*.

I stumble backward, expecting a fight, but Thanatos spits blood onto the carpet and grunts. He doesn't move to return the punch. "Get out."

Rage stands between me and Thanatos while I zip up my boots and grab my purse. I've lost my bra again, so I'll have to leave without it. The cold is gonna be a *bitch* when the sun goes down. Thankfully, neither of them speaks to me as I grab Rage's hand and pull him toward the door. Rage doesn't look at me until we're two blocks away, his own anger still simmering just beneath the skin. He takes a steady breath before grasping both of my hands in his.

"Are you okay?" he asks, searching my face, then my body, like he's expecting to find bruises. "I didn't know he would show up. I'm sorry."

I shake my head. "What was that about?"

"Thanatos?" Rage pulls a face. "He's got issues like the rest of us."

"No, I mean—" I take a breath. "How does he know those things about me?" The divorce, sure, that's common knowledge at this point. But my dad? That was *years* ago. The official story is that he committed suicide, but I suspect that it was an inside job. Someone within the bratva took him out.

It's the way all criminals die, in the end. Backstabbed by one of their own.

A shiver rolls down my spine, making my teeth chatter. I don't like to think about my father, because he's a reminder of everything that's wrong with the world. *My* world. I left the bratva because a good man died for someone else's sins. My brother and I lost our father, my mother lost her husband, and for what?

Money?

Shaking my head, I try to clear the oncoming headache before it starts. "The bratva, I—" I wince. "I know they were upset when Valentina left the city, but I stayed. I'm still here."

Rage clenches and unclenches his jaw for a moment. "You married an outsider." It's a fact, not an accusation, but it still sounds like one. "You only got away with it because your dad was already dead. If I were Mikhail—" he grips my chin, pushing his thumb against my lips, "—

I would have married you off to some rich, eligible *vor* the moment your ex dared put a ring on your finger. Because, Celia, you *belong* in the bratva. You belong with *me*."

"If he married me off, I wouldn't be yours right now."

Smiling, Rage slants his lips over mine, humming into our kiss. "Trust me, mama, *nothing* would stop me from taking *this*." He grabs my ass and spins us around, pressing me against the cool metal of his car. "You're just as mine now as you would be with another man's ring on your finger. Which there wouldn't be, because I'd kill him before he could ever get to you. The only reason it took me this long," he murmurs, slipping his hand beneath my skirt and palming my ass, "is because I didn't realize how perfect you were for me yet. That came later." He brushes his lips over mine with a sigh. "I'm only sorry it took me so long."

A question wriggles in the back of my mind. I've asked it before, and now I have even more unanswered questions about all three brothers. *Four*, if I include Thanatos, which it seems like I have to now. They fight for attention, each question needing answered, but I stick to the most pressing for now. "Rage…"

He kisses me, slow and sweet, despite the hand curving between my thighs to feel the cum leaking around my panties. "Yes?"

"When did we first meet? Did I know you back when…" I think to what Thanatos said earlier. "…things were different for you and your brothers?" If what Thanatos said is true, they've had a tougher life than I'd realized. The image of Rage's bare chest flashes through my mind, the mottled skin pink and raised, and I wonder what happened to him. I wonder what happened to *all* of them.

"You mean *harder*, not different," Rage muses, grabbing the thick flesh of my thigh. His palm skates up and down my skin, teasing me. "Maybe we knew each other back then. It's difficult to know for sure. I kept my focus on our family once things went—" he scrunches up his face, like there's a bad taste in his mouth—"south." He nips my bottom lip. "But things are *much* better now."

"So we met at *Midnight*," I try to clarify, grabbing Rage's wrist to keep his hand from wandering. "Right?"

He groans, mouthing my jawline. "What does it matter? The past doesn't change anything."

"Why are you avoiding the question?"

Lifting his eyes to mine, he presses his lips into a thin line. "Because you won't like the answer. Let it go, Celia."

Now I'm remembering why I find this man so infuriating. I slide my fingers into his hair and pull, tearing his face away from mine and enjoying the pained grunt he makes. "Rage," I warn, "tell me the truth. Was it at my dad's funeral? Before? Did you know me when I was in high school? College?" I run through the possibilities in my head, but that has to be too far back. "You didn't know you wanted me until I was already married."

Rage's hands slide up my sweater, one palming my naked breast while the other closes around my throat. My sweater catches on his arm, exposing me to anyone who walks by. The cold winter air makes me shiver, my nipple pebbling between Rage's fingers. He squeezes both of his hands, the smile on his face the cruelest I've seen all day. "Keep digging, *krosotka*, and you'll only get hurt."

"Why?" I swallow against his palm. "Did we meet each other *during* my divorce? Did you know that I locked myself inside my house for months? That my husband was cheating on me?" It *sort of* fits, but I have a feeling that Rage would have broken my door down and forced his way inside my life sooner, had he known the extent of my depression. Still, I run with the idea. "That's it, right? You didn't come rescue me after my divorce. You're afraid I'll hold it against you."

Rage stays silent, which prompts me to look harder. He never attended one of Ted and my house parties, so those years are off the list. I didn't do much between the time my husband cheated and the divorce was finalized. I barely left the house, so that theory doesn't work. The only thing that kept me busy in those months was my design work or my brother.

My breath catches on a sharp inhale.

Mikhail is part of the bratva—one of the captains, actually, in charge of projects involving real estate and finances. Rage, Rebel, and Ruin don't work directly under him that I'm aware of, but somehow, our paths still crossed. We know each other because of my brother. Something he did? Somewhere I went? A party or a funeral or a—

A wedding.

"You were at the chapel. The wedding." *The Bara-*

nova Butchery or *Baranova Massacre*, as it's now known among inner circles. Ice floods my system, freezing me from the inside out. "But I didn't see you among any of the guests. I haven't forgotten a single face from that day."

Or a single scream.

Rage's eyes bore into mine. "I wasn't exactly on the guest list."

I blink up at his infuriating, handsome face.

He wasn't on the guest list.

I struggle against him, pulling his hair, slamming my knee into his thighs, whimpering as he holds me down and grabs me with enough force to bruise.

"Celia," he hisses, "calm down."

"You were there!" I dig my nails into his scalp, hoping he bleeds. "You heard all of those screams! People were scared for their lives! How could you do nothing? Where were you—"

Masks. There were at least a dozen men wearing armor, masks, and face shields rounding up the guests for interrogations, holding guns to people's backs, shouting orders in both Russian and English. "You weren't a guest," I repeat, my body shaking as adrenaline courses through my veins. "You were on a *job*." I hurl the word at him, spitting flecks of saliva in his face. On a job just like Thanatos, another huge, muscled, *angry* man, waiting to take out his problems on the next unsuspecting victim. "You tortured innocent people."

Rage's expression goes eerily still. "None of them were innocent."

I bark a laugh, my throat burning as it claws free. "Tell that to the children. The mothers. The wives. I spent *hours* protecting them from men like you—brutes who were scaring them to death!"

"Exactly!" he snarls, cutting off my airway with a twitch of his wrist. "You were the *only* one in there not losing her fucking mind once everything went to hell! Do you know how rare it is to find a woman tough as nails before she's eighty? It's fucking impossible. The old bats keep their cool because they've lived through shit, but *you*, Celia Monrovia, you *fight*. You protected every single child in that church for hours, not letting up for a single second. You fucking *snarled* right at me, like you wanted to kill me." A shudder courses through Rage's entire body, easing his grip over me.

I wheeze for air, coughing from the burn. "Maybe I should have."

Rage laughs, his dark eyes sparking with joy. "It's too late for that, mama, because you're fucking *mine*. You gave your word *and* your body. Soon, you'll lie beneath my brothers, too, all three of us pumping you so full of our cum, you'll be pregnant every nine months." He moves his hand from my breast to my stomach, scraping his nails along my ribs, making me hiss from the flash of heat, the sting of pain.

"I can still kill you." I move my hands to his throat, and he doesn't stop me. I squeeze as hard as I can, feeling his Adam's apple bob beneath my palms. "Then none of you will have me."

"I'll always have you." His voice scratches against my

skin, burrowing in, latching on. "Because you'll always have me. Right *here*." His fingertips dig into my abdomen, making me gasp. "I own you, mama, in this life and every life after. Killing me won't change that."

Fury melts the ice freezing me in place. I squeeze harder, enjoying the way his eyelashes flutter. He could break free. He's stronger than me. We both know it. Why isn't he stopping me? Why isn't he shoving me hard against the car so that I black out? Why isn't he fighting back?

He smiles, lifting a hand to brush his bruised knuckles against my cheek. "You're beautiful, *krosotka*. Have I ever told you that?"

I press my thumbs harder, deeper, closing his arteries, his windpipe, anything I can. My heart leaps in my chest, making my arms shake. *Dammit.* I can do this. I can kill a man.

I can kill Rage.

But when his body finally goes limp and he drops to the ground, I fall with him, a sob tearing through my throat as all the hope I had for the future—the tender smiles, the bubbling laughter, the children running up and down the halls—fades into smoke.

Chapter 19

Ruin

It's unusual for Rage to be late.

One of his most prominent traits is punctuality, because he's obsessive about keeping a schedule. When the schedule is kept, everything else that follows runs smoothly.

The fact that I'm standing at Jimmy Morrel's doorstep with a bouquet of flowers in hand is *not* an indication of things running smoothly.

He's late.

And I'm the one suffering for it.

Mrs. Morrel is an older woman, well-known within the bratva for her husband's accomplishments and her son's failures. The former died a respectable enough death in a shoot-out that took half a dozen enemy lives, but the latter found himself tied to my chair while I ripped his tongue out with rusted pliers. The differences between the father and son duo could not be understated, and Mrs. Morrel, as a woman of average intelligence, understands this.

It's why she isn't surprised to find me on her doorstep.

"Come in," she says gruffly, not bothering to hold the door open for me. "Wipe your feet on the mat."

Her home is average, too, with decor I've seen dozens of times in houses all across the city, arranged in exactly the same way, at the same height on the walls and paired with the same colored knick-knacks. I could tell her that she has a lovely home, but that would be a lie.

"Your son died."

I don't tell her that he died honorably, because he didn't. She likely understands that, too. I leave out the part about him praying to God, though, and the part about him begging for forgiveness around what little remained of his cracked teeth. Most people don't want to hear the details. They only need the most basic of truths.

"I figured when he didn't come scurrying home, that he was gone for good this time." She doesn't sound too sad about it. Sitting in a rocking chair by the roaring fire, she eyes me from across the room. "You're one of those brothers," she murmurs. "Can't say we haven't met, because I recognize you from somewhere. Lord knows where, though, in this city. You must handle the tough jobs, on account of the mask." She nods toward me like she understands, but this part, she's faking.

No one knows the full extent of what I do, because it's always changing. I float in and out of the spaces my brothers leave empty, removing body parts wherever I go because I can't help it, while our clean up crew silently mops up the mess. They don't complain, so neither do I. It's not a bad life.

It's just not a normal one.

"I brought you flowers." I hold out the bouquet. The petals are all different shapes, some soft, some prickly, with varying colors from one flower to the next. People are like that too, on the inside. Some parts soft. Some hard. Different colors bathed in reds and blues and pinks, changing with every slant of light.

"Put them in a vase with some water. They're in the lower left cabinet by the kitchen sink."

There's only one vase. Tall, blocky, bland. As white on the inside as the outside. I fill it with tap water and stare out into Mrs. Morrel's backyard. It's a tiny square with patches of dead grass sprinkled across bare earth, enclosed with a chainlink fence that's seen better days. It's rusted where the metal links cross one another—like my pliers.

The problem with Rage not being here is that he handles transitions best. There's an easy way to move people from one room to the next, and it's by using your words. He's good at that. Talking.

"No dog?" I ask, staring out at the empty doghouse in the backyard. The paint chips off the sides, blanketing the ground like snow.

"He died shortly after my husband."

I stick the bouquet inside the vase, the plastic wrap crinkling as it slides through the lip. "How did he die?"

Mrs. Morrel appears at the refrigerator door, refilling

her glass of iced tea from a plastic pitcher. "Got run over in the road. That how my Jimmy die? Car crash?"

"No."

She sips her tea. "Didn't think so."

Silence stretches between us. "They sure didn't teach you anything about conversation, boy. Your mama run off?"

The scars crawling up my neck itch. "She died."

"My condolences."

I don't think Mrs. Morrel means it.

I really wish that Rage were here. Then I wouldn't have had to speak with Mrs. Morrel at all. Truthfully, I could have broken in through her back door or any of the bedroom windows, but Ezra told me to be polite. She lost her son recently. She might scare easily.

Nothing about the old woman in front of me looks scared.

Why would Rage be late? Why wouldn't he call? The cell phone in my pocket feels heavy. I tap my fingers against my thigh. "Can I sit with you, Mrs. Morrel?"

She waves her hand toward the living room. "I'll pour you some tea."

The ice clinks in my glass, condensation dripping down the sides. The entire house is warm from the fire, making my palms sweat. The glass slides down my fingers. I set it on the coffee table and lean back on Mrs. Morrel's couch. "I've never had iced tea."

Her face twitches. "Why don't you try some. Jimmy loves my tea."

"Jimmy's dead."

"How did he die?"

I lick my lips, a shot of adrenaline coursing through my veins. "I killed him."

The confirmation rocks through her body like a bullet, jolting her backwards, the chair rocking into the wall. "Oh, Jimmy. You fool." She shakes her head, but I catch the swell of tears in her eyes. Jimmy cried too, near the end. Mother and son have that in common.

I rise from my seat and cross the rug toward her. It's also white. So much of this house is white. And beige. And cream. Wicker furniture. Things that stain easily.

"Where is your brother?" Mrs. Morrel asks suddenly, her hands shaking around her glass. "He's supposed to be here, isn't he? He's supposed to speak with me. You don't go on these visits alone, do you?"

"I don't know where he is."

"Then call him!"

"He's probably busy."

Which can't be right, because he picked Celia up this morning. Neither of them have come home yet, and the sun will set within the hour. He can't be busy, because there's nothing for him to be busy with when he's with Celia.

"I'm not supposed to hurt you," I tell her. "We're supposed to talk."

"You're bad at talking."

"I know."

She exhales heavily, slumping in her rocking chair. "Jimmy did his best, you know. For the bratva. For this family."

I know that she believes that, so I don't say otherwise.

My phone vibrates in my pocket while I'm standing in front of Mrs. Morrel. When I'm on the job, I usually leave it in the car, on the floor, on the counter. Somewhere out of the way, where it can't buzz at me. But the only ones who contact me are Ezra or my brothers.

And lately, Celia.

I take the few steps back to the couch and sit down. Mrs. Morrel visibly deflates like a balloon, flattening into her chair, forgetting to rock. Her breathing is shallow, but she keeps her eyes on the fire, like its presence is going to make a difference for what happens tonight. Or maybe she's trying to see the future. Forget the past. People do strange things before they die, so I keep my eyes on Mrs. Morrel to find out what she's going to do next.

My phone buzzes again, so I fish it from my pocket and squint at the screen. Rebel is spamming our group text with messages.

> REBEL:
>
> you mofo
>
> where are you?
>
> its been all goddam day
>
> hello???

Then, in our group chat with Celia:

> REBEL:
>
> baby, u ready 2 come home?

> I can cook u dinner

Rage remains silent. Celia doesn't reply. It's like they're keeping us out—which goes against our new rules. I send a message to our private chat without Celia.

> did she choose you today

REBEL:
> fuck no, she didn't choose Rage
>
> she chose me
>
> fucker locked me in my room
>
> im still here u know
>
> i told u to let me out ruin
>
> y is no one home??? im starving

I call Celia's phone, and it goes to voicemail. The same for Rage's. I call Rebel, and he starts yelling at me the moment he picks up.

"It's about damned time! How far away are you? Can you bring me a burger or a taco or something?"

Mrs. Morrel's eyes move from the fire back to me. Watching. Waiting.

"Rage isn't answering his phone."

"*I know.* I've left him ten fucking voicemails."

"Celia won't answer either."

"*Tell me about it,*" Rebel snaps. "You send a girl *one* fucking dick pic, and she ices you out!"

"She won't answer me, either."

Rebel snorts. "Because she *definitely* wants to talk to the guy who smears blood all over her thighs."

I grunt. Celia could like it.

My phone pings again.

> RAGE:
> don't come after me
> I mean it

"What the fuck does that mean," Rebel groans. "Do you think he's high?"

"He doesn't get high."

"Maybe he would if Celia asked him nicely."

Well. Maybe.

A picture comes across the group chat, and my heart thumps hard. Rage is crumpled on the ground, his head caught at an awkward angle against a car tire. *His* tire. I recognize the color and trim of the vehicle.

"What the *fuck* is this?" Rebel yells.

Rage's skin is paler than usual, and there are dark shadows around his neck like he's been choked. But there aren't any other signs of a struggle—no ripped clothing, torn fingernails, blood or bruises. It's like he got choked out by a ghost.

Any sign of Celia is also nonexistent, like she vanished into thin air.

"Maybe an ex-girlfriend went after him," Rebel guesses, his voice muffled as he shuffles around his room. I can picture him pacing, agitated, clawing his way out. It's bad enough that he's been locked up all day, but to be locked up while something's going on will drive him crazy.

I think about Rebel's theory. It could be an ex-girlfriend... or a new one.

Blood rushes through my veins. *Exhilaration.* Pumping its way into my limbs, coursing through every chamber of my heart. Did Celia try to kill Rage? Did he hurt her first, or did she crave that look of fear in his eyes the same way I do?

Rage wouldn't give it up for just anybody. I doubt he'd even give it to Celia. No, he was probably grinning up at her while she tried to strangle him to death.

Key word being *try.*

If it *was* her, there's no way she finished the job. She's too green right now, inexperienced in the art of death.

I can't wait to paint her in deep shades of red.

"I'm coming to get you." I'm already halfway across the room by the time Rebel replies.

"Wait! I'll let Liara in. She can handle it."

"Rage doesn't like other people in the apartment."

"Does it look like he's gonna care who I let in the apartment? Go get him, Ruin!" He hangs up the phone and I jump to my feet, already dialing Rage's number again. I'm out the door without saying goodbye to Mrs. Morell, but I doubt I'll ever see her again. If she's smart, she'll leave town after tonight.

There aren't any defining features in the picture to clue me in on Rage's location, and we don't have tracking devices on each other in case one of us gets kidnapped. We've made a pact: brothers first, then ourselves. We don't want to lead our enemies to the rest of us, even inadvertently. When the phone rings and rings, I hang up and call Thanatos. He picks up on the first ring.

"Ruin," he greets, unable to hide the surprise from his voice. We aren't very close on account of being nearly fifteen years apart in age. "What is it?"

"Rage is missing." I jump into my SUV and start the engine. "Someone strangled him."

There's a beat of silence. "Is he dead?"

"Not likely." Although he was pale and unconscious, he didn't look *dead*.

Thanatos makes a sound that I can't decipher over the phone. "He was with Celia an hour ago. Shit, maybe two. Or more." He huffs into the receiver, making rustling sounds as he moves. "They left the safe house in *The Backyard* together."

The safe house? "What were they doing there?"

"Fucking," Than grunts, then adds, "and ruining my good sheets."

My cock swells, but I ignore it and pull out onto the street. I bet Rage has been on cloud nine all day, while Rebel's been miserable with jealousy over *breakfast*. When he finds out they had sex, he's going to explode. I saw the group text—Celia wasn't clear on who she wanted to see, but that means they both should have gone.

If they had gone to see her together, Rage wouldn't be lying on the asphalt right now.

"Which way did they go?" I ask.

Thanatos grumbles. "I don't know. I wasn't with them. We got into a—" something slams in the background—"an argument."

I'll have to ask about that later. "I'm on my way there. Text us when you find him. I'll tell Rebel we're going to *The Backyard*."

"Call Wren. Is he still practicing?"

"He's still living." That'll have to be close enough.

I'm about to end the call when Thanatos stops me. "Ruin, wait." He exhales harshly, crackling the line. "Do you know why I'm back in the city?"

I haven't guessed, and no one has told me. I answer honestly. "No."

He clicks his tongue against his teeth. "I tracked him here."

There's only one *him* that Thanatos would follow past city lines—it's the reason he left five years ago. To find him. Capture him. *Kill him.*

"Are you sure?"

"Yeah, I'm sure."

Nerves spread down my arms, tingling every dead and broken cell in my body. I'm not scared of anything, especially if it's something I can kill. But dormant emotions don't follow the rules. They crack through the layer of rock around my heart and break free one small sliver at a time, infecting the present with the past.

I'm not afraid of my father like I used to be.

But some feelings are burned into the flesh.

And grudges are born from scars like ours.

Chapter 20

Rage

When I was five years old, I saw my father kill a man. There was no finesse about it. The guy walked up to my father with a baseball bat slung over his shoulder, and despite the busy street and dozen witnesses, my father tore the bat from his hands and beat him with it. Brutally. There was brain matter on the pavement, blood spray on my clothes, and a feral gleam in my father's eye. I used to wonder what was going through my father's mind, but now that I'm an adult, sometimes I can *feel* it. That same pulse of frenetic energy courses through my veins whenever I beat information out of someone or remind them what happens when you miss paying your dues two months in a row. The world tilts. My heart sings. For that brief moment, nothing else matters but the feel of flesh beneath my knuckles.

But the difference between me and my father is that he would lash out at us, too. His children. His wife. Anyone who dared give him a funny look. He wasn't in control of it—the impulse took him over in a frenzy until he was too exhausted to continue.

When Celia first wraps her hands around my throat, I can feel the buzz of it in my fingertips. That wild energy sparking, seeking an outlet. I know that it's some kind of fight or flight response, something about the body's need to preserve itself and keep on fighting, to make sure we don't keel over just because we're too weak to fend off an attacker.

Celia isn't attacking me, though. It might look like it to anyone else, but she's not happy about it. Her hands shake. There's a tremor in her voice. Yeah, she's furious at me for being involved in the Baranova wedding bullshit, but that doesn't make her a killer. Even when I forced her to her knees in front of a hundred people at the club, she might have hated me for it, but she wouldn't kill me. The difference involves two things:

Control.

Preservation.

I understand both. I'm in control of when I release my pent up energy in a fight. I know when to pull back before snapping someone's collarbone or breaking their ribs. It's a gut instinct, sure, but there are indicators for when it's time. Signs that the other person's body gives off to let me know *this is it,* they're too close to the edge, and I need to pull back.

Preservation is part of survival. We all have the ability to stay alive—it's why adrenaline is such a bitch when it hits. Your body is fighting to stay alive, giving you one final push of energy so that you can either fight for your life or get the fuck out of Dodge.

When Celia wraps those beautiful, talented hands around my neck, she still has control. Strangling me isn't about letting out her anger—it's about preserving her own life, saving herself from a perceived threat.

Me.

I've known that I'm a threat to others.

But to Celia? I guess I'm her *Public Enemy Number One.* Maybe it's because I told her that I wanted to hurt her. Or the thought of being tied to me, literally, legally, or otherwise, is too fucking astounding for her to accept —*no,* for her to admit that she might not hate it as much as she thinks she should.

I saw the look in her eyes when I promised her a baby. That's not the look someone makes out of *hate.* There was a bright fucking star of hope shining in her gorgeous eyes, and I know that she believed me.

She has no reason *not* to.

So she strangles me not because she hates me, or because she wants to kill me, but because she's scared that I might actually give her what she wants—and her mind hasn't caught up to the fact that being with me is a *good* thing.

Preservation first.

Then control.

Because she could have killed me. Easily. With her hands. With the gun tucked into my waistband. With the half dozen weapons I keep stored around my car—hell, there's an even smaller pistol stuck under the front fender that'd fit in the palm of her hand like a glove. She had options.

And she chose to spare me.

Just like I chose to spare her.

Falling unconscious feels a lot like drowning. No one talks about it, but being unable to breathe can make the world go fuzzy. Your lungs burn. Your heart races. That bitch, Adrenaline, kicks into high gear. It would have been easy to break Celia's hold over me, toss her ass into the car, and tie her up for being a brat.

She *promised* that she was mine.

We don't break our fucking promises.

I need to get her a goddamn collar so that every time she swallows my fat load down her throat, she remembers who she belongs to.

This shit won't happen again.

A growl rumbles in my chest as I check, *again*, for the spare key to my handcuffs. She must have found them and took 'em with her. Clever girl. The gun I took from Thanatos is missing, so she snagged that, too, before cuffing me to the rail I had custom-fitted beneath my sedan. I normally use it to drag people a few hundred feet down the road. She used it to keep me here while she ran away from me.

I wish I could have glimpsed those skimpy red panties while she high-tailed it out of here.

The need to *take* roars in my ears. It's only a matter of time before I find her. Before *we* find her. Ruin will bust a nut at the mere mention of chasing her down, and Thanatos, despite his goddamn issues with her history, can track her anywhere. Rebel will have a fucking field day simply because we're doing something out of the ordinary.

I don't have to worry about my brothers.

I don't even have to worry that they'll want to kill her for hurting me. Resistance to change is normal. It's part of the process. Denial. Resistance. Then acceptance, or what-the-fuck-ever the steps are. Point is, she'll come around.

Especially after we fuck a baby into her. Then preservation won't just be for herself, it'll be for our child.

And what loving mother wants their child to grow up fatherless? Surely not our girl. I can tell she was a daddy's girl up until he died, and I can be the same for our child. Loving. Supportive. *Present.*

Celia hit the fucking jackpot with me and my brothers, because we won't fuck around with affairs, or secret lives, or boring nine-to-five jobs that keep us stressed and impotent. When one of us is busy, the other can slide right into place to pick up where the first left off. She won't have just one husband, but several. Not one partner, but three.

Point being, she doesn't realize what she's running from, so we'll have to remind her. As many times as it takes.

Chapter 21

Celia

There isn't much I inherited from my father after his death. The house went to my mother, all of his business assets and contracts went to my brother, and anything else within our home was either given away or sold when my mother finally moved on. But while Mikhail was swept away by new responsibilities and my mother consumed by grief, I spent countless hours inside his office. Sitting at his desk. Fingering through the books on the shelf. Pretending to answer the landline. The thing about sudden, unexpected death is that it hits everyone differently. For me, I wanted to uncover secrets my father kept. It's how I learned that in addition to his extensive real estate contracts and connections, he kept a ledger on the side. Although I never cracked the code for what he bought, sold, and traded his life for, I *did* find something much more valuable to a girl whose path diverged from the role of *submissive bratva wife* she was supposed to fill.

It was a place to hide.

The house my father kept in secret is under another man's name. I haven't the faintest idea who he was—my father bearing a false name or some other long-forgotten soul whose identity he stole—but I took the key hidden in a side panel in my father's office and claimed the safe house as my own. I spent the latter part of my teenage years going back and forth between our family home and this one. I haven't changed much in the time I've spent there—it's a bachelor pad through and through, with shag carpet and a huge TV in the sitting area, enough canned goods to feed a small army in the pantry, and a single bed that creaks with the slightest shift of weight. Nothing luxurious—just enough to get by for a night or two before the appeal of alone time wears off. It's the opposite of the luxury my brother and I grew up in.

That must be part of its charm.

I kept this property a secret from my ex-husband—in fact, I haven't been back in years. It's only when I'm panicking in the street that it even comes to mind. A place to run. A place to *hide.*

You can't hide forever. They'll find you sooner or later.

A shiver runs down my spine, and I resist the urge to look over my shoulder. I'll have to go back to my house to get the key. If those texts I sent from Rage's phone have done their job, none of the boys will be waiting for me at home. Hopefully, they're too busy looking after Rage to spend even an ounce of their attention on me.

I move on stiff legs as I cross a busy street, considering my next steps. Am I fleeing the city? Or am I going to stay and fight for the life I've built?

I think of Valentina and wonder how she made the decision to flee not only the bratva, but her position as our princess. Had she been planning it all along, or was it a spur of the moment decision? How did she get away—and *stay* away? Did she have help, or was she alone?

Staring up into the gray winter sky makes me feel as small as every speck of snow flurrying down. Calling anyone for help will only put them in danger. Mikhail is the exception, but as much as he might support me getting away from Rage and his brothers, he wouldn't support leaving the city altogether.

Is that what I want? To *leave*?

I catch my reflection in a storefront window and place my hands on my stomach. Flutters of hope stir in my chest, and I fight the tears welling in my eyes. If I become pregnant, which option is the best for my child? To stay within the city—within Rage, Rebel, and Ruin's sphere of influence—or to leave? I clutch my stomach as another idea emerges.

Is it better not to become pregnant at all?

The last time I let Rage in, I took a morning after pill. At the time, having sex with a stranger made the consequences a bit too permanent. But now that I know Rage, has that really changed? Or is it worse knowing who he is and what he's done?

Bile rises to the back of my throat and I duck in an alley and throw up my breakfast. Conflict wars inside my body, the future uncertain, my path unclear.

Rage seemed like he wanted to have a baby.

With me.

But as much as I want a child, bearing *his* child feels like a noose tightening around my neck. I'll be at his mercy until the baby arrives—and even then, once I'm under his complete control during the pregnancy, will he ever let me go once it's over?

Me *and* the baby?

I shake my head, already knowing the answer. Having Rage's child will tie me to him permanently, and a baby born into the bratva will become a weapon just like its father. I can't let that happen, or all of my dreams of a perfect, normal, happy family will go up in smoke.

The walk to the pharmacy around the corner is frigid, chilling me to the bone. I'm shivering as I step up to the counter and ask the pharmacist for a *Plan B*. Forty dollars and a numb journey home later, I'm standing in my master bathroom with a tiny cardboard box in hand.

I will give you everything you've ever wanted, everything you've ever dreamed.

For a moment, I believed him.

But only for a moment.

Chapter 22

Rebel

Thanatos calls to inform me that they've found Rage passed out in the cold and handcuffed to his car. Who knows how long he's been there. An hour? Two? Longer?

If the fucker hadn't locked me inside my own goddamn room all day, none of this would have happened. I would have gone to breakfast, smoothed things over between them, and reaped the benefits.

Because once Rage and Celia finally get together, then it'll be *my* turn.

Rage is just too goddamned stubborn to let things go any way other than his own. It's going to put him in an early grave. I grimace as the picture of Rage passed out on the ground flashes to mind.

Okay, not the best turn of phrase... but that doesn't make it any less true.

While Ruin and Than rouse our brother and take him to see our very own Doc-in-a-Box, I make my way to where Celia should be—*her home.* Despite how little time we've spent together, Celia's house has become one of my favorite places. Unlike our apartment above the club, it's spacious and open, with enough wide windows to bathe every square inch in endless natural light at all hours of the day. Sunlight, moonlight, and any other kind of light in between. I love it, and that's the most surprising part.

If I could steal it from her, I would.

That's why I spend hours searching its every nook and cranny, taking little knick-knacks and shiny things when I can fit them in my pockets. The problem with driving a motorcycle is that it doesn't lend itself to much cargo space without saddlebags—and those bitches are *ugly*. Meaning, if I want to take something, it has to fit in the palm of my hand.

Swiping her keys was easy. Making a double of every single one and slipping the originals back into place was even easier. The thing about Celia is that she's oddly trusting for a woman whose life we bulldozed through all of a sudden. Scratch that—she's oddly trusting for a woman raised within the *bratva*. Maybe that's why she's complacent about it, though—she knows how inevitable we are.

The bratva creates the kind of person that's impossible to refuse. Despite all her fussing, Celia hasn't put a gun to our heads and demanded we leave her alone.

I'd be impressed if she did.

It's why I'm not the least bit concerned when I bound up her three little front porch steps and unlock the main door to her house. She has a shotgun hiding in the hall closet and a pump-action rifle beneath her bed, but she wouldn't dream of using them on someone as charming as me.

I'm her favorite.

"Celia!" I call out, scanning her living room for her first. Then I jog to the kitchen and find it empty. I click my tongue and swipe a bottle of her favorite white from the wine cooler, then pinch two wine glass stems between my fingers.

A little romance can't hurt.

She *did* try to kill my brother—allegedly, if we believe Ruin's theory. Unless Rage antagonized the fuck out of her and she suddenly snapped, I don't see Celia as the killing type

What the hell did he do to her?

Rage won't fess up, too stubborn to admit when he's done something wrong, so it's up to me to smooth things over with our girl.

I kick the cooler door closed and shiver at the chill. Jesus, is the heat off? I turn on my heel to check the thermostat down the hall when movement in the corner of my eye grabs my attention.

The back door is ajar, letting in the cold evening air. Curtains hanging over the window scratch against the glass as a breeze blows them back and forth.

I set down the wine glasses and reach for my handgun. "Celia? You home, baby?" Carefully rounding the corner to the dining room, I check the corners before stepping inside. Rose petals flatten beneath my feet, with even more of them covering the entire dining room table. A heavy vase sits in the center, its crystal spiraling and sharp from the base to the lip. Two taper candles flicker on either side, like someone set the table for a romantic candlelit dinner.

Although I wouldn't oppose dinner with our girl, I doubt she has romance on her mind after this afternoon. I set the chilled wine on the table and continue moving through the house. The ground floor is clear, so I head to the stairs. Bottlenecking in a stairway is the worst idea ever, but it's the only way upstairs unless I feel like climbing the giant oak in the front yard.

Not fucking happening.

I keep my footsteps light as I pad upstairs. Once on the second floor landing, I make a beeline for Celia's bedroom. The door is wide open, and so are her dresser drawers. Clothes are thrown inside an open suitcase, like she's planning to make a run for it.

Also not fucking happening.

She isn't in the room. I glance inside her bathroom and find a little purple box torn open on the counter, but still no Celia.

A *thud* through the wall makes my heart race.

Lifting my gun and storming into the room next door, I finally find Celia.

Eyes wide.

Duct tape over her mouth.

A masked stranger with his fist wrapped around her gorgeous fucking hair and a gun held to her temple.

"What the *fuck*," I hiss, aiming straight for the dude's

stupid fucking face. Plain white hockey mask with a half dozen holes I can slam a bullet through. But then he jerks, making me aim for Celia instead of him. *Shit.* "I will fucking *end* you." The vow hammers through my heart like lead, heavy and final. This motherfucker has *no right* to touch our woman.

Who the fuck is this guy?

Celia always locks her doors. I just happen to know my way inside. He must have broken in. I should have checked the back door for signs. Broken glass, smashed handle—

He skirts the room, sidling toward the jack-and-jill bathroom that leads to the other guest room. Motherfucker is trying my patience.

"Let her go, asshole."

His dark eyes never leave mine as he inches closer to the bathroom.

"Wearing a mask? What a fucking coward." I bare my teeth at him. Ruin has a valid reason for wearing one—he's the exception to the rule. Everyone else should walk around with their real fucking faces on display. Be held accountable for their actions. "I bet you're so ugly under there that Celia dumped your ass." Or *old*. Man's got a head of grays. I bet his dick's as limp as a wet noodle. "Better yet, I bet she wouldn't even go out with you. That's why you're here, isn't it? The roses, the candles—you'll do anything for a taste of her. Too bad I interrupted your fucking dinner plans, bitch." A sneer curls over my lips. "You'll never fucking have her. She's *mine.*"

The next few seconds happen in slow motion.

Cowardly motherfucker shoves Celia at me so fast that I'm barely able to get a shot in before she's tumbling into my arms. Our bodies collide to the hard *thud* of bone and flesh while Limp-Dick literally *limps* across the bathroom and slams the door shut behind him.

"You good, baby?" I brush her hair from her face and search her eyes. When she nods, I breathe a sigh of relief. *Thank God.* "I'm gonna go after him. Stay put."

I skip the joint bathroom and jump into the hallway, following the man's thundering footsteps down the stairs. He's out the front door in record time, because *shit,* I never locked it when I came in. "Dammit!" I hop over the porch steps to the front sidewalk and pound the pavement after him, lungs burning, pistol raised. I fire off a few shots but he skirts into the short stretch of woods that leads to the neighborhood pond. Clearly, I fucking missed.

The motherfucker never even *tried* to shoot me.

Bet he's a shit-fucking-shot, too. Has to be on some kind of drugs to move that fast with a limp. Did I shoot him?

I call Thanatos while I run after him. "I need eyes on Celia. I'm chasing some motherfucker who broke into her house."

"Kind of busy," Thanatos grunts. I hear a car horn in the background. "Stay with her. I'll send a team over."

"Fuck. Okay."

Limp Dick won't come back with me there, *I think,* so I head back to Celia's house. The front door is wide open. This time, I shut and lock it behind me, then I check both back doors and lock them up tight. The kitchen door wasn't broken, just unlatched.

Maybe Celia walked inside and forgot to lock them back because...

Oh yeah, because she was about to fucking *run from us.*

I storm upstairs and slam into her bedroom door. It flies open, banging against the wall. "Celia," I call out, shoving my gun back into its holster, "you better have a good fucking explanation—"

My eyes ping to the bed, all the random clothes strewn about, some even scattered to the floor, but no suitcase. Her favorite perfume is missing from the top of her dresser, and the six-inch hunting knife I snuck inside her nightstand is gone, too. The rumble of a car engine sounds beneath my feet, and I jerk to the window to watch her peel out of the garage in her pale blue Porsche —the one she rarely drives. She rams into my motorcycle on her way down the driveway, punching it to the ground before course-correcting and barreling down the street and out of sight.

Far the fuck away from here... and far the fuck away from *me.*

What little air I have in my lungs evaporates, leaving me choking on the bitter taste of betrayal as I imagine the girl I just saved running away from the cute fucking future I had planned for us.

The mental image of the two of us smiling at each other while we joy ride through the city on my bike at sunset before having a private fucking party for two on a blanket beneath the stars pops like a bubble, making me realize just how flimsy it all was to begin with.

Because things like *easy* and *happy* don't belong to men like us. I was fooling myself into thinking things with Celia could be sweet.

We're men created from shades of gray. I will never be able to meet Celia in her world of light—the two don't mix.

If I'm going to keep her, I'll have to drag her into our box of shadows and throw away the key.

Chapter 23

Thanatos

The red tracking dot on my phone stays perfectly still, like it has for the past week. No quick trips to town or fleeing the city boundaries—the bitch has decided to stay, for better or worse.

Unluckily for her, things are about to get really fucking *worse*.

I crack every joint in my body before walking up to the tiniest ramshackle house I've ever seen. It's unobtrusive but offensive, the paint peeling on the outside, the flowers and bushes in the front garden long dead, the patches in the roof needing repaired at least two years ago. Whoever owns this place doesn't give a shit if it falls apart.

How Celia Monrovia can stand living somewhere less than perfect is easy to answer: desperate people break their own rules all the time, and our prima donna princess better be damn near falling apart.

She tried to kill my brother.

I'll never fucking forgive her.

There are a lot of things I can overlook—being a bitch, okay, a lot of people suck. Being prissy *also* sucks, but it's not a death sentence. Marrying outside the bratva, even, I don't give two shits about.

It's the lack of loyalty. The way she leads people on, only to throw them away once she gets bored. I don't give a fuck why her husband left—only that she didn't fight to keep him. From what I understand, she collapsed into a puddle of pathetic tears and went crying to my brothers' club, climbed into their laps, and joy rode them with some S-tier, magic pussy, because they're bending over backwards to make her love them.

But I know for a fact that a girl willing to run out on a man after he saves her life from a home invasion isn't worthy of their love. She isn't worthy of the spit in my mouth. The fact that she gave Rage hope that she would *choose him* over everything else and then walk away because of a *job* he couldn't have—and rightly shouldn't have—refused...

It's enough to make me want to kill her.

After witnessing the hell Valentina Baranova went through to stay loyal to her men, I know a strong woman when I see one.

And Celia fucking Monrovia?

She isn't worth shit.

Walking up to the front door of her hideaway and busting the lock in, therefore, is satisfying as hell. I'm not usually the kind of guy who likes to terrify girls—I'll leave that to my brothers—but *this one*... I enjoy every shiver of fear her body makes. The way her wide, doe eyes dilate as the adrenaline kicks in, and she scrambles for the gun resting on the counter behind her.

Bratva lesson number one she clearly failed to learn: keep your gun within arm's reach.

I'm on her before she can load the first bullet into the chamber. Tearing the gun from her hand and flinging it across the room, I bear down on her hard, pulling her arms behind her back and locking her wrists into handcuffs. She fights—I half expect her not to, so it's a welcome surprise—kicking and thrashing against me.

"Easy, princess—"

"Get off me!"

Rage told me not to bruise her. All of my brothers have some kind of fetish for marking her body for themselves. Fine, whatever, I'll give the man room for what he's due. I work carefully, then, shoving a gag between her teeth without getting my fingertips chomped off, then tying a rope around her ankles and looping it through her cuffs. It takes a few minutes for her to realize that she's been bested, and even when she does, she looks like she wants to scream about it.

Her smooth skin glistens with sweat, a delicate flush curving down her neck.

If she weren't so venomous, I might actually agree with the rest of the bratva that Celia Monrovia is *the pretty one.* Everyone knows who she is—and there are a lot of men who would cut off a finger if it meant they could marry someone as pedigreed as her.

But there's nothing pretty or desirable about a traitorous bitch.

"Don't worry, I'm not here to kill you." *Much as I'd like to.* "My brothers are convinced that you're worth something, so it's up to them to realize how little that is. A few weeks with you in a cage might change their minds. Once they realize you're nothing but flesh and bone instead of some kind of goddess, everything will go back to normal."

She trembles in my arms as I carry her out to the gutted cargo van. Tossing her into the back, I watch her hit the metal floor with a heavy *thud*, satisfied when her face scrunches up in pain. She has no idea what real pain is.

My brothers are too blind to teach her. I can see it in the plans they make—cages and satin and handcuffs, like she's an unruly pet they're fond of, when all they really need is to put her down.

I could drive her to the cliffs and throw her over, watch her sink to the bottom of the icy ocean.

I could put a dozen bullets in her right here, bury her in the backyard of this little hovel, and tell my brothers that I never found her.

But we are a family with a history of being denied our grudges—this one, I can actually deliver.

While we drive across town to the club, I keep an eye on her in the rearview mirror. She keeps still, no longer wriggling to free herself, just... *silent.* Eyes shut. Blocking out the world.

Maybe planning retaliation, if she's smart.

I slam my hand on the dashboard, enjoying the way she jumps. Loose tendrils of hair wisp around her head, stick to her neck, and billow out in a delicate halo of honey brown. The scarlet flush on her cheeks is a delicate thing—too light to be considered a bruise, but too dark to be mistaken for the embarrassed excitement of a blushing bride being delivered to her future husband. It's something in the middle, some kind of new, ruddy color, which does something to me. My gut twists, and my glare turns steely.

It's kind of *pretty.*

"I don't understand it," I laugh, my shoulders bouncing. *God,* I so don't get it. "What's so great about a bratva reject?" Shaking my head, I take a breath. "See, even after I left, Ezra took me back in a heartbeat. Andrei, too, of course, since I'm of use to the bratva. But you?" I tilt the mirror to get a better look at her. Long legs stuffed into tight, black leggings, a pale pink sweater that rides up her sides, exposing a nude bra underneath. Her stomach is showing, and I force my eyes back to the road.

That's another grievance.

The Plan B.

"If we tell the bratva what you've done—" I click my tongue against my teeth—"not even your brother can save you. It would have been faster to put a bullet in your brain, you know, if you wanted to kill yourself. Messy, but fast. You would have been gone like *that*." I snap my fingers. The sound echoes through the empty drum behind me, making Celia flinch. "But now?" I whistle, taking the next turn at a red light. "Now, you won't escape my brothers, not even to death. You realize that, don't you? They're gonna lock you up so they can play a game of pretend—but let me tell you a little secret." I meet her gaze in the rearview. "The only games they know are the brutal kind, and even when they're gonna try to be nice to their fake little *wife*—" I spit the word, resentment flooding my system—"none of us have seen what a happy marriage looks like. Our dad was one mean bastard, especially to the things he *loved*." I roll my eyes on that last part. I doubt my father ever knew the meaning of the word *love*.

"Anyway, you should have offed yourself." I run a hand down my face, fighting a sudden wave of fatigue. The long nights are catching up to me. Not only does Ezra have me running protection for the *real* bratva princess—excuse me, *Queen*—but I'm combing the streets for a real threat every other waking moment of the day. Exhaustion is a persistent mistress, riding my ass from dusk till dawn.

But at least I won't have anything more to do with Celia Monrovia after this drop-off.

She'll be my brothers' problem to solve.

It takes an hour, but we finally make it back to the club. During special swinger events, they call it *Midnight*, but during the day, it doubles as a gentleman's club serving alcohol and pussy to anyone with enough cash to pay their way through the door. Most of our clients are fellow mafiosos—Russian, Irish, Italian, whoever we're dealing with that day—so it's rare to have guests we don't entertain with our specially-curated staff.

I swing around to the back entrance. Ruin is waiting at the door, arms crossed, looking as menacing as ever.

Most of the time, I think it's a shame that our father fucked him up so badly, but it's times like these that I know we're better for it. Stronger. More resilient.

It's a fucked-up kind of gratitude, but maybe that's the only kind we can afford to have.

Anything else—the softness, the sweetness, the genuine thankfulness someone might have for any number of life's blessings—never makes it to our doorstep.

I throw open the back of the van and drag Celia to the edge. "Brought you a present." Smacking the metal floor next to her, I watch her for signs of panic, but she's completely collected, the long drive giving her time to think and process her future.

Ruin stares at her for a long moment, unmoving. The seconds tick by while I wait, exhaustion creeping in on me, its needles stabbing the backs of my eyes. "We good?" I ask.

My youngest brother breaks out of his trance and nods. "Did you drug her?"

"Didn't have to. She wasn't much of a challenge."

He grunts, then takes his time getting to the van. He fingers the ropes around her ankles and follows a trail of red up her calf, likely from where she was pressed against the ridges in the floor for so long. Goosebumps break out across her skin, and I watch as they bleed from one inch of skin to the next. Ruin traces their path with his gloved fingertips, a reverence to his touch that I simply don't understand.

How can he still like what he sees?

How isn't he strangling her right now?

But if I know my brother like I think I do, he already has plans for how and when he touches her next. Ruin is deliberate, methodical, liking to take his time to ensure he experiences every raw detail of the moment.

If anyone will stay Rage's temper and curtail Rebel's impatience, it'll be Ruin. He could keep the bitch alive for days. Weeks. Hell, *years*.

That might even be his plan—dragging things out as long as possible, denying her death even if she begs for it.

I hope she does.

I hope my brothers deny her wish.

After all, she denied them something precious, too.

A baby wouldn't have solved our family problems, but it might have brought us a ray of hope in this dismal fucking world.

I glare at Celia as Ruin picks her up and cradles her against his chest. Leaning down to meet her eyes, I throw every ounce of my hatred into these words: "I hope you never get pregnant."

She flinches like I've slapped her.

"A bitch like you would poison your child before it's even born. They're better off dead than with you as a mother."

A silent tear tracks down her cheek. I brush it away with my thumb and swipe it over her gagged lips, hoping that she not only tastes its salt, but that she remembers this moment as much as I will.

Because every time she cries, I want her to think of me—and choke on her regrets as much as the rest of us.

Chapter 24

Rage

I run my hand down the gilded bars of my new cage, admiring how they shine in the light. It's a new addition to the club floor—a cage for someone to dance in. Lounge in. Get fucked in. Bolted down right next to the padded throne I use to survey the crowds. There's a smaller one in the middle of our apartment, taking up what used to be our living room floor. We never used it for much beyond quick meetings before or after jobs, so this is a much better use of the space.

Together, my brothers and I will teach Celia what it means to break promises.

You don't get a fucking choice but to keep them.

I wrap my fist around one of the bars and tug, satisfied with its sturdiness. All three of us hold matching keys, but we decided that if one of us puts her inside, another one isn't allowed to take her out. I wanted to commission a smith to create three different locking mechanisms so that if one of us locks her in, the other won't be able to unlock it, but time was of the essence.

We couldn't risk Celia actually *running away*.

To think that she stayed within city limits this entire time...

A hum catches in the back of my throat as I wonder, for the hundredth time, if she was waiting for us—*for me*—to come after her and bring her home. If she didn't really want to leave, but she was scared of how angry I'd be with her after our little strangulation incident.

I don't blame her for it. In fact, I'm proud that she acted out of passion instead of shoving it deep, deep down to bury it. Most men within the bratva are taught that emotions are weaknesses—but my brothers and I believe that they're weapons.

Hate. Fear. Excitement. *Love.*

They fuel us to be better versions of ourselves—versions that our enemies can't use against us. If we harness our emotions, we control our reality.

It's when we act out recklessly that we lose control.

Which is why the cage is necessary. It will keep me in check as much as it will keep Celia safe. Being around her, knowing that she aborted our baby before it ever had a chance to take root... My fists clench hard enough that my bones scream.

She *promised* to have my baby, to love and cherish it.

A mother who loves her children doesn't throw them away. Not *ever.*

Now that Celia will be under lock and key, she won't be able to get rid of my gifts so easily. It was an error of judgement to trust her the first time, but it was also an error to tell her anything about the Baranova wedding and my involvement in it. She doesn't understand the circumstances. I don't even know if Mikhail—or Valentina—has told Celia the truth about what happened that day.

Guessing from how violently Celia reacted, I'd say, probably not. It's something I'll explain to her while she's behind bars.

But not *these* bars. First, I'll need to train her how to behave and be grateful for our generosity—*then*, we'll upgrade her to the cage on the club floor.

Until then, she'll stay where she belongs—under constant watch, all hours of the day, in the heart of our home.

Full of our cum.

Becoming the mother she's always dreamed of being.

As beautiful as the first time I laid eyes on her.

I leave the club's main floor and head up the lavish front stairs to our apartment, my body thrumming with anticipation. She's close. I can feel it. A week apart has felt like an eternity—especially after burying myself inside of her and leaving a piece of me behind. It's not just about the sex—although fucking amazing—it's about the promise we made to each other.

I will give Celia everything she needs to be happy.

It's up to her to decide how she receives it.

With a diamond ring on her finger and a baby in her belly... or locked in a cage, collared in leather, until she learns how good it feels to be ours.

Are you ready to rebel?

Find out in book two, *Tempted to Rebel*, coming early 2025.

If you enjoyed *Claimed by Rage*, please write a review! 🩶 They feed Misti's soul better than her favorite chocolate chip cookies.

For another dark read, check out my MFM serial killer standalone romance coming in July 2025: *Theirs to Take*

Two unhinged brothers make me the target of their twisted game. The ending? *Death.*

If I thought being a college student was hard enough, adding in two psychotic misfits definitely ups the ante. They're both obsessed--one with hating me, the other with teasing me. At first, I think it's a flirting game to get into my pants.

Then someone brings out a mask, a knife, and an ultimatum, and the alarms bells in my head start screaming. This isn't just a game--it's a death sentence.

There's only one way to win:

Know Your Enemy
Seduce Your Enemy
Don't Fall for Your Enemy

Meet Kane, Zane, and Mercy in the preview prequel on my website:
https://mistiwilds.com/pages/theirs-to-take-preview
Or meet all the killers from this multi-author series in our free anthology.

About the Author

Just a smut-lover listening to angsty love songs on repeat.

Misti Wilds loves watching characters pine after one another from afar--until a tall, dark, brooding alpha male says *fuck this* and claims his woman. But one man isn't enough these days--Misti's got her hands full when it comes to writing multiple dark and delicious men with violence in their hearts and a declaration of love etched on the barrel of their guns.

Why choose one when you can have them all?

Also by Misti Wilds

Baranova Bratva:
Rule of Three

Reign of Four

Brutal Beauty:
Brutal Beauty (prequel)

Claimed by Rage

Tempted to Rebel

Bound by Ruin

Born to Riot

Serial Killer Romance:
Begging for Mercy

Printed in Dunstable, United Kingdom